Henry Cholmondeley-Pennell

Fishing Gossip

Stray leaves from the note-books of several anglers

Henry Cholmondeley-Pennell

Fishing Gossip
Stray leaves from the note-books of several anglers

ISBN/EAN: 9783337277598

Printed in Europe, USA, Canada, Australia, Japan

Cover: Foto ©Andreas Hilbeck / pixelio.de

More available books at **www.hansebooks.com**

FISHING GOSSIP

STRAY LEAVES FROM THE NOTE-BOOKS

OF SEVERAL ANGLERS.

EDITED BY

H. CHOLMONDELEY PENNELL,

AUTHOR OF THE 'ANGLER-NATURALIST,' THE 'BOOK OF THE PIKE,' ETC.

EDITOR OF THE LATE 'FISHERMAN'S MAGAZINE AND REVIEW.'

EDINBURGH: ADAM & CHARLES BLACK

MDCCCLXVI

DEDICATED

TO

HENRY FENWICK, ESQ.

LATE M.P. FOR SUNDERLAND,

WHOSE ENERGETIC AND SUCCESSFUL

EXERTIONS IN THE CAUSE OF FISHERY REFORM

MERIT THE GRATITUDE OF

ALL ANGLERS.

CONTENTS.

CONTENTS.

DUM CAPIMUS CAPIMUR.

UDGEON,— Hurley,— Julia ;— Nothing particularly exceptional or congruous surely in these three substantives that they should insist upon presenting themselves to my mental camera in such pertinacious juxtaposition ? Nice, silky, euphemistic words they are, no doubt —words naturally suggestive of gurgling water, whispering willows, and what Barney Maguire calls the " laste taste in life" of *dilettante* sentimentalism ;— but is that any reason for their ringing the changes in a sort of " grand chain" through my head all night, and taking me a regular slap in the face this morning the moment I opened my eyes upon the quadrangle of old Trinity Hall ? Heigh-ho ! who'd have thought that a week's gudgeon-fishing would have produced such psychological manifestations ? And am I not lying, too, in saying that " gudgeon" is a euphemistic word ? Distinctly : one more *un*-euphonious it would perhaps be a puzzler to name; and so evidently thought Izaak Walton's poet, **Jo** Chalkill, when he was driven to find a rhyme for it in *sturgeon.* Poor Jo! "gudgeon" was evidently altogether too much for him. Elsewhere he tries **his** hand at it again with even worse success :—

> " Roach or dace
> We do chase,
> Bleak or gudgeon
> Without *grudging*."

Awful! He might at least have improved upon this, by adopting the spelling of Davors :—

> " And thou, sweet Boyd, that with thy watery sway
> Dost wash the cliffes of Deighton and of Week . . .
> In whose fair streams the speckled trout doth play,
> The roach, the dace, the *gudging*, and the bleike."

How much more neatly "John Williamson, gent, temp. 1740," manages the matter :—

> " Tho' little art the gudgeon may suffice,
> His sport is good, and with the greatest vies ;
> Few lessons will the angler's use supply
> Where he's so ready of himself to die !"

Well, be the difficulty great or small, there certainly *is* a peculiar fascination in catching, if not in poetising, gudgeon. Doesn't Salter tell us of an angling curate who was engaged to be married to a bishop's daughter, lingering so long over his twelve-dozenth fish as to arrive too late for the ceremony, whereupon his lady declined to be wedded to a man who preferred his basket to his bride?

Wasn't Sir Isaac Newton, like his great piscatorial namesake, master of the art of catching gudgeon? as well as Bacon, Gay, Cecil, Hollinshed, and a host of other celebrities? Why, even our neighbours over the Channel take naturally to it. Moule's *Fish Heraldry* tells us that it was the cognisance of John Goujon, one of the first French sculptors of the sixteenth century; and old Salter says that in the waters round Ghent "it is the general practice to angle for it with a bit of raw sheep's liver." (How a Thames gudgeon would turn up his nose at such a plebeian bait!)

In a gastronomic point of view, *gobio* gives precedence to none: a fry of fat gudgeon, eaten piping hot, with a squeeze of lemon-juice, is a dish "to set before a king," and as superior to anything that Greenwich or Blackwall can produce, as Mouet's champagne is to gooseberry pop. John Williamson, gent, aforesaid, who seems to have had a keen eye to the good things of this life, commends the gudgeon "for a fish of an excellent nourishment, easy of digestion, *and increasing good blood.*" Nay, even as a cure for desperate diseases, the gudgeon is not without his encomiasts; for Dr. Brookes says, in his *History of Fishes*, that he "is thought good for a consumption, *and by many swallowed alive;*" though it is to be presumed that the fish so disposed of were not of the same size as the four from Uxbridge, **to which the** doctor refers immediately afterwards **as** " weighing **a** pound" each.

Dr. Brookes' remedy reminds one of Madame **de** Genlis' prescription **for a less** serious attack. **On** being charged by her companions, one day when out fishing, with being **a " fine Paris lady,"** she suddenly **snatched** up a fresh-caught gudgeon, **and** exclaiming, " This will **show** whether I am **a fine Paris** lady !" **swallowed it alive, to the utter discomfiture of her tormentors, who** declined **to follow her in so** vivisectional a test of fashion.

Galloway, the **fisherman at** Chertsey, **tells, I re**member, a good story **of two** old gentlemen, " mighty gudgeon-fishers," who were in the habit of betting **heavily on their** respective " takes ;" till at last **the** old fellow **who almost** always won was discovered with a *silk casting-net* stowed away under the boards of his punt ! Almost as great a sell **that,** as the parson losing his wife ! This piscatorial clergyman, by the way, lived at Hampton ; **and if any** Cockney wishes to remember the best gudgeon grounds, let him not forget his *H*'s. **Curious how many** there are of them scattered **up and** down the Thames—Hampton, Halliford, Harleyford, **Hurley, Henley,** all beginning with the eighth letter of the alphabet, and all redolent of gudgeon-fishing. Gudgeon-fishing! which I maintain to be, *par excellence,* the sport **of** the poet and the philosopher.

Some men there are, I know, who prefer a helter-skelter rush, thorough flood thorough fell, after a burly salmon, with a moral certainty of breaking either their tackle or their necks, and a very fair chance of taking an involuntary header over a cataract, or being soused plummet-wise into a whirlpool ; others again rejoice in a tussle with that grim cannibal the pike, or a solitary stroll, trout-rod in hand, by the banks of the arrowy Dart, " shut in, left alone, with themselves and perfection of water ;" but of all sports and spots commend me to a good gravelly swim on the Thames in July, a punt, a rake, a pretty companion, and a day's gudgeon-fishing.

> " A league of grass, washed by a slow broad stream
> That, stirred with languid pulses of the oar, .
> Waves all its lazy lilies and creeps on." . . .

What can be more jolly ?　A fellow has come back, regularly done up, perhaps, with grind, to spend "the long" at the Grange with the cousins (Julia is a ward in Chancery, I fancy ?)—one of those broad white houses to be found nowhere but on the banks of Thames, with a skirting of pheasant-cover or wooded cliff as a background, and a lawn as smooth and green as the finest Genoa velvet, sloping down from the drawing-room steps to the boathouse. The moment breakfast's over, " Now then, come along girls !" some one shouts ; and out you go, through

the window **or** over the balcony : a scamper to the
boathouse, a vigorous shove or two with the punt-
pole, and in five minutes the ripecks are fast, and
everything snug in the very perfection of a "pitch"
—not that one out there over the shallows, for the
sun will soon have done washing his face, and in an
hour will blaze up dazzling enough for Phæton himself—but the other under the island yonder, and just
within the dip of the chestnuts, where you can see
the "golden gravel," **as** Tennyson calls it, about four
feet below, and as bright as a new **guinea**.

Splash ! in goes the rake, leaded at the end like
a constable's staff that it may sink well out over the
swim,—three minutes' vigorous raking—another **for**
comfortably **shaking down into** places, and you **are
about to set to work with a will,** when you probably
discover that Blanche has broken her line, or that
Julia's hook is off (it was yesterday !) But lines are
not difficult to mend, and there are more hooks than
one in the world, so everything is **soon** *en règle,* and
at it you go. Ha ! a bite the moment the float touches
the water, bob—souse !—you have him,—so has Julia
—(Blanche and Charley aren't baited yet)—two fish
in two swims,—that looks well ; for if gudgeon don't
come on to bite at first, they often don't do it at all.
"Julia, a pair of gloves on the first dozen ?" "Done !"
—and done you are, for Julia nobbles twelve unsus-
pecting *gobiones* in as many swims, before you have

bagged your fifth, and triumphantly informs you that her size is "sixes, sir!" "Again, come,—double or quits?"—If you are lucky you may possibly win; but if you are not only not lucky but in love, you **lose** to a dead certainty. Something must be wrong: you examine your little red worm with an unloving and critical eye, and you find that your No. 9 Kendal is minus its barb! Well, that's soon remedied :— "Come, one more pair?" but Julia declines with thanks the proffered "glove," and hints that when she accepted it before "your *hand* wasn't in!" The little sharper! Well, so she is—sharper than you at all events ; and she might have accepted your challenge, sir, with the utmost safety if she had chosen to "bleed" you ; for she is one of the best gudgeon-fishers on the Thames, and when ladies *do* take in earnest to catching gudgeon, let me tell you they beat the lords of crea- tion into fits. "Bless you!" as a Smithfield butcher once observed to me *à propos* of sticking pigs, "it comes nat'ral to 'em!"

But how's this? the gudgeon have all of a sud- den left off biting? half-a-dozen swims without **a** nibble—"give them another Rake." You do, till your arms ache. But you might just as well give them another Spade for any effect it produces. Stay—I **see!** My friend Mr. *Perch* is down below, and the process of biting, so far as the gudgeon are concerned, is taking a passive instead of an active form. Try him with a paternoster ; whilst he stops there nothing will bite, depend upon it ; you might as well tempt **a** snake-fascinated paroquette with a **cater**pillar ! Ha ! I have him . . . a *John,* by all the powers !—a big bullying pike, come here to make a breakfast.—Julia, the landing-net—quick—don't wait till he's done up, **but pop it under** him the moment **you** get a chance, for whilst he **can show** fight he keeps tail towards you and his head down, with the gut in the corner of **his** great mouth where he's got no teeth ; but as soon as he's beaten, his mouth slews round, and the line will be in the " breakers" **in a** moment. So—bravely done : a six-pounder **at the** least, and in capital condition !

But what on earth **can** Charley and Blanche be **about all this time ? They** actually haven't begun **yet ! Well, the fact is that Blanche and** Charley have contrived to get their two lines into a most ingenious tangle, and somehow the juxtaposition of so many pair of taper fingers doesn't seem to have much expedited matters.—

*   *   *   *

But there ! what's the good of talking and making myself melancholy—one can't eat one's cake and keep it : it's all **over and** done with, and here I am back at my venerable Coach's again—**Homer,** Horace, Livy—Livy, Horace, Homer—the old grind ! Adieu **to** gudgeon and gudgeon-fishing, **Hurley** Bucks,

Harleyford Woods, cool breezes, murmuring rivers,
and pretty cousin Julia, until—the next long vacation.

> " Glide gently, thus for ever glide,
>   O Thames ! that anglers all may see
>   As lovely visions by thy side,
>   As now, fair river, come to me.
>   Oh, glide, fair stream, for ever so,
>   Thy quiet soul on all bestowing,
>   Till all our minds for ever flow
>   As thy deep waters now are flowing."

H. C. P.

IRISH LOACH-TROLLING

ITS ORIGIN AND PRACTICE.

On Lough Neagh's bank, as the fisherman strays,
　When the clear **cold** eve's declining,
He sees the round towers of other days
　In the waves beneath him shining.
Thus shall Memory often, in dreams sublime,
　Catch **a glimpse of the days that** are over ;
Thus, sighing, look through the waves of Time
　For the long-faded glories they cover !—MOORE.

IN a mood somewhat **kindred to the** spirit of **these** beautiful verses, it occurred to **us** to " catch a glimpse of the days that are over ;" and to rescue from " the waves of time " a few recollections of Irish angling half-a-century ago.

The particular description of fishing indicated was practised for some time as a secret in the larger **lakes** of the midland counties ; and in its early stages the harvest reaped was certainly great, and **the motives for** concealment proportionate. It is not to be supposed, however, that the value of a practice so fertile in results, and conducted in **the open day,** could long remain **undetected.** . If the rivalry of contemporary anglers **be** potent to conceal, **the** jealousy of their brothers of the rod is equally powerful to discover, the quality of **a** favourite lure. The veil, con**sequently, with** which it was sought to guard **the art of** loach-trolling from the knowledge of the **unin**itiated was not long **in being** penetrated. The following account of **the** event is derived from **the** principal actors **in the** transaction, **with whom the** writer, in his **youth, was long** and intimately **ac**quainted. He merely uses the author's privilege to reduce the information he received to a more **connected form.**

It is, **then,** about fifty-five years—*si rite remetior astra*—since **two** men met on the high road which tangentially touched the northern extremity of Lough Lane—a lake of moderate extent in Westmeath, but famed at that time for the number, excellence, and sporting qualities of its trout. One of these men belonged to the old Irish constabulary, the other was the occupant of some twenty or thirty acres of land, overlooking the lake. They were proceeding in opposite directions, and might have passed on without further recognition than that implied in the usual salutations of Irish peasants on such occasions. But both being anglers and old friends, the meeting led to a more protracted interview. The elder of the two carried in his right hand a two-piece rod and a landing-net of ample dimensions ; a cast of lake flies in his hat ; and, suspended in his left hand, an old tin kettle, very much the worse for the wear. A potato, firmly impaled on its nozzle, helped to keep the contents from escaping ; corks being a luxury not always at hand in those days in out-of-the-way places. The regard, however, with which he grasped the handle of this part of his equipage would appear to attach greater importance to the contents than the exterior seemed to justify. To the junior figure in the scene the article was an entirely new item in a fly-fisher's *impedimenta*, and forcibly attracted his attention. He had rowed and fished in the same boat with the most aristocratic anglers of the county ; but amongst the superfluities of their tackle he had never observed a utensil of this kind. Had it been a flask of " mountain-dew," or a sandwich-case of smoked beef or ham, he would have thoroughly comprehended its congruity with the occasion ; but an old tin kettle !—the very thought filled his mind with mingled sensations of wonder and ridicule. Yet he had far too high an opinion of his friend's sagacity to believe that he would thus burthen him-self with such an incumbrance on a hot summer's morning without some sufficing reason. His acquaintance's success, too, of late, when other fishers were becalmed, or unfortunate in the selection of their flies, had reached his ears, and served to awaken

his suspicions. Assuming, therefore, an air of in-
difference, he diplomatically approached the subject
of his curiosity by remarking : " Well, Tom, if it
isn't bad manners, or making too free, might one ask
what you've got in the kettle ? A horn of Cruise's
' Castle Billingham,' or a ' cropper' of Jim Flanigan's
' double-shot' that never saw the face of a gauger,
wouldn't be a bad beginning of the day's work."
Quite prepared for the question, and alive to its sig-
nificance, Tom coolly replied : "Snipes, Paddy !" and,
suiting the action to the word, applied his fore-finger
to the point of that prominence in the " human face
divine," usually appealed to in responses of this kind.
Paddy was fairly " sold," " bothered out and out," without a chance of making another attack on the suspected
" kettle." They accordingly parted good-humouredly
in the flash of the repartee—Tom to his boat, which
lay higher up the lake, Pat to tend his potato-beds
on the hill. The latter, however, did not wholly
relinquish the chase, and muttered as he went along :
" A kettle of snipes, indeed ! Did anyone ever hear
of snipes in such a lardther afore ? The ould thief-
catcher ! I'll be even with him yet !" and so passed on
to his work. Looking down occasionally from the hill-
side, which commanded a view of the whole lake, he saw
from the track and pace of Tom's boat that he must be
trolling for something. But then nobody trolled, at
the time, for trout ; pike were fortunately few in the

lake then, and Tom, besides, was not much in that way. Still the landing-net **could** be dimly descried in the distance in operation from time to time ; **and,** combining these facts and conjectures together, he concluded there was a new fishing dodge of some kind "in the wind." As a last resource, it occurred to him that the examination of Tom's boat might throw some light on the subject. **Some** traces of the slaughter might be found where the deed was done. When he saw Tom depart for the night, he accordingly descended to the boat, and there discovered, to his surprise, not only fragments, but a living specimen of the *Collaugh rhua—Anglicè*, the "red-hag"— the veritable stone loach **of** systematic writers, swimming about merrily in the bilge-water of the ill-caulked **craft, and which** doubtless found its way there accidentally from Tom's "kettle of snipes." The secret was now out, and soon **to** become a fatal fact to the fly-fishing of the district, as will appear hereafter.

Before proceeding to the practical details of this paper, I may be permitted to offer a few general remarks on the appearance, haunts, and habits of the Great Lake trout, or *Salmo ferox*, **to** which these details apply. Into the science of the subject I shall not enter, though well aware of the wide and seductive field of observation which the natural history of the fish opens to the amateur essayist. But the subject is one which **will** be approached with greatest caution **by** those who are most deeply impressed by **its extent and** complexity. At a moment, indeed, **when the** very principles and methods to **be** pursued in the investigation are called in question, and keenly **disputed** by the ablest minds, the prudent observer will pause ere he mingles in the conflict. Anatomical research, which superseded the systems of classification by external characters alone, and which was long considered to rest on a firm basis, has failed in its turn to satisfy the objections of later discoveries. Either of these methods, or both combined, may be usefully employed in the discrimination of living beings one from the other, not because they meet the requirements of every case, but because we know no better at present. Till the exigencies of an exact science then are adequately worked out, it must suffice to assume here that there **is** such a being as the Great Lake trout, distinct from the other species and varieties of the *genus*. **I** would however, *in limine*, object to the very improper liberty taken with **one of** my earliest piscine acquaintances in giving him the inappropriate *specific* name of *ferox ;* for **I can** safely aver, from long familiarity with him, that he **is** neither savage nor ferocious, except indeed when he resents the prick of a fish-hook, or the too close proximity of a landing-net to his nose. We swam the same waters together from youth to manhood—with **Burns I might** literally say—

> " We twa ha'e paidelt in the burn,
>   Frae morning sun till dine ;
>   **But** seas between us braid ha'e roared,
>   Sin' auld lang syne"—

and never observed a single trait **of the** defamatory character with which he has been branded in systematic works. On the contrary, we shall see presently that he is quite an epicure in diet, and playful as a kitten on his own domestic hearth. In no stage of his existence can he **well be** confounded with his cousins of the river. Even in his infancy there is **a** breadth and freedom **of** outline in his configuration, **which distinguish him at** once from relatives of the same age in brook or streamlet. When viewed play-**ing** at their favourite game of entomology, one of them exhibits a promise of future expansion never presented **by** the other. Not **but that** the latter, under favourable circumstances, is capable of reaching a considerable weight and size ; but the larger he **grows** the less he really resembles the Great Lake type. His increase is lateral rather than longitud-**inal, as if the vertebræ** refused to **be** parties in the **process** ; and I have seen quadrilateral monsters of **this kind taken** in small bog-lakes, which weighed **from** 9 lbs. to 10 **lbs.,** though not more than a dozen or fifteen inches long. But they were nasty tenchy creatures to look at ; bad for sport, and worse for the table. Our old friend *ferox*, notwithstanding his bad name, **never** makes a beast of himself in this fashion. **No matter** to what stature he grows, he never, **till** age overtakes him, loses his noble **athletic and** artistic proportions. In these characteristic qualities, he vies with *salar* and *trutta* themselves. Into rivers or brooks, except for the purpose of making **them** tributary to the propagation of **his** young, he never condescends to wander. Even in the lower reaches of rivers discharging into the lakes he inhabits, I have never met him **in** the summer months. Neither will he answer the calls **of inquisitive** naturalists who expect to find **him at** home in small loughs, though contiguous **to** or connected by stream **or river** with **large ones.** Elbow, or more correctly fin-room, he must **have**, or he will not prosper. There would appear, indeed, a certain ratio always to exist between **him** and the extent of water he requires. In this he, of course, **only** conforms **to the supposed law of har-mony which** is said to prevail **between all** organisms and external circumstances. But **why other little** fishes in the same waters **do** not conform **in the same** way the philosophers **don't tell us.** **It is** probably certain, **however,** that in **lakes** less than **three** miles **long, and half** that in width, a genuine specimen of *ferox* will **not be found.** The physical features, too, of the ample **basin** he loves **to** sport in, besides mere extent, **have** doubtless **much to** do with his health and happiness. Shingle beaches, marly bottoms, precipitous rocks, fathomless water-valleys, and **cor**-responding elevations of sharps **or** sunken islands, **to** which in the summer months **he resorts** to have a charge at the sticklebacks, or a **tumble at** his favourite Ephemeridæ, constitute **some of the domestic** requisites for his full development. **As a variety he has no objection** to a certain amount of bog-shore ; **but** it is obvious it does not agree **well** with his **constitution**—his fine colours suffering there, and **his whole** physiognomy becoming bilious and jaundiced. **If** brooks or rivers are not at hand, he and **madam** *ferox* provide **heirs to** the estate in some nice gravelly **or sandy** creek of the **lake.** For this **I can answer,** having **frequently been a witness** of their connubial happiness, standing **with hymeneal torch** in hand **over the** nuptial bed **on a** dark November night. How many seasons the amiable **couple may live** to visit the gravel beds is rather a difficult question to answer. The registry of births, deaths, **and** marriages in such remote and obscure places as **the** depths **of a** "great lake" **furnishes but** doubtful data for the **sta**-tistics of the **ages of the** population. Neither **have we, in** this case, **the** " equine marks" of the teeth, **or** the " annual **vegetable** rings" **to** appeal to. **The pro**-bability is that the happy pair live to a good round age, though it might be imprudent to reduce it to cyphers. The pounds **avoirdupois** which they are found to weigh **after** they attain a respectable size, may possibly **give** a fair approximation **to** their respective **ages.** Sooner **or** later, however, the day of **decline** arrives. Fly-fishing **or** trolling, I have hooked **during** the season occasional specimens **of a** long, tapering, huge-headed **animal**; all skin, bone, and fins, like **a flying-fish, but languid in** his movements, **voracious in** his **appetites,** and seemingly indifferent **to his fate. Shall the** melancholy fact be recorded ?—**it is our once gallant** friend *ferox,* who could in better **days run out forty** yards of line in a breath, **spring from the lowest** depths of his domain above **the surface with fly or** loach in his mouth, and contemptuously **turn up** his nose half-a-dozen of times **at net or gaff; but** now, alas! wabbling about like **a** miserable snig **in** his dotage and decrepitude. **And** as **if** this **were not** sufficient humiliation for the **pride and** paragon **of inland waters, the rustic** fishers, **no more** respectful **of his character than the** ichthyo-**logists, have** combined **to** call him in this state a "piper." ***Date obolum*** *Belisario*—gently remove the hook **from his aged jaws;** return him safely to his native element, and crown the deed of charity by sending after him **as many** loaches as you can spare. When **you next visit** the lake you will probably witness **his** obsequies performed and his bones picked **by** a merciless group of gulls and scarecrows, scream-

ing and howling over his remains, as they are buf-
feted about by the waves. Such is the natural end
of *ferox*—full of indignities indeed, but from which
it is consoling to reflect that the insensibility of
death has plucked the sting!

The food of this distinguished member of his
family, like his place in systematic arrangements,
has been a matter of doubt and dispute. That his
whole bill of fare cannot be correctly filled up is
very probable. But sufficient data, I think, exist to
make out a tolerable *carte* of his favourite dishes.
Oh! those words of learned sound, and little meaning, that must be used to describe this food in the
jargon of science, make one almost shudder. That
he is, then, *insectivorous, vermivorous, molluscivorous,
piscivorous*, and probably *herbivorous*, is all but certain.
I have taken him with at least twenty different kinds
of lake flies. I have seen him in his junior state
dragged up like a malefactor amongst slimy eels on
a night-line baited with worms. He has risen to my
hook baited with five species of little fishes—namely,
the loach, stickleback, fry of trout and pike and
the gudgeon. His addiction to these dainties has
been proved to me numberless times by a very unwilling visit to my net. There is, however, as far I
have been able to observe, one condition necessary to
his indulgence in these luxuries. They must be in a
comparatively minute form, and presented to him on

a link of clear, **clean** gut. **As a** general rule, the
limit of his **taste in** this respect does not exceed
baits **of three or** perhaps four inches. He must be
hard up for a dinner if he goes beyond these dimen-
sions. To be sure it has been stated—what indeed
of fishes has not?—that, like the pike, he attacks
prey of a considerable size. Possibly this may be
so. There are cannibals amongst our own species who
will finish a missionary at **a** meal ; but these are
fortunately exceptions to the general tastes of humanity. I have trolled with pike-tackle and larger
baits, how **often I know** not ; but never, **in** any
instance, **did** *ferox* favour me with **a** call while
engaged in this **kind of work in** the waters which he
inhabits. **Of his** feeding on small shells and larvæ,
which are to be found in large quantities on the
bottom of lakes, the evidence, though inferential,
assumes **a** look of certainty, on examining the contents **of** his stomach. **The** *débris* of these semi-
digested creatures is there **to** be seen and felt
clearly enough. Amongst **the** mass are traces of
apparently green vegetable matter ; but whether
these are the remains of a salad of aquatic herbs is
problematic.

The dietetic tastes of our subject being thus disposed of, **so far as** I have observed, the selection of
the best bait, and the mode of using it, follow in
order. Of those which I have stated, the loach will

be found the best, at least in Irish lakes. **It** might be asked at the outset, why this should be so, as the loach is seldom a denizen of lakes, and not consequently a part of the natural food of the large trout which these lakes contain. The only answer that can be practically given to the question **is** that which *ferox* himself instructs us to **give—namely,** that he likes it. The first thing then to be done is to catch your loach, if you expect *ferox* to follow *suit*. **This** is not a difficult task on the Irish side of the Channel. There are few streams or rivers here in which "beardy" does not abound. The smaller the stream or brook, the easier to find and secure him. If you do the business yourself, the **only** weapon you require is an old-fashioned, three-pronged, steel meat-fork. With **this** little instrument in the right hand, just cautiously raise with the left any flat stones you see in stream **or** shallow pool where "beardy" is **known to frequent.** You will probably see his nose or tail projecting at the edge of the said stone. Then with quick eye and steady stroke transfix the little victim with the fork against the bottom of the stream, otherwise he darts off as fast as lightning, and you see no more of him for that day. He is tenacious of life, and if not badly wounded will survive for the time you require his services, by placing him in a supply of fresh water. He is not easily driven into a net, being quite as obstinate in this respect as a young porker. For persons whose backs have passed the period of bending freely, and whose feet don't take to the water kindly, the duty had better be performed by deputy. For a few pence **any** young " Patlander," whose shoes and stockings **are no** hindrances to aquatic exercise—being those only which nature provided him with at birth—will get your " Honour" as many of them, any morning, as you may require. I may add, before concluding this part of the subject, that the loach sometimes outgrows the measure of the best-sized trout-bait. If you have an option, select the smaller greenish specimens from $2\frac{1}{2}$ to 3 inches long, in preference to the larger reddish variety, which is not so much relished by *ferox*.

I will now assume that the intending loach-troller is supplied with a stock of the necessary baits ; and that they are carefully provided for with fresh water in some more commodious vessel than Tom's kettle. The next subject for consideration is the rod and gear to be employed **in** the experiment, and here I must premise that my observations will apply to tackle used for the purpose fifty years ago, without any reference whatever to tackle and resources of a later date. The rods, lines, and reels then used for loach-trolling **for** trout were precisely the same articles used in fly-fishing. Persons who had a choice between pike and salmon rods seldom if ever employed the latter for this purpose. It was obvious to them, as it must be to everyone, that a rod and tackle equal to contend with a fish of 8 or 10 lbs. weight, taken **by** a fly, would be competent to master the same fish caught by a loach. There was no casting in the case, the whole process being conducted in a boat, so that no advantages were to be gained by additional length or strength of the rod. The foot-line, however, was entirely different from that employed in angling with flies, except in the fact of its being made of gut. If of single gut, as was sometimes the case, the gut should be of the very best and strongest of that kind sold as salmon-gut. On the other hand, if this material was not procurable, the gut-twister was called into operation ; three fine, long, and evenly matched hairs were twisted together in lengths, and these united as follows :—Four or five such lengths usually went to make a foot-line of 4 or 5 feet long. Fine double swivels were placed at each end and in the centre. These were attached to the gut-links by the latter being simply drawn through the eyes of the former, the points of the protruded link being thinned a little with the knife, turned down on the main link, and then carefully lapped with silk rubbed well with shoemaker's wax ; the union of the other ends of the **lengths** or links of gut was by a single water-knot, the waste ends of the gut being trimmed and neatly tied down as in the case of the swivels. The double water-knot on twisted gut makes clumsy work, and should be avoided if possible. The single gut foot-line is made up precisely in the same way, except that here **the** double knot may be employed. We have then a foot-line, single or treble as the case may be, the upper end attachable to the fishing-line by the eye of the swivel there and a suitable knot of the line, in making which caution is required. To the other end of the foot-line is to be attached the single link of gut carrying the hook and bait, which is next to be described. This separate link should be in all cases of the very best gut, and always single. To one end of it was attached a single hook of lake-fly size, or smaller, used for salmon-flies. It was also some-times called a drake-hook, somewhat larger than those used for common lake-flies. At the other end was knotted a longish loop, by which it was readily united to, or disunited from, the lower swivel. One small but indispensable item was to be added to the finished foot-line—the weight. This was generally composed of a swan-drop or two, or a single buck-shot, cut nearly in half, and squeezed fast on the upper third of the length of the foot-line. The shops sold an article made for the purpose, but it was apt to become entangled in weeds and stones on a foul bottom. The precise weight of the lead can of course be only determined by actual experiment—the quality of line, hook, swivels, etc., used, influencing the amount of weight required. It is of importance, however, that the adjustment be nicely effected, otherwise the loach may float too high or run too near the bottom to attract the attention of the fish. One operation more —the attachment of the loach to the hook—and the mount is complete. **This was** effected in various ways. I shall describe but one of them : the hook in this method was simply introduced into the mouth of the loach, carried down superficially in the flesh of the little animal along the mesial line **of** its side, as if putting on a common worm, and the point made to protrude as far as the bend, at a little less than two-thirds of the whole length of the bait from the head. Making the whole straight, a bit of fine waxed silk was knotted round the nose of the little creature, **then** knotted round the gut of the link, and the job **was** completed. **Two and** sometimes three small hooks were employed, but they were found more complex and less efficient in practice than the single hook. The season for this description of fishing presents an extensive range for selection. One of the largest fishings with the loach which I recollect to have seen made, was about the middle of February. Eleven fish, from 3 to 7 lbs., were taken by one rod ; but it was a gratuitous and perhaps unjustifiable slaughter, the fish not having entirely recovered from spawning, and being of inferior quality. The season may therefore be considered to extend from March to September inclusive. On any day during this period, calm or stormy, overcast or even moderately bright, this kind of fishing can be practised with success. There is **no** variation of weather within the period stated, in which I have not seen it successful. But **anglers who** were not mere poachers seldom resorted to it except when fly-fishing was impracticable. Amongst the former there was an impression, and one I know to be well founded, that the large and breeding trout of any lake may be injuriously diminished by the practice ; and the fly-fishing properties of the water thereby considerably reduced. It was then in fact considered not reputable, and a proof of ignorance of the art, for any respectable angler **to put out** a loach when trout were to be caught by flies. It was therefore only in the intervals, when flies could not be employed, that the legitimate angler had recourse to the loach. And these intervals were not only the best, but the most agreeable, for the practice. A fine calm summer or autumn evening from three or four o'clock to nine or ten, may be assumed as the appropriate time for loach-trolling. From the mode of mounting the bait on the hook, it will doubtless have been inferred that its vitality was neither likely nor essential. It will also have been understood, though but incidentally stated in the preceding remarks, that this kind of fishing was exclusively conducted through the medium of a boat. Wading, casting, spinning, or

shore-fishing there was none in this case. A boat
alone could adequately command and reach **the**
favourite haunts of the fish sought for. Two rods
may be conveniently worked from the same craft :
but I will take it for granted that there is but one
to be used ; and that the angler, single-handed, is
launched into deep water, with **the tackle** described, to
row, fish, and land his trout. Giving a few smart strokes
with the oars in the direction to **be** taken, the boat
receives sufficient momentum to give time for letting
out the bait and a portion of the line. This operation is
repeated till about forty yards of **line** are drawn off
the reel. This length of line will be generally found
sufficient ; **but is of** course subject to **variations**
according to **the depth of** the water and other cir-
cumstances.   The rod is next carefully stretched in
the boat on the right-hand side of the angler, with
the point projecting some five or six **feet**, as the case
may be, beyond the stern of the boat. Care should
also be taken that nothing impedes the free revolution of the handle of the reel when called into action.
The loss of bait, hook, and a large fish, may be con-
sequences **of** the neglect **of the** precaution. Nay,
the rod itself, if carelessly placed, may in such case
be jeopardised. The strength of the tackle, it should
be recollected, is not greater than its weakest part,
which in this instance is a single strand of gut ; and
the shock of the first charge of a hooked *ferox* or

fario, either of full growth, if not moderated by the action of a check-reel and the elasticity of the rod, may be greater than that weakest part is able to **resist.** To an angler acquainted with the subaqueous **topography** of a lake, no instructions as to where he **should** fish would be necessary. But the stranger, ignorant of this knowledge, would be on a level with a philosopher groping in the dark, or the mariner sailing without a compass. Neither can the best and fullest written directions ever compensate for the absence' of this information. Some few remarks, however, upon this obscure subject, and the proper trolling pace of the boat, may not be wholly useless. Around the shores **of a** great lake, and of its islands and sharps, if it contain these latter, there is a certain line or boundary at which, looking down perpendicularly from a boat, on a fine bright summer's day, light and darkness will be observed to stand face to face in well defined and fearful contrast. On one side are seen the sloping sides of the great basin **itself,** sleeping in sunshine ; **on** the other, nothing **but** the impenetrable wall with which darkness shrouds the mysteries **of its** depths. To follow this line as nearly as circumstances permit, should be the first object of the angler trolling for large trout. There are of course exceptions ; and in some lakes the central parts may be trolled with as much success as the shores. But in all such cases the depth of the water will be found not to be great. The rate at which the angler propels his craft should not be fast nor yet too slow. There is a happy mean which keeps the bait in its proper relation to the bottom, and which can only be learned by experience.

But ere theory has concluded its precepts, practice has stepped in to teach us something better.

The reel sounds the alarm; the rod "chucks" convulsively from butt to point; and before the oars can well be drawn in, old *ferox* has shot bolt-upright **out** of the water at fifty yards' distance, shaking his open jaws violently as if threatening his antagonist, but in reality struggling to disgorge bait and hook; and I am sorry to say for the amusement of the reader, has succeeded in his dodge and is gone. The line **lies** listlessly on the wave, the rod **has** recovered its wonted composure, the reel has ceased its enlivening click, and nought is heard save that **heavy** sigh with which the young angler meets the loss **of** his first chance.

But let him cheer up; he may have better luck next time. Life has many disappointments, and angling has its share. In fact, when, in either **fly-**fishing or trolling, a large fish thus works on the surface immediately he is struck, it is an inauspicious symptom, and there **is a** strong probability of his being imperfectly hooked. **The** line, however, must now be reeled in, and the bait, which will be generally found run **up** on the link of gut, is to be put in proper trim **if** not much damaged, and the whole paid out **as before.** Perhaps in rounding that point of land in the distance, or coasting the sheltered creek **beyond it,** you may meet one of *ferox's* blood relations **out** on **an** evening cruise for his supper. Ha !— there he goes ! and **at** lightning pace ! But be not over-anxious. **He** keeps to the bottom this time ; and is probably well entered for the race. You have **therefore only to sit** quietly **for** the present ; giving him yarn **enough,** but at the same time letting him **understand** by a certain strain of **the rod** and tackle, that angling is not exactly what it has been sarcastically **described :** " **A** worm at one end **of a** string, and a fool at **the other."** At the risk of coming under the latter denomination, permit not the line to wholly slacken ; **if** you do, *ferox* may not stretch it for you again. **After** a few more charges and as many sulky **huggings of** the bottom, **he will rise and** come near enough to reconnoitre the enemy's **resources ; but not liking** appearances, **and considering prudence the better half of** valour, he **will make a last** attempt to escape **difficulties** which **he begins to** feel him**self** unable **to overcome.** When he reluctantly re**turns again to the** light, you **will** probably observe his **gill-covers to** quiver, **and his** maxillaries to ex**pand more than** befits **a** subject at ease. Then **standing up, and** poising yourself steadily in the

centre of the craft, let the rod and landing-net move
in opposite directions ; and in quicker time than the
brain can give the word of command to the muscles,
let the translation of poor *ferox* to his last home be
a *fait accompli.*

Perform the honours of the occasion, I pray you,
gracefully—or, as sweet Will **says, "Do** your spirit-
ing gently." There are many **less poetic and pic-**
turesque sights than the vigorous young **angler**
standing, rod in hand, in his light skiff on the blue
unfathomed waters, skilfully performing the exciting
operation I have essayed unworthily **to describe.**
Some fair eye, too, interested in your success, may
be pressed to the telescope in **the** drawing-room
window of that snug box on the hill-side. Having
played your part well, you may expect, on your
return, to be complimented on **having** "won your
spurs," and claim the decoration **of** the Order of
ferox, **or the** *loach.*

E. N. M.

A PLEA FOR TOURISTS.

THE only disadvantage that we know of, following on the late enormous accessions to the brotherhood **of** the gentle craft, is that it **is** now extremely difficult **to** get a day's salmon-fishing in any part of the country. Once it was truly "the poor man's recreation ;" but that day has gone by, and in no part of the kingdom is it less practicable for a stranger to get a day's **sport than where** salmon rivers are most numerous and fish **most** abundant—namely, in the Highlands of Scotland.

The railway runs some two hundred and fifty miles north of Edinburgh : before the grilse season is at its height, **the heart of** Sutherland will be accessible by train, **and in that long stretch of country the** traveller **is scarcely ever out of** sight of **some noble** stream, **teeming with salmon.** But **how few are the stations** at which **he can pause with the assurance** that for a moderate **payment, or, indeed, for any pay-ment at all, he can have a day** or two's fishing with the **chance of taking** salmon **or** grilse. **Even** trout-fishing **is not** unfrequently refused, which is **a** mistake on the part **of** salmon-breeders, as there **is no** more

deadly foe to the ova and young fry than a lusty
yellow trout.   Happy they who can afford to keep a
snug box by a Highland river, and warn off intruders !
But may they be happier still—and with the memory of
former courtesies before us, we freely admit that there
are many such—who, having this power, have also
the heart to use it liberally ; who make glad the soul
of wandering fishermen in the north—men willing to
pay either in coin or gratitude for a day's sport,
though they cannot rent a river.

In the grilse season—in July and August—when
most folk love to go a-pleasuring, at least some parts
of these northern rivers might be made accessible to
the tourist without prejudice to the sport of the legitimate proprietor.   The fish are all on the move ; you
may see them in shoals rushing over the fords, and
sunning themselves in joyous leaps, as they plunge
into the deep water above.   Do you think they are
to stop there?   Not they.   On they go, further and
further every day, up the rapids, through the long
silvery pools, over the cataracts, into the narrow
glens among the birches, where the water is all white
with foam and the sound of its broken fall is inces-
sant.   There—the exuberance of their joy sated at
last—they "skulk" among the rocks in nooks and
crannies known only to themselves, impervious to the
wiles of the fisher, until the time arrives when they
proceed to the great business of their life, and the

law of the land throws over them its protective shield. But in those days of rapid ascent, what sport is open to the fisherman! With a "bit of a fresh" in the water, a stiff westerly wind blowing, the air as exhilarating as a dram, and tackle in order, these running fish will take as gaily as a kelt in spring, and there are plenty of them for all. The millionaire who rents a river, and who might throw open part of it to the fishing public on such terms as should prevent the water from being robbed, will naturally reserve the best pools ; he has thus the best chance of sport ; but every angler knows, or will come to learn, that with fresh-run grilse the chance amounts simply to that of coming over the fish when they are in a taking humour. They may be sullen in one pool and lively in the next : if they pass on scatheless the chance is gone, probably for ever. Last summer, in the month of July, there was a most opportune flood in the river which passes the writer's door. The grilse tasted it afar off, and instead of coasting along the shore as they usually do, with the certainty of falling into the traps of stake-net and bag-net fishers, they struck at once into the channel of the estuary, and bounded up stream like school-boys to their playground. Great was the sport while the "run" lasted. When it was at its height, a friend took an evening cast, and literally, as fast as he could land them, he laid on the green sward by the river's bank, eight splendid grilse from 7lbs. to 10lbs. each, and might have taken we do not know how many more, but that an accident put an end to his fishing for the time. The whole affair was over in less than two hours.

Now suppose such a piece of luck happening unexpectedly to a young Englishman, not overburdened with cash, who had gone to the Highlands for a month's excursion,—why, a thousand pounds in his pocket would not be equivalent to the gratification; years would not dim the recollection of it, his heart would beat warmly to the North every time he spoke of it; and, let us add, *per contra*, it might cost him a good many thousands before he saw the end of it; for, if fortune proved prosperous, a salmon river would never be far distant from the scene of his recreation. Clipping a salmon is like "taking the shilling;" it enlists you for life. Of course one does not take eight "fish"—Scotticè for salmon or grilse —every two hours one wields a rod; but it is hard to see the long swirling pools of a Highland river unoccupied day after day when the fish are taking, and when it would do no perceptible harm to the sport of the lessee if a tourist had leave to try his luck in some of the pools. Of the eight fish that we refer to, probably not one would have been in the same pool next morning, and they were but a small part of the shoal brought up by one tide to replenish the river.

The harm done by rod-fishing in a well-stocked river is quite infinitesimal.

It is a different matter when autumn begins to tint the leaves. Then fish enter the pools sedately, as **becomes the** " gravity " of their position. They have been probably kept hanging about the mouth **of the** river, waiting for a fresh flow of water, until their sides have become tinged with gold instead of silver. If veterans, they advance cautiously, not caring **to** seek the surface **in** the glare **of** day. **They** select the big pools **to** rest in, and the near fords for spawning. To catch a fish that has "potted" (to use **a technical** phrase), the fisherman must exert his utmost skill, and we **cannot** blame the proprietor, who, at that season, preserves his pools undisturbed. But with fresh-run grilse it is quite different ; they are almost like birds of passage on their flight—if not shot in Kent to-day, they will be over the border to-morrow ; and if it be so, as, with some experience of what is pre-eminently a grilse **river, we believe it is, surely it** is not pressing an unreasonable request upon **owners** and lessees of Highland rivers, to ask some little more freedom for strangers than they have now in the matter of fishing. It is **not** a small privilege to be able to give legitimate pleasure to one's neighbours ; and Highland gentlemen have a character to support for more than common hospitality. A " Highland welcome" has become proverbial throughout the land, and we hope that, within reasonable bounds, it may hereafter include access to **salmon** rivers in those quarters which are accessible to tourists. Englishmen who rent Northern rivers will **also,** we hope, look favourably on the case of their countrymen who long to know the pleasures of running a fish, and may have the opportunity of obtaining it only once or twice in a lifetime.

W. C.

A SEASIDE YARN.

"SMASHED everything and gone, by Jove!" "Yes, Major, and so they allers will, if so be as you tries on that 'haul devil, pull baker' sort of game with big bass. Fishes ain't hosses by no manner of means, leastways they won't be sarved as sich." Such was the exclamation of my hasty fishing companion, the Major, and such the stricture passed on his misfortunes by old Bob, our boatman; and Bob was right. Fish are not " hosses," notwithstanding the laborious efforts made by so many of their would-be captors to treat them as if they were. Few sea-fish there are, perhaps, more generally misunderstood and coarsely fished for than bass, and few are there with whose habits I am acquainted that feed so differently according to the position and circumstances under which they are placed, thus affording a wide scope for the skill, ingenuity, and research of the fisherman, who shall, if he pleases, accompany me on a short voyage, and peep, Asmodeus-like, at the bass " taking his divarsions " **in** his own sea-garden, and **lend a hand** at ensnaring him.

Let us then, drift quietly away, with the flowing

tide, to one of those old sunken hulks, so **much** like Noah's Arks retired from business, beneath whose submerged timbers lie crag and rugged ledge, gorgeous with many an animal and vegetable wonder. Upward like giant flag and rush stream the fronds **of** the *Laminaria digitata* and countless whip-like lashes **of the** *Chorda filum ;* whilst **groups of** corallines and algæ glitter about like brilliants in **a** sapphire setting. Here too, amongst the secret crannies of the soddened oak, might be seen, **if we could look** close enough, creeping annelids, little lurking gobies, and other pigmy **haunters of** submerged leviathans. Tiny crabs, shrimps, and other crustaceans scramble in and out, through what was once the window of **a** **state** cabin ; whilst clusters of mussels, and whole **beds of serpeda and balanus,** grow everywhere around.

Here, then, is one of the chosen hunting-grounds of the bass, and here we **will watch him** engaged in what is to him the main business of life—the chase ; thrusting his strong nose by a **sudden** upward dart into the tufts of weed, and then by a sweep of the tail, retreating on winnowing fin ready **to** pounce **on the dislodged prey.** Catching him when thus engaged is by no means as easy as it looks, but may be thus attempted :—A strong rod of average length (almost **any** strong rod will answer the purpose), fitted with a large winch, having plenty of fine strong prepared line on it, should be used. To this append a six-foot trace of strong twisted gut, armed with two No. 3 Limerick trout-hooks, after the manner of a common paternoster; with a sinker or lead at the end, light enough to be carried by the run of the tide well under the hulk, but of sufficient weight to keep your line tight.

Bait with a small fish, such as a sand-launce, smelt, or sprat, or in lieu of these a strip of cuttle-fish; a couple of large mud-worms, which will be found figured in my little work, *Sea-Fish, and how to catch them;* or a strong strip of pilchard gut, hooked by the hard end. These tempting morsels should then be allowed to sink away, quietly carried by the run down which you are fishing until well among the bass, then by a series of short "lifts" bring your bait back again; when, if fortune favours, and the fish prove a large one, some little care and management will be needed. Bear well in mind that fish are not "hosses," or you will come to grief to a certainty. Keep **the** top of your rod well up, and don't give an inch of line unless it is *taken.* A wide strong landing-net is far better than a gaff for this kind of sport, and it should be always at hand. Large polluck, and a variety of other fish, are taken when fishing in this way; and here perhaps a few words touching the question of the superiority of fine over coarse tackle may not come amiss before pro-

ceeding to other branches of our subject. I broadly
assert then, as I have elsewhere expressed it, that
" the finer the tackle is, consistently with the requisite strength to hold the fish, the greater will be
the chance of testing its powers."   Fine tackle is not
necessarily weak tackle, neither is a straw band of a
goodly size as strong as a small wire rope.   Some of
my readers will no doubt remember a most amusing
account of an experimental fishing-match by my
friend, Mr. Frank Buckland—" Fine *versus* Coarse
Tackle," which appeared in the columns of *The
Field*, I think last August—champion knights, Mr.
Cholmondeley Pennell, fine gut paternoster, dressed
silk line, and jack-rod : Mr. Frank Buckland, ordinary coarse tackle and hand-line ; " Robinson Crusoe,"
ditto.   The results were, as our friends who find
" Jordan such a hard **road to travel**," would say, " the
tallest kind of caution ;"—the knight of the jack-rod
and gut-line being triumphantly victorious, *and
beating both his antagonists, together with the united
crews of two boats anchored near them, out of the
lists !*

A little contest of a somewhat similar kind which
I once watched the result of, amused me much at the
time, and may be worth referring to here.   During
one of my hunting rambles in the East, I was, rifle in
hand, forcing my way through a belt of tangled vines
and underwood, **on** the banks of one of those large

but comparatively unknown rivers, which serve to minister to the mighty giant streams in whose floods their waters and names are together swept away. It was morning, and the sharp call of the jungle-cock **and cry** of the pea-fowl sounded shrilly from the depths of the forest, whilst the wheetle-wheetling and chirping of myriads of tiny creatures called into activity and insect bustle by the rays of coming day came up from amongst the tufted yellow reeds and feathery grass. **Just** at the point at which I broke cover, the river, after thundering over a high ledge, took a sharp turn round **a** huge pile of black rock, and then, with a wide sweeping eddy, formed as glorious a pool as the most exacting of fly-fishers ever waved wand over. But, alas! no lordly salmon, or agile speckled trout, leaps here. What those unknown depths contain, who shall say? Alligators probably, and what besides I fancy few would care to dive for the purpose of ascertaining. Just by the shoulder of the rock, under the shade of some trailing plants, sat or rather perched some half-dozen dusky " gentry of the neighbourhood," whose united **tailors'** bills would have barely paid turnpike for a walking-stick, each on his own particular stone, much like some of the grotesque figures the Japanese delight in representing fishing. After the first start of astonishment at my sudden appearance on the scene of action, friendly relations were at once established, and I had

an opportunity of investigating their sporting operations. The lines, with one exception, were composed
of grass cord, which was exceedingly strong, and
about the size of ordinary whip-cord; the hooks, of
European make, of the description we use for eel-
lines; the sinker, a small heavy pebble with a hole
in it; the bait, a flat ugly little worm, not unlike a
juvenile centipede. There was but one rod, which
was owned by the possessor of the exceptional line,
who was about as ill-looking an old ruffian, grizzled
and mummy-like, as you would find in a long day's
march, even through an Indian country—and that
is saying a great deal. A very few minutes passed
before I had examined his gear, overhauled his
catch, patted **him on the** back, and pronounced
him in my own mind a master hand, which during
the couple of hours I passed in his company he
fully proved himself to be. **His line** was, I think,
of pine-apple fibre, or something very like it, beautifully twisted, very little stouter than salmon-gut, a
large even coil of which was placed in a gourd shell
at his feet; the sinker, a single buck shot; the
hook, the same pattern as the others, but covered
with some kind of hard varnish, and sharpened at
the point like a needle. The rod was a shoot from
a tough shrub, about six feet long, and of very light
proportions; this was ingeniously looped by each end
to the line, forming, so to speak, a mere continuation

of it. On a fish biting, being struck, and making
a rush, the stick was instantly cast into the water,
where it acted as a float, the line was allowed to run
out from the gourd, and the scaly victim dexterously
humoured, until pitched high and dry on the sand
by the nimble fingers of this ill-favoured but artful
old nigger, who managed to catch more than all the
rest put together. "So much for fine tackle!" said
I. The greater number of fish caught appeared to
be a species of barbel, of very fair size and condition.

The mouths of rivers, open beaches, and sand-bars,
are favourite resorts of the bass, where, feeding in
with the coming tide, at times barely covered by the
creaming surf, he may be successfully fished for with
rod and "ledger," "hand-line," or "ground-bolter."
Spoon-bait trolling may also at times be practised,
with considerable success, near his haunts, particularly
in the evening, when bass are most disposed to feed.

A rising tide is by far the best for sea-fishing.
Each feathered roller of the young flood, as it thunders
on the strand, tolls the dinner-bell of our scaly gourmands the fish, and in they come accordingly.
Curious it is to watch the extreme state of bustle,
wriggle, and hungry activity that this same flood-tide
brings with it. Our submarine acquaintances have
evidently decided, one and all, that "the good time
coming, boys" is, on this occasion at least, in the present and not the future tense, and as the first inward

rush eddies round the stony pools, cunning old crabs, of acquisitive but unsociable habits, bolt from their hiding-places like misers out for a holiday. Prawns and shrimps sail about "promiscuously," making their appearance as **if** by enchantment from the deep clefts into which they retired as the tide went out. Myriads of tiny mouths **and star-like** discs open, and the flowing water is filled with waving arms and fringed legs. Now will be the **time** for us to enjoy a few hours' sport, at anchor **on some good** set of "marks" laid down from former observation. And here let me give a word of advice. Mark **well** fruitful spots by conspicuous objects, such as rocks, headlands, or buildings on the shore, noting **the** season and state of tide when good takes are secured. **A** great variety of fish **may** be taken when fishing from a boat anchored **on good** ground, and as a number of modes may be had recourse to at **the** same time for ensnaring them, much variety and amusement are often the result.

Some diversity of opinion **prevails as** to the particular strength and arrangement **of the tackle** requisite. As already stated, however, **I** have generally found salmon-gut strong **enough to** hold **anything** in reason, **provided a** landing-net **is** used. When there are not too many **in the** boat, a short stiff **rod,** fine prepared line, and strong gut paternoster mounted with hooks No. 2 Kirby trout-pattern, will be found in tolerably skilful hands as destructive an engine as can be well devised. In using it the great point is never to let the line *slacken*—indeed the point of the rod should always be kept a little bent by the strain on the lead. When fish of moderate size are hooked, the line should not be reeled up but drawn in from below the first ring above the winch by the hand, keeping the rod well up. The weight of the sinker must be proportioned to the current of the stream and depth of tide running, and different depths should be tried if the fish cease biting as the tide rises. " Chop-stick lines" are also used for boat fishing.

Without any comparison, the best bait for all small fish, as generally fished for on our coasts, is, in my opinion, the mud-worm (*Syllis monilaris*). These should be kept in water-tight wooden boxes, lined with pitch, which may be easily run into the seams with a hot iron. The ordinary puzzle-box shape is best, and the sliding cover must have a few small air-holes made in it. Clean sea-water, just sufficient to cover the worms, should be poured into the box every day, after thoroughly cleansing it, and removing every dead and injured worm. A little bit of wood nailed under one end of the box, so as to raise it about an inch, will be found advantageous, as it will keep the water always at one end, and enable the worms to crawl high and dry if they think proper,

thus prolonging their lives and improving their quality as bait. In the absence of worms, strips of cuttle-
fish, or small portions of any other fish, may be used.
When fishing at anchor, it is well at all times to lay
out one or more float-lines (*i.e.* without any sinker);
these should be composed of fine prepared line
mounted with yard traces of strong salmon-gut and
one No. 5 Limerick trout-pattern hook each. This,
baited with a "lask" or strip, cut from **the tail of a**
mackerel, should be allowed to drift away with the
stream to some considerable distance from the **boat**.
The inner end may be conveniently held by **one of**
the cane "gunwale blocks," described in my little
work, *Sea-Fish, and how to catch them*. In fitting
all my sea-lines, large or small, a brass swivel at the
union of the trace and line is never omitted ; an arrangement which I can strongly recommend. To the
allurements of ground-bait sea-fish are by no means
indifferent ; and to its enticements many **a** scaly
victim owes his fall, or rather rise. It **is** to be prepared thus :—A piece of old worn-out fishing-net
must be procured—say of about three feet square.
Into this put all the fresh fish offal, refuse bait, etc.,
you can get, provided that the net will hold it ; mix
this with about a gallon of bran, and beat them well
together with a stout stick ; put a heavy stone in **the**
middle, tie it up after the fashion of a dumpling
compounded with a view to tickling the gustatory

nerves of an ogre, and sink it by a piece of line to within three feet of the bottom, and be assured your trouble will not be thrown away. I remember some few years ago, when visiting the island of St. Helena, having great sport with the mackerel, which are at times to be taken there in large quantities, provided the proper method is pursued. Whilst busily occupied in (on this occasion) my by-no-means-profitable piscatory operations, a canoe-like boat, paddled by a perfect specimen of a "coast of Guinea nigger," made its appearance under the stern, and I was addressed as follows : "Suppose massa wants for catch um fish, an Massa Teward gib um plenty biscuit-dust an lilly bit ob pork, massa come along ob me, plenty catch um berry soon." Right welcome was my sable friend, "a man and a brother." Massa Teward was found equal to the occasion for once. Pork and biscuit-dust were procured, embarked, and we started. After paddling about half-a-mile from the ship the tail end of an eddy or run was reached, and the canoe was anchored by letting go a heavy stone at the end of a rope made fast to the midship thwart. The gunwale was thus brought down almost to the water's edge, a proceeding rather unpleasantly suggestive of sharks, which at times, to quote from a bucolic friend, "show in this district a capacity for feeding and increase of bulk perfectly amazing." My sable gondolier produced from some secret nook four lines, composed of fine strong thread, each **mounted** with three hooks of small size; these **were respectively** baited with a **strip** of pork rind. The biscuit-dust was thrown **over, and allowed to float** (a small portion at a time) away **with** the stream. In less than ten minutes the **surface for a** space of fifty **yards** was covered **with mackerel, all head** to stream, **darting** here and **there at every** fragment as it floated by, and **like** Oliver "asking **for** more." No Mosaic law **in**fluenced these fish of **sunny** seas. Two and **three at** a time **in they** came, fluttering with stiff **fins** and ultramarine tints, as mackerel alone can, until from sheer weariness I cried "Hold, enough," and indeed **we could not well** have held **many more.** I lighted **my old black pipe,** the cherished (and still spared) **comrade of many a ramble** and scramble by flood and through **forest, and with the** gurgling water rushing under the canoe, and **the lip-lap of the** current making dreamy music as it fleeted by **our** smooth sides, yielded myself to the guidance of my sable oarsman, until the hoarse challenge, "**What boat** is that?" and the dark loom **of my ocean home, called me** abruptly back from dreamland to waking realities.

W. B. I.

A STREAM IN ARDEN.

I SING a stream in Arden.   It might be
The selfsame stream, to which our Shakespeare led
His melancholy Jacques, and eased his soul
With contemplation,—for the feathery boughs
Of immemorial trees droop o'er its course,
And shed their pensive shadows on its sward.

On moorland levels, 'mongst the purple heather
And golden gorse, my brooklet hath its birth.
It bubbles into life and song together—
Crows, purls, and prattles to its reeds and ferns,
Then gambols down the vale, and frisks along,
Full of fair changes and fine fantasies,
And pretty breaks of temper,—now a pool,
Clear, calm, a mirror for the clouds and stars,—
Now a sharp shallow, rattling o'er the rocks,—
Now fairy cascades, passion-white with foam,—
And now a stream, careering, strong and steady,
As with a foretaste of the open seas.

The pastures love my brook, and press it close,

With velvet cincture, and the hoary hills,
Though clov'n in the midst to let it pass, and smit
As with a Parthian arrow, silver-barbed,
Toss their green tops with joy at sight of it,
And whisper a *non dolet* to the winds.

And I, the angler, love it well, and croon
Its praises in spontaneous undertones,
What time I pace its paths at summer dawn
'Ere yet the morning star hath left the sky,
And all the world is young; or else, at eve,
My pastime o'er, when through its leafy roof
The sunset glory shimmers, and the trout
Dimple the violet water with their rings.
Oh! then old dreams beset me, and I sink
Silent, in some green hiding-place, and hear
Dryad with Hamadryad hold discourse,
Naiad with Naiad, pagan dreams, with dreams
Of later superstitions interfused,
Kelpy and Kobold, till the rose and pearl
Fade, languish—till a solemn hush descends
From starry heavens, and sudden o'er the hills
Rises, familiar, the full harvest moon.

T. W.

ETYMOLOGY OF BAIT & ENTOMOLOGY OF MAY-FLIES AND STONE-FLIES.

BAIT.

Not the least important, and certainly the most widely-extended subject **falling under** the legitimate cognisance of the fisherman, is comprised in the small **word of four letters that heads this** chapter. The whole practice of "fysshinge with an angle," as Dame Juliana Berners, our **earliest** piscatorial authoress, **terms** the gentle art, is founded on the expressive word *Bait*. As well might we go **to the** mart without money, **to** the camp without **courage, to the court** without courtesy, as to lake or river without **bait. He who** might be simple enough to do so would truly " be in **very like case to the** gentleman angler, that goeth to the river for his pleasure, **and** returneth **home lightly laden at** his leisure," **as so** described by **Mr. Thomas** Barker in his **fishing** treatise entitled *The Delight*, published **more than two** hundred **years ago. At** *Banco Regis* **a man may,** it is said, sue *in forma pauperis*, **but** it **is utterly useless to go** empty-handed to the bank **of** the river ; the fishy nation are, in more senses than one, a scaly set, and obstinately refuse to render any assistance towards filling the fisherman's basket, without at least the proffer of a comestible bribe.

According to the *Diversions of Purley*, the word "bait," in itself, is simply the past participle of the verb to bite. We offer a bait to the fish, which in turn bites it, thus denoting the acceptance of a line of invitation to dinner, not indeed to eat, but like Polonius to be eaten. It is the ancient and often repeated case of the biter bitten, daily occurring on land as well as in the water, and causing old Guillim, the herald, shrewdly to observe that there are many more fishers in the world than are members of the Worshipful Company of Fishermen. " A man," says the moody-minded Prince of Denmark " may fish with a worm that hath eat of a king, and eat of a fish that fed of that worm." Shakespeare, by the way, shows himself to be as familiar with the pleasant sport of fishing, as he was with almost everything else, frequently making direct and metaphorical allusions to it. Claudio, in *Much Ado about Nothing*, says : " Bait the hook well, this fish will bite ;" and in *Measure for Measure* we may read—

> " O cunning enemy, that to catch a saint,
>   With saints doth bait thy hook ! most dangerous
>   Is that temptation that doth goad us on
>   To sin in loving virtue."

Milton, **too,** uses the word in a similar sense, when speaking of

> " Fruit like that
> Which grew in Paradise, the bait of Eve
> **U**sed by the tempter."

This last quotation, sad to say, has most probably given rise to the assertion made by some irreverent reprobate, that Satan was the **first** fisher ! **What** would good old **Izaak** Walton have said, if he had found the following **lines inscribed on the window of** his favourite hostelry, Bleak **Hall,** after passing a night in the **ever** memorable " fresh sheets **smelling** of lavender ?"—

> " **When Eve** and Adam lived in peace,
>   *Sans* either brawl or jangling,
>   The Serpent, from his brimstone den,
>   Thought he would go an angling ;
>   He baited his hook, with fiendish look,
>   Says he, This **will entangle her—**
>   And **so, my** friends, **you all may see**
>   **The Devil was the** first angler."

The Honourable Robert **Boyle, in** his *Occasional Reflections,* improves, as some people would say, upon the idea, thus :—" As the Apostles were fishers of **men, in a** good sense, so their and our grand Adversary is a skilful fisher of men, in a bad sense, and too often, **in** his attempts to cheat fond mortals, meets **with a** success as great and easy. Certainly that tempter, as the Scripture calls him, does sadly delude us, even when we rise **at his best baits,** and, as it were, his **true flies."**

Horne Tooke's derivation of bait from **bite is supported by** the **well-known use of** the **word to** signify a refreshment, taken either by **a** horse or man when travelling, thus alluded to by Spencer :—

> **" The Sun,** that measures heaven all **day long,**
> **At night doth bait his** steeds the **ocean waves among."**

A local joke in connection with the word is attached **to** the saddle-making town of Burford, in Oxfordshire, not unknown to the fisherman, from its position **on the trouting river** Windrush. **The common phrase, " a Burford** bait," however, does not **imply a light repast to stay the** stomach, as quaint old Fuller informs us, but one **to** lose the wits thereby, and resolve at last into **drunkenness.**

Bait, in short, consists of the **animal or vegetable** substances that generally form **the food** of fishes, or the artificial representations of **such substances.** Fly-fishing, by the use of natural or artificial insects for bait, being almost universally conceded to be **the** highest branch of the art, and this month being remarkable **as the** one in which **the** May-fly, the most notable of all insect baits, springs into its short-lived existence, the first portion of this paper may not inappropriately be devoted to so far-famed a bait, famous not only in itself, but also as the representative type of a host of others, **all well** known **to** fishermen and entomologists, still not so well **known as they might** be.

May-Flies.

Fishermen generally believe that the May-fly, the *Ephemera vulgata* of naturalists, is represented **by two** individuals, respectively termed the green drake and the grey drake, the one being the male **the other** the female of the same species **of insect.** This is an error, though a very natural one, under the circumstances. The writer, being both fisherman and entomologist, would like to bridge over the gulf formed by this difference in opinion, and there could scarcely be a more eligible place for setting such a question on its true basis, for probably the first time, than in these pages, devoted alike to natural history and fishing.

For considering this subject minutely, no apology need be requisite ; it has been well said that

> " Each crawling insect holds a rank,
> Important in the plan of Him, who formed
> This scale of beings ; a rank which, lost,
> Would break the chain, and leave behind a gap,
> Which nature's self would rue."

The remarkable metamorphoses undergone by many of the insect tribes are generally known to the most unobservant. There is, however, a peculiar feature connected with the last change of the May-fly tribe, unparalleled in the history of any other insect, that compels a kind of recapitulation of insect phases, before it can either **be properly** explained or understood. Take a butterfly, then, **for** instance, and **we** first find the insect in the form of an egg. This, when hatched into life, becomes a caterpillar, scientifically termed larva, from a Latin word signifying a mask; Linnæus, the bestower of the name, knowing that in the crawling caterpillar were masked or concealed the full-winged glories of the future butterfly. In this state the insect remains a longer or shorter time, till at last, ceasing to eat or move, it fixes itself in **some** obscure corner. A kind of skin then spreads over its body, enclosing it like a mummy, or as babies **used to** be swaddled **in folds of cloth**; from which circumstance it is now called pupa, from a Latin word signifying an infant. Some pupæ, having a golden colour, were anciently termed chrysalides, from a Greek word having a similar signification; and thus it is that the pupa of a lepidopterous or butterfly insect, whatever its colour may be, is most generally termed a chrysalis in England at the present period. After remaining **in the** chrysalis or pupa state for a **certain time, the** enclosed **creature,** becoming **mature** in all its parts, bursts its swaddling bands, and shows itself to the light of **day a complete** winged insect in its ultimate state of perfection; this last is called its imago state. **Thus, as** we follow it from the egg, we perceive that it successively lays aside its mask and throws off its bonds of pupilage ; consequently, **being no longer** disguised, confined, or imperfect, **it becomes the** imago, literally speaking, the **image and true** representative of its class and species. Though the word metamorphoses has been **already** mentioned here to designate these changes of form **and nature, it was** merely used in accordance **with the popular** mode of expression; for these are not metamorphoses or transformations, in **the true sense** of the word, but merely **a series of embryonic** developments. Many animals, much **higher in the scale of creation than** insects, pass through as strange a series.

The general analogy existing between **the trans-** formations of some insects, and the life, death, and resurrection of man, has been most happily treated by the late Rev. Mr. Kirby, in his delightful *Intro- duction to Entomology.* The subject is rather, perhaps, beyond the scope of this article, still **it may** just **be** noticed, *en passant,* that **the ancient fable of " Cupid and Psyche"** seems evidently to have been constructed **on** the same foundation. The word Psyche, **in** Greek, signified not alone the human soul, but also a butter- fly, **and** in painting and sculpture the material object **served** as the symbol of the immaterial. And even to the heathen mind nothing could, **in** a more forcible **or** familiar **manner, denote the** survival and freedom

of the soul after bodily death, than the representation **of** an animal which, first a voracious, unseemly, ground-crawling grub, next falls into a state of **complete** torpitude, and then, casting off its temporary slough, becomes a light, **lively,** beautiful winged creature of the air.

The May-fly passes through **a somewhat** similar series of developments to those **just** attributed to the lepidopterous insects, **but** with **the important** difference **that it undergoes an** additional **fourth** change, which they do not. Instead of **at once** springing from the pupa* to the imago **form, it** passes through a short intermediate stage, **termed by naturalists the** pseudimago, **or** false image, before **it attains** to the imago, **or** perfect insect. Hence arises the confusion between **fishermen** and entomologists on this question, the former **terming** the insect in its pseudimago state the green drake, **in its** imago state the grey drake, and, ignorant of the natural change that takes place, forming erroneous theories—such as the one being male, the other female, etc.—to account for the slight difference in hue presented by the insect in **these two** states. **Dr.** Hagen, in the *Entomologist's Annual* **for 1863,** says, **that** " Pictel first

---

* **The** pupa of the May-fly **does not assume** the torpid, mummified, swathed condition, **from which the name** is actually derived. It has limbs, can crawl and swim, but not fly, and thus comes under the class of pupæ termed semicompleta.

rendered the essential service of pointing out the characters **by which the** sub-imago (pseudimago) can be distinguished from the imago; they consist in the dull membrane of the wings, the presence of delicate fringes of hairs on the margin of the wings, **and the** distinct hair of the caudal filaments. The **form** of the sub-imago is analogous to that of the imago, but the caudal filaments and legs are shorter. The colouring often differs essentially ; **that of the body** is generally paler, with greyish **tinge;** that **of the** opaque wings is always darker, yellow, grey, or **even** blackish, but not **bright."** The structural differences referred to are shown **in** the illustration. To put **the** subject in its simplest and clearest form, **it may be** tabulated thus :—

ENTOMOLOGIST.	FISHERMAN.
Ephemera vulgata (pseudimago) **(1)** .	The Green Drake (3).
Ephemera vulgata (imago) (2) . .	**The** Grey Drake.

The May-fly **belongs to the class of** insects known to entomologists as the Ephemeridæ, **the name derived from** a Greek word **signifying diurnal—their short span of life, as perfect insects, seldom exceeding the** space **of a few hours.** Many readers must recollect Dr. **Franklin's** beautiful address, **alleged to** have been delivered **by** an aged ephemera, **that had lived** four hundred **and** twenty minutes, **as one of the** most profoundly humiliating lessons ever read to proud human **nature.**

Scarcely do any other genera of aquatic **insects furnish so** many baits for the fisherman. All the multitudinous varieties of "duns" and "spinners" belong to the Ephemeridæ, the former representing the pseudimago, and the latter the imago states ; and though of so short an individual existence, some one **or** other of the tribe may be found on the water from February to November. Whatever may be the time of day, or month of the year, whether the locality be north or south, the water river or lake, the fisherman cannot be far astray who has one specimen of a dun on his line, resembling of course in shape and colour the natural fly on the water. Ask a Scottish fly-fisher of long experience what fly in the course of **his life he** has caught most fish with, and, ten to one, he will answer, "the **hare-lug.**" To the same question **an Irish** fly-fisher **would** reply, "the ash-fox ;" both **being** representative types of a large sub-class of duns. All the Ephemeridæ are readily recognised by each species possessing what may popularly **be** termed a tail, consisting of three long hairs, or, as fishermen name these appendages, "the whisk."

To trace the Ephemeridæ *ab ovo*, the eggs are **dropped** into the water in such immense quantities **that** although they at once become the welcome prey of every kind of fish and aquatic insect, yet numbers escape to advance in due course of time to the larvæ **state, when** they, **in** turn, commence vigorously to devour **the eggs of** other insects and fish, thus maintaining the grand **cycle** of extinction and re-production which obtains over the whole wide domain of nature. The larvæ, being essentially aquatic animals, must be furnished with organs, analogous to the gills of fish, for the purpose of respiring the **sur-**rounding fluid. They are a series of fin-like fringed appendages, extending down each side of the abdomen, and by and in **these,** which are continually in motion, the air is decomposed or separated from the water, and conveyed through spiracles to the tracheæ. Besides the lateral appendages, the larvæ have three **pairs of** limbs on **the** forepart of the body, which **enable them to crawl and** swim about at pleasure. The pupæ differ little from the larvæ except in their larger size, and that in the more advanced state the future wings can be perceived carefully encased over the thorax. In no instance, as has been erroneously asserted by some writers on fishing, do any of the Ephemeridæ form a case **or caddis to** dwell in, as their neighbours the Phryganidæ or stone-flies do ; but, in both the larvæ and pupæ states, the Ephemeridæ **form holes** at the bottom and the sides of the stream, wherein they can avoid the too officious attentions of **their fishy friends.** The length **of** time **they** remain **in** these states is unknown, probably it extends from **one to two, or** even three years. At the period of their penultimate transformation, the pupa, **rising** to the surface of the water, almost instantaneously assumes the pseudimago or green drake form, and makes shift to fly to the bank, alighting on a bush, stone, rush-stem, or any appropriate object, not rejecting a man's hat or arm. The bathing-robe, if it may so be termed, is still upon the insect; the thin membranous pellicle, that protected its full dress from the water, still enfolds it. But, in a few seconds after alighting, the case seems to split up the centre, the wings are unfolded and drawn out of their covering as a lady takes off her glove, and the insect flies off in full bridal dress to seek its appointed mate. The aërial nuptials being consummated, the female drops in the water, lays her eggs, and dies from exhaustion, if not snapped up by bird or fish. The male hovers at a higher altitude over the water; being destitute of eggs, and inflated with air, the fish care little about him, and thus he obtains from the Oxfordshire anglers the opprobious epithet of bastard.

The astonishing number of Ephemeridæ that start into existence in the space of a few hours is almost incredible. Reaumur thus describes a scene of this kind he witnessed on the banks of the Marne:—

" The myriads of Ephemeræ which filled the air over the current of the river, and over the bank on which I stood, are neither to be expressed nor conceived. When the snow falls with the largest flakes, and with the least interval between

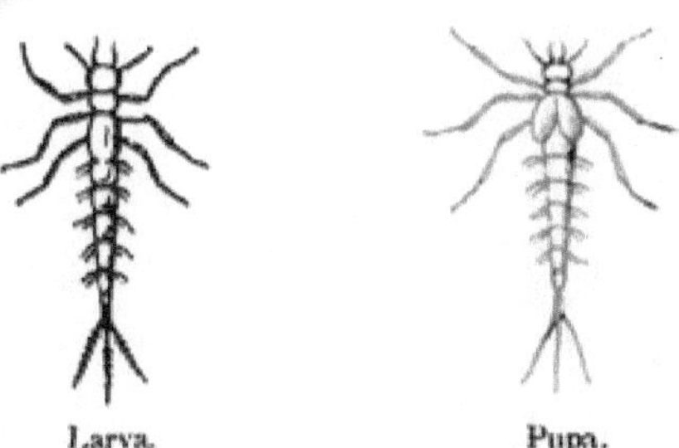

Larva.   Pupa.

Pseudimago.

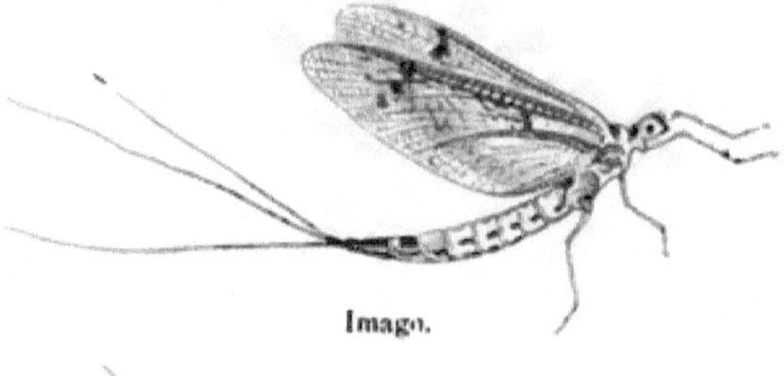

Imago.

The Green Drake.

them, the **air is not so filled as it** was around me with Ephemeræ ; scarcely had' I remained in one **place a** few minutes when the **step on** which I stood was quite **concealed** with a layer of **them from** two to four inches in depth. **Near the lowest step** a surface of water of five **or** six feet dimensions every way was entirely and thickly covered by **them, and** what the current carried off was continually **replaced. Many** times I was obliged to abandon my **station, not** being able to bear the shower of Ephemeræ, which, **falling** obliquely, struck every part of my face, filling **my eyes, mouth, and nostrils."**

The **writer once witnessed a very** similar scene in **England, when** passing **one morning in early** summer, a little after sunrise, along a path **not a** quarter **a mile** in length **on the** bank **of the** Thames between **Teddington Lock and** Kingston. The particular spot alluded to is bounded by the wall of Sir Byam Martin's grounds, and in that short distance the face, hat, **and** clothes were covered by the cast-off skins of Ephemeridæ. The myriads of insects in their full dress, gaily disporting **in the** beams of **the** morning **sun, and** the local associations of the **neighbourhood, for**cibly brought to the writer's recollection Pope's description of the sylphs in his inimitable *Rape of the Lock :—*

> " Some **to** the sun **their** insect wings unfold,
>   Waft on the breeze, **or** sink in clouds of gold ;
>   Transparent forms, too fine for mortal sight,
>   Their fluid bodies half dissolved in light ;
>   **Loose to** the wind their airy garments flew,
>   Thin glittering textures of the filmy **dew,**

> Dipped in the richest tincture of the skies,
> Where light disports in ever mingling dyes,
> While every beam new transient colours flings,
> Colours that change whene'er they move their wings."

A trout-stream with the May-fly on, as its brief season of existence is termed, is a remarkable sight not readily to be forgotten by any lover of nature. The hosts of insects springing into life, the luxurious trout sucking them down into the jaws of death, the circling swallows taking their share in the upper regions, and the rich quiet beauty of our English river-scenery forming, as it were, a frame of still-life to the busy picture. The May-fly affords the most nutritious and acceptable of all food for trout, imparting a rich flavour to the fish, as well as vigour and spirit to its muscular development ; thus rendering it more delicious on the table, more gamesome, gallant, and less easily conquered in the river. In local distribution the insect is limited and uncertain. It generally affects small streams and shady brooks, especially in the midland counties of England. It reigns over the Hampshire and Derbyshire rivers, it revels on the Middlesex Colne, but shuns the Surrey Wandle, and is seldom seen on the Axe. It generally avoids the English lakes, while the Westmeath lakes in Ireland derive their principal value as fishing-stations from this insect. It mostly makes its appearance on the water between, say, the 18th and

22d of May, and between the hours of 12 **and 3** o'clock **in the** day. The May-fly **is** readily recognised by its tail and mode of flight; it generally rises to about the height of six feet, beating the air rapidly with its wings, and then descends, its wings extended and motionless, the tail elevated reversely over the body, and the two lateral whisks separated so as to form right **angles with the central one.** It is from **this kind of curl** in the tail **that the** name of drake **has been** applied **to the insect**; for **the** same reason, in some counties, **it is called** the "tilt-up," the "cock-tail," and in Ireland **the** "caughlan."

The trout does not spring up to the May-fly as it does to other insects. Knowing that the fly will descend on the water's surface to deposit its eggs, the fish just watches its opportunity, and sucks the delicious morsel in as a man gulps down an oyster. For this reason artificial floating May-flies have been formed, and, when not too clumsy, **have proved killing** baits. The May-fly varies its tints of yellow in different localities, and it is generally as **well** for the fisherman to procure his artificial flies in the district where he may be fishing. There is **no** certain rule, however, for such matters; a river may be dotted with May-flies, the trout, probably sated, may reject any imitation of their favourite food, but eagerly snap at an artificial nondescript, **that** would puzzle a Westwood to assign it a local habitation and a name as a natural insect.

The natural May-fly is not unfrequently used for dibbing or daping, as it is termed, which is merely fishing on the surface of the water with a real fly. It is scarcely possible to fasten a natural fly on the hook so that it can be thrown like an artificial one, and consequently, where there is any space of water to cover, and a nice gentle breeze, recourse is had to what is called blowing the fly. A blow-line is formed of a very light, fine kind of floss silk, sufficiently strong for its purpose, and yet so light as to be susceptible to the influence of almost the softest zephyr. With **but a** light air, in the right direction, and a little judicious manipulation of the rod, **as** easy to be imagined as **described,** the angler manages **that the fly shall** fall softly as thistledown **on** the **desired spot,** where a trouty triton is observed eagerly swallowing down his insect dainties. The lure, if at all adroitly managed, seldom fails ; the fly is sucked in, a smart twitch fixes the well-tempered steel barb, and after a short struggle, the finny prey is successfully brought to bank. To bait a hook with the natural fly is **a** rather delicate operation, but, with care and dry fingers, it can readily be accomplished. **The** hook should be inserted under **one** wing, and the point brought out upwards between the two wings **on the** back. Two flies generally are **used,** placed on the hook tail **to** tail.

It is true that some enthusiastic fly-fishers denounce blowing the fly as a rather unsportsmanlike mode of angling ; when practised with an artificial fly it cannot well be defended on any grounds what-**ever** ; and in all rules for fishing clubs it ought to be forbidden. There is another mode of dibbing, however, free from any such objections, for which the natural May-fly answers admirably. It not unfrequently happens that a large trout takes up a position under the spreading branches of **a** tree, beneath **a** natural *chevaux-de-frise,* formed by a straggling evergreen thorn, or in some similar position, utterly unattainable by an artificial fly, though thrown by the deftest hand. Here, too, that large trout, the best in water, will remain till forcibly ejected by man, otter, or a stronger fish than itself ; and if the tenant of one of those acquatic castles be captured one day, the next best fish in the neighbourhood will be in full possession on the day after. Randal Holme had probably a fish of this description in his mind when he wrote, in his extraordinary *Academy of Armory,* that " trout are emblems of quiet, calm, and gentleness, such as love not to be in troubled waters, or to be tossed to and fro by the blustering of wicked and malevolent spirits, but rather live quiet at home, than enjoy abundance through labour and trouble." Whatever the trout may love, however, is beyond the question ; man likes **to** catch it, and the way to achieve a consummation so devoutly to be wished is as follows :—The position must be carefully reconnoitred from the opposite bank, or nearest point of vantage, and the most eligible spot for dropping a fly before the trout's nose carefully selected. If there should be no suitable opening for the rod, one can be made by a bill-hook, and another lower down to admit the protrusion of a landing-net may also be not disadvantageous ; and lest the fish should be unnecessarily alarmed, the openings may be made the day previous to that of action. A short stout rod and line are used for this purpose ; and the line, to avoid any obstruction or entanglement, should be lightly wound round the top of the rod. With the stealthy silence of a mole the **point of** the **rod** is pushed out through the opening, exactly over the trout's haunt, the line is gently unwound **by turning the rod** in the reverse manner to that in which it was wound on, and the fly suffered to light on the surface of the water as softly as the hand of a sacrilegious thief might glide into the pocket of a Lord Mayor. If the operator from his position cannot see the water, a person on the opposite bank, in view of the spot, can guide every movement by waving **his** hand either to the right or left, up or **down, as** these signals may have previously been agreed upon. **The result** is almost a certainty, the trout being speedily transformed into that form of flesh known in the United States as a gone coon. No delicacy must be used after the hook is once fixed ; the line, as previously mentioned, being strong, the fish's head must be held up to the top of the water ; play in such circumstances being out of the question, nothing but work, energetic work, can be allowed. A long-handled landing-net, adroitly slipped below the trout, removes all doubt of safety, and he is at once transferred to the basket. On a very wooded water, once in possession of the writer, a dish of fish could be ensured at almost any time during the season by this means.*

The keeper called it "circumventing 'em," and it differs little from what Mr. Kingsley, in his entertaining *Chalk Stream Studies*, terms "foxing." Whoever may try it successfully will no doubt agree with that reverend author and angler that there is a considerable amount of pleasurable excitement in "foxing a great fish."

Stone-Flies.

The class of insects known as the Phryganidæ, spring or stone flies, are, as bait, only second in importance to the Ephemeridæ or May-flies, while both genera are equally remarkable in their natural economy. The word "Phryganea" or "spring-fly" has little more actual reference to the history of the class than "Ephemera," for all the Phryganidæ are not peculiarly

* Using, **of** course, other insects when the May-fly was not on the water.

insects of the spring, any more than all the Ephemeridæ are limited to the existence of a single day.
The history of the Phryganidæ forms one of not the least
strange chapters among the manifold wonders of entomology. The mature female insect generally deposits
her eggs on the leaf of a tree overhanging the water.
Here the eggs are retained by a kind of glutinous
substance until hatched, when the larvæ, strange
little six-footed creatures, drop off into the water. **In**
this new element, each larva, prompted by the un-
erring instinct of nature, commences to collect around
it a case composed of parts of plants, leaves, pieces
of stick, small stones, sand, and even small fluviatile
shells with their living inmates. These materials are
collected and secured by loose threads of a glutinous
kind of silk spun from the mouth, as practised by
several caterpillars. **The larva** first collects a suf-
ficiency of materials before it attempts to enclose
itself, for it is obvious that the longer it builds, the
less constructive action it can maintain. A remarkable
instance of adaptation of materials is seen in those
cases constructed of small stones, of all shapes, full
of angles and irregularities, out of which the larva
forms a tube as straight, smooth, and uniform in the
inside as a gun-barrel. **Nor is this** all ; as the case
is a movable house, which the insect drags about at
will, the under surface must **be as smooth** and free
from projecting inequalities as the **inside. The larva,**

thus secured from fishy enemies, protrudes only its head and two rudimentary fore-legs out of its case, and so it can readily roam over the bottom of the water, seeking for its food. The case, it must be observed, has almost invariably a seeming irregularity about it, to the curious observer. If made of small stones, it will generally be perceived that a small piece of lighter material—wood, leaf, or bit of rush—is attached to it. Again, when constructed of lighter substances—such as pieces of wood, leaves, or aquatic plants—a stone or two will be found adhering to the structure. Though at first sight this seems a rather incongruous sort of architecture, where so much ingenuity is displayed, it can nevertheless be satisfactorily explained. The larva being of the same specific gravity as the water in which it lives, it follows, as a matter of course, that the case must be as nearly as possible of a similar weight. For if the case be heavier, the larva could not drag so weighty a house with it when roaming and feeding at the bottom of the water ; whilst, on the other hand, if the case should be lighter, it would raise the larva from the ground, to be carried away by the current. Thus our little hydrostatic engineer, if it finds its case too light, ballasts it with a stone or two, but if too heavy, instead of discomposing the case by throwing off ballast, the insect merely attaches a bit of wood or other light material, to give it the buoyancy required. **In** this state the larvæ of the Phryganidæ are the cadis, case-worms, or cad-bait of our old writers on angling. But, as the venerable Walton says, "to know these and their several kinds, and to know to what flies every particular cadis turns, and then how to use them, first as they be cadis, and after as they be flies, is an art, and an art that every one that professes to be an angler has not leisure to search over."

When the period arrives for the larva to assume the pupa state, it securely anchors itself to the bottom, and closes up the mouth of its case with a network of strong silk, leaving but a few apertures to admit a current of fresh water for the purpose of breathing, effected by the spiracles of the pupa; Reaumur having actually observed this network in motion, alternating from concave to convex, as the water passed out and in. After passing its due time in this state, the pupa, endowed with greater powers of motion than are possessed by any other incomplete pupa, with its stony mandibles cuts its way through the network, and leaving its case, throws off a filmy skin and becomes a fly. There are slight differences in the transformations of the many Phryganidæ. Thus the pupa of the *Phryganea grandis,* the stone-fly of fisher-men, leaving its case makes its way to the shore, and lives several days in an incomplete state before it becomes a fly. In this state it is the water-cricket or creeper of the north of England and Scottish fishermen. It lurks among stones till its wings be fully grown and it assumes the form of a perfect fly.

In this last state the stone-fly has a thick body, of about an inch in length, of a brown colour, with yellow markings underneath. It has four wings, which lie flat on the back, the two upper ones of a speckled grey, reticulated with darker coloured veins, folding back over the lower ones. It greatly resembles a moth, but its wings are not covered with the fine scales that give a powdery appearance to the lepidopterous tribe of insects. The cadis-flies are ranked in the order *Trichoptera*, and Mr. M'Lachlan, at a late meeting of the Entomological Society, described 124 British species, arranged in 43 genera. As an artificial fly the wings are formed by the matted feather of a hen pheasant. The body may be of almost any kind of a dark brown fur mixed with yellow camlet or mohair, so as to show the most yellow near the tail and belly of the fly. A grizzled hackle wrapped round under the wings affords a good imitation of the natural insect's legs. Two hairs from the whiskers of a black cat may be employed to represent the antennæ, but, considering the gut itself quite sufficient, the writer never uses them. The stone-fly has no whisk or caudal termination, as is erroneously depicted in Ronald's *Fly-Fisher's Entomology*, and in the edition of Walton's *Complete Angler* edited by Ephemera.

The natural **fly is used** for dibbing or daping, as I have already described in my observations **on the** May-fly. **And it** should **be** observed that **among** Scottish fishermen **the** stone-fly is almost invariably termed the **May-fly.** Stewart, **in his well-named** work, *The Practical Angler*, **falls into a curious error,** contending that the cadis-worm **is not** the larva of **the** stone-fly, **as** he has observed **the cadis** in rivers **as late** as the **month of August,** long **after the** last stone-fly has disappeared. **And so he** might, for besides the stone-fly, the Phryganidæ afford many other lures **for the use of** the fisherman ; **the** grannam **or** green-tail, **the** cinnamon-fly, the alder-fly, **the oak-fly,** the large **fetid** light brown, the silver horn, **and several others, all belong to this** interesting **class of insects.**

The creeper is a favourite bait in the north of England **and** Scotland. The author of a work called *The North Country Angler* endeavours to make us believe that he first discovered the insect, though it was correctly described by Cotton, under the local name of a jack, in the *Complete Angler.* It is by no means a fascinating creature ; Stewart says that it is " the most venomous-looking insect **that the** angler **in** pursuit of his vocation has to encounter." It runs **fast, moving with alternate** inflexions of the body, **that give it almost** a kind **of** serpentine character, **and** when taken **up for the** first time into tender hands, **its six** bifurcated legs tickle **the holder** so alarmingly, that it is frequently thrown **down with a** malediction that may be imagined better than related. It **is,** nevertheless, a famous bait, **both as regards the** quantity and quality of the fish **it** catches. **A** person may have threshed the same pools for **years** with the artificial fly, and never seen anything larger than half or three-quarter **pounders. When** lo! **the** creeper brings **out its one** and **two pounders, to the** great surprise **of the** fisher **who never** imagined that there **were such trout in the** water. I am alluding **particularly to the** many tributaries **of the** Tweed where the trout, though delightfully **plentiful,** generally run small—that is **to** say, small **in comparison to** those said to be caught **near Fairford,** where, according to a recent letter in *The Field,* **there** are none under three pounds, and these **only in a** certain season **of** the **year termed Tib's** Eve, which the learned **editor of** *Notes and Queries* explains to be neither **before Christmas nor after it. The** creeper is **baited by placing two on a largish-sized** hook, **and is fished in what is termed the sinking and drawing manner. The line** must be **short,** and worked very **gently, or the bait** will very **soon be** destroyed. The Scotch method of fishing **with the creeper** is much **superior,** as the bait lasts longer, and **the** fish **are hooked** with a greater certainty. Two **No. 7 or 8 hooks are** tied with yellow silk to the **same** piece of gut, **so** closely together, that **the barb of one** hook may be about half an inch distant from the barb of the other. The lower hook is put through the creeper crossways a little above the tail, and the upper hook is put through about the shoulder, according to the size of the creeper. The yellowest baits, and not the largest, are generally considered to be the most attractive. **A** short line is used, the bait thrown up stream, and allowed **to come** down gradually with the current. The creepers are or ought to be collected the evening before fishing, and an old powder-flask may be conveniently used for keeping them in, and **carrying** them to the river.

W. P.

"EARLY" & "LATE" SALMON RIVERS AND CLOSE SEASONS.

THE regulation of the fence months for salmon-fisheries has long been a difficult one to adjust in such a manner as to give general satisfaction, and it still continues to be a vexed question. Too many of those engaged in fishing seek to obtain what they conceive will be best suited to their individual interests, and do not consider the subject upon broad principles as affecting the general welfare. You find very frequently men whose knowledge of the habits of the salmon is so contracted that they are incapable of arriving at any sound conclusions, either with regard to the interests of the country at large or their own, and yet who are dogmatic to the last degree in giving their opinions ; you find others who may have extended their observations somewhat further, yet have not learned enough to escape the dangers which a "little knowledge" proverbially entails ; and again, a third class there are who assume a knowledge which is not their own, but borrowed—gathered up in scraps from others, and consequently superficial and worthless. **This is one of** the most troublesome elements in the **discussions which arise in** Parliament or elsewhere, **when the close and open** season **for** salmon-fishing is the **question to be settled.**

It was long since **determined by the** Parliaments **of** England, Scotland, and **Ireland, that salmon should not be** taken during a certain portion **of the year.** The first Salmon-Fishery Act **on the English** statute-book is the 13th Edward **I. No. 1, cap. 47.** It prohibits the taking of salmon "from the **nativity** of our Lady" (8th of September) "until **St. Martin's** day" (11th of November). Many Acts were subsequently passed. Power was given to magistrates **at** quarter-sessions **to fix close** seasons for **different** rivers, and the final result was as pretty a kettle **of fish** as could well **be desired. For the** Commissioners of 1860 found that there **was not one day** in the year on which, in some river or other throughout England, fishing was not **open! In** Ireland, **under** former legislation, interested persons induced Parliament to open the river Lee at Cork all the year round, because a good salmon, it was alleged, might be found **in it** any day **in** the year. In Scotland **the outrages** allowed **to be** perpetrated against the **unfortunate** Salmonidæ **were not quite so bad ;** however, **at one** time, and indeed **up to a recent** period, the fisheries opened on the 14th of December—and that was bad enough.

Having **thus glanced at** former legislation, **to** show what a **contrast it presents** to that of the present day, I would **call attention to the** fact, that although men's minds **have been** brought **to** agree to **much less varied limits in** close and open seasons—or rather to **concur in the** opinion that a longer close season **is in all** cases required **than** that before generally adopted—still there **is much** controversy and **a great** difficulty **in fixing periods which** will meet **with the** approval **of all, and it is now of** great importance that the close **and open season question should be** considered **attentively** and become **better understood.** With **the view of inducing those who may be in**terested **in the subject** to give it a more dispassionate and careful investigation, it has occurred **to me** that it may, perhaps, be of use to call attention briefly to a few facts which may possibly not be generally known.

The **time** then of the spawning of the salmon is to a **great** extent uniform. **In** no river does it **com**mence before October, **or** continue after February ; **this I state broadly. A few** very rare cases **may be found in which these limits are** exceeded, and I **once** took **a salmon in** June so full of far-advanced spawn, that **it poured** out of the fish when landed. **I have** also heard **of a few** fish spawning in September. But these are **the** exceptions that prove the rule. The fish *enter the rivers*, however, for the purpose of spawning at all seasons of the year ; and **the** fact should **be** borne in mind, that some, and those not a few, make the fresh water their habitation for the whole of the summer; the majority ascend in April, May, June, July, and August; whilst others remain again in the sea, and only enter the fresh water a few weeks, or it may be a few days, before they spawn. The object of this natural law, I think, is quite clear. It is intended that the fish should distribute themselves throughout the whole of the waters of the largest rivers, the upper as well as the lower; and this they will do, if not interfered with by man. The fish which ascend the earliest will choose their position in the deep pools or lakes on the higher reaches of the waters, and there be ready to take possession of the gravel beds in the vicinity when the time has arrived to sow their seed; whilst those which remain in the sea will, and always do, spawn on the lower beds. The earliest spawning is always the highest up; the latest the lowest down. In small rivers, without lakes or deep pools, the fish will not ascend at all until autumn approaches, having divined by a marvellous instinct that they would not find water enough in summer to shelter them. There is no such thing as "clean" newly-run fish with the roes scarcely developed to be found in December, January, and February, except in rivers connected with lakes, or large rivers and deep pools. Where those December and January fish have been captured in any considerable quantity, it has occurred only in places where there is a facility afforded for arresting their upward progress, and it is supposed that fish of this description frequent only those rivers; but I am strongly of opinion that they may be found to frequent all large rivers, especially where lakes exist, and that their supposed absence in some may be accounted for. In Scotland they have been taken in the cruives at Invershin where no fish could pass when the cruive was closed; and on the Thurso in the same way. In Ireland, at Waterville and Cara, with impassable cruives in the tidal-water at the mouth of the Cara, and on the Lann with stake and bag-nets; on the Liffey, where the fish were stopped by the Island Bridge weir; at Rathnuthin, Murrin, Brundronst, and some other places where the fish could not pass up, and could not fail to be taken in the cruives. In all these places lakes are in question, where the fish which ascend in November, December, and January, would remain and spawn in the adjacent streams, but not until the following autumn. Of this fact I have no doubt, from my own observations. The lessees of fisheries connected with some of those waters will tell you that spawning operations are all over before Christmas, and that therefore January may be opened without injury; but I have found this not to be the fact, as I have seen fish spawning on some of them in February when I went to look for them and see for myself. The lessees of **the Shin** and Thurso fisheries in Scotland will tell **you that the** clean-run December and January fish are **barren** and never **will** spawn, but they will admit that the same description of fish which ascend in February will spawn the following October.

The following is an extract from the *Angler-Naturalist,* which illustrates the influence of the source **of a** river upon the earliness or lateness of its fish :—

" This " (the early ascent of salmon) " is often the case in rivers issuing from large lakes, in which **the** water has previously undergone a sort of filtering process, and has become warmer, owing **to** the greater mass and **higher** temperature **of its source ;** whilst, on the other hand, **streams which are liable to be swollen by the** melting of snows, **or cold** rains, **or which are** otherwise bleak and exposed, **are later** in season, **and** yield **their** principal supply where **the** great lake **rivers are beginning** to **fail.** Two **of** the Sutherland streams offer good examples of these operating causes. One, the Oikel, springs from a small exposed alpine pool some half mile in breadth ; **the** other, the Shin (a branch of the Oikel), takes its rise in the deep sweeping waters of Loch Shin and its tributary lakes. The Shin joins the Oikel about five miles from the sea. Early in the spring, all the salmon entering this common mouth diverge at the junction, pass up the Shin, and thus return, it would appear, **to their** own warmer stream ; whilst very few keep the main **course of** the Oikel until **a much later** period."

I now propose to explain the circumstances under which January fishing, **in** particular, has been sanctioned in Ireland, and which **some** still advocate, though by the many it is objected to. I shall **also** endeavour to show that five months of the year at least should be closed for net-fishing. That some " clean " fish can be obtained in some rivers **during** January is an undeniable fact ; that others may **be** obtained in December and November is equally **patent,** and for that matter throughout every day in the **year,** as I have already stated **in my former article ;** but these are exceptions to the general **rule—"** oddfish " **in** fact—and it cannot be denied that the three months in question comprise **the period** when **the** great bulk of the spawning process is accomplished in *all* rivers, and hence, *primâ facie,* all rivers should be closed during them.

The exodus upwards is to a certain extent perpetual; that downwards is not so—the fish which have spawned commencing their descent in January and continuing it through February and March, when it **may** be said to be all **over,** or nearly so.

There are two simple considerations then to be observed in determining the times for open and **close** seasons : the first is as to the period of time requisite to desist from killing your fish, to ensure the reservation of a sufficient number for reproduction ; the second is to fix the most suitable time to allot for that object. The Act of 1861 has fixed the close season for England from the 12th of **September to the** 1st of February ;

these five months comprise 153 days, and constitute decidedly the period when the fewest fish in good condition are available as food for man, and the soundness of this rule is so far manifest. . By the Act of 1862 for Scotland, **168** days are required to be closed ; and in 1863 Ireland followed suit, and by the Act then passed required the same number to be observed ; thus an addition of fifteen days to the time fixed for England has been made for the other portions of the kingdom, and it may be well for England to consider whether she will not take the hint from her neighbours, and move with them in the same provident direction.

Having so far disposed of the question as applying **to** suitable legislation, I would call attention to **some** of those circumstances connected with the migrations **of** salmon, which it may be interesting for naturalists **to** consider and useful to investigate ; and in doing so I shall confine myself on the present occasion to the rivers of Ireland, for as they were my earliest companions, I am bound and not unwilling to acknowledge them as my most familiar acquaintances.

On **the** south-west coast of Ireland then, in the *Kingdom*[*] of **Kerry,** lies the Bay of Ballinskelligs, not far from the famed island of Valentia, **from** whence the cable of the Atlantic Telegraph Company was started. **The river** discharging from Curraune

---

[*] *Vide* the man who inquired what part of Kerry *Ireland* was in.

Lake enters it at Waterville ; the distance from the lake to the sea being not more perhaps than 800 yards. A cruive-weir has been placed across the narrow river time out of mind, and latterly a considerable number of salmon have been taken in it in January, and, before the law restricted it, in December and November also. Many **of** these fish were found to be in the highest state of edible condition, bright, firm, fat, well-flavoured, and with roe and milt in the earliest stage of development, and they were ascending during the time that the earlier-run fish were actually in full spawning in the streams tributary to the lake. It was often urged that all spawning operations terminated in these Curraune waters before Christmas, yet I saw a pair of salmon myself in the act, on the 3d of February, above the bridge at Waterville. It was the only opportunity I had had of seeing for myself, and I would suggest to those who may wish to arrive at facts in natural history, and especially in the somewhat intricate history **of** the salmon, that it is far safer *to go and see*, than to rely upon what you only hear.

The river Inney enters the same bay within a distance of about two miles from the mouth of the Curraune ; there is no lake connected with it ; the floods or spates discharge quickly, and during the dry summer months it affords no " deeps" sufficient for the protection of salmon, which are **therefore** far **too**

" cute" to enter it until the Lammas floods set in. They hang about the tideway, biding their time for the journey to the spawning-beds until they can undertake it with some degree of safety, and when they have accomplished their object, skedaddle away back to the sea again as quickly as possible.

Westward of Ballinskelligs is Dingle Bay, at the head of which the rivers Laun, Cara, and Main discharge. The first is the outlet from the celebrated Lakes of Killarney, and there some salmon, such as those before described, are obtained in January. **The** Cara is also connected with lakes, and holds a prominent place in the list of " early rivers." My colleague in office Mr. Barry, and myself, upon one occasion—a **23d** of November—assembled the local board of conservators, **lessees** of fisheries, proprietors, etc., having caused **the cruives to be set** in fishing order the night before in Michael Foley's weir below Cara lake, **and** eighteen salmon were found to have been taken **in the traps.** They all looked bright and beautiful, but on a *post-mortem* examination we found that two were so far advanced in roe that they would have spawned that season, and that sixteen were in **the** early stage which would suggest their non-spawning before the following autumn.

The third river, the Main, **is very much** of the same class as the Inney, though larger ; no lakes, and **little deep water.** Into this river the **fish** will not

come until they have some rational hope of security.
And they are quite right ; for if they relied upon the
tender mercies of the passers-by, who could not fail
to discover them in their unsheltered situations, they
would be wofully disappointed.

In the Lee, some of those " early spring fish," as
they are called, though they anticipate that season in
their ascent, are found. They enter the fresh waters
at Cork in December and January, and rush through
them to the Lake of Inchegeela, which by the river
course is at least forty miles above. There they sojourn in security until the autumn following, when they
spawn early. So much for the south ; we now come
to the north of Ireland, round by the east coast. In
the Liffey, at Dublin, without a lake, but with some
deep pools of refuge for the fish, we find some early
" springers" ascending in January. While the Island
Bridge Fishery was closed during that month, the
proprietor was sure of his *best* haul on the first day
of February.

So far shalt thou go and no farther, said the impassable weir at that place ; and there the poor emigrants were detained, in the hope of some favourable
opportunity occurring to enable them to surmount it.
Vain hope, alas ! for on the first of February out came
the great net and mercilessly enclosed them, after
which the fatal operation of crimping terminated
their earthly, or rather watery, career !

After turning round the north-eastern corner of the island we come to the Bush, similar in every particular to the Liffey—no lakes, some deep pools, a barrier in the shape of a cruive-weir, and January **fish** as long as the trap was allowed to operate during that month. We proceed westward to Rathmelton river, at the head of Lough Swilly—Lough Fearn above—December and January fish trying hard for it, but impeded by a weir and captured below. Westward, at the head of Sheep Haven Bay, is Doe Castle river, lake, and weir with trap—January fish. **On** the north-west coast, in Donegal Bay, we find the small river Bundrows, running from Lough Melville, with a barrier and traps, said to yield a good clean salmon every month in the year except November; **while** in the Great Earn, at Ballyshannon, connected with the broad lake of the same name, and debouching within two miles of Bundrows, no such fish can be found until March or April, and I am very much disposed to think that the secret is that they cannot be detected. The waters are large at all times, generally greatly swollen in December and January; there is no complete impediment, or anything approaching to it, to interfere with or arrest them in their upward progress, and it is quite possible that they pass up unnoticed.

Proceeding southward **we** arrive at Sligo. The river there discharges the waters of Lough Gill, a lake of nine miles long, and from one to three broad

— December and January clean fish entering it, *when they can;* but the state of things here is pretty much like that described with regard to the Island Bridge Fishery in the Liffey. The upward fish have been stopped by the weir in the town of Sligo, and accumulated below it, where on the 1st of February an ample haul is generally effected. There are other instances of the " presence " as the naturalists say, of these early fish, besides those to which I have referred, but it would be too tedious a proceeding to enumerate them ; so I shall finish my yarn, which I fear I have already spun to an unwarrantable length, with the Munin in Mayo. This river and the Owenmore unite just above the head of the tideway. The Munin flows from Carramore lake ; the Owenmore is not connected with a lake ; " clean " and " foul " fish come up the estuary in company in December and January; *all* the clean fish turn up the former, *all* the foul fish up the latter. From the close connection of these two towns, they are often quoted as the great example in Ireland of the anomalous proceedings of those fish, after all comparatively very few, which take up their quarters in the fresh-water lakes or deep pools of rivers to sojourn there so long before their spawning-time arrives.

And now, to sum up for the jury of naturalists, who it **is** expected will give the case of the migrating of salmon their attentive consideration. I would beg for their best endeavours to enlighten the **public** upon the two following interesting points to be **considered** :—1st, The why and the wherefore with reference to the fact, that while a great many fish disport themselves **in** the cool briny exhilarating waters of the sea, luxuriating in the greatest variety of delicious food, during far the greater portion of the year, others betake themselves to the vapid waters of the inland rivers, there to dwell in apparent discomfort, stuck under weeds and banks to shade themselves from the scorching sun of summer. 2d, Whether all, and if not, what proportion of the salmon spawn every year, or every alternate year. There is evidence to show that kelts, going down in February, having spawned in the course of the previous winter, which **have** been carefully marked, return to the rivers in the course of the ensuing summer for the ostensible purpose of spawning the following winter ; while it is quite certain that those exceptional **fish** which ascend in November, December, and January—assuming that they do not spawn until the following autumn—must allow a season to elapse between the events. Now, gentlemen-naturalists of the jury, you will, it is to be hoped, well and truly try the issues submitted in this case, and true verdict give according to the evidence.

W. J. F.

BAGNALL'S BUNGLES.

A REVIEW.

" HAS this book a sufficient excuse for existence—is it wanted, in short?" That is a query which all authors, and angling authors emphatically, would do well to put to themselves when proposing to lay a fresh burden upon our already groaning shelves. Assuredly it is a question which the critic must ask, and get answered too, even before that of, "Is the book good, or is it bad?"

What then is the excuse for the existence of the *Piscatorial Rambles?* Let us turn to the preface. To the preface we turn, but search through it in vain, we will not say for any excuse, but for any apology for an excuse for its coming into being. There **is** not a word which conveys the smallest idea to our mind as to why this small volume of microscopic type and aspect uninviting should now be lying in bodily presence before us—why we should be called upon to review it, and why others (as we may presume that every book has some one or more purchasers) should be called upon to read it. We are sorely tempted to doubt, indeed, whether the author himself had any ideas to convey; the few vague generalities, such as that it is his aim to " render the fisherman all the assistance in his power "—that his writings were " eagerly sought for and favourably noticed "—and that he has acted upon the advice and suggestions of those " several literary and other friends" (save us from our friends !), who always come in so opportunely on these occasions, indicating rather the consciousness of mental haziness than lucidity on the point.   But stay ; we have an idea (envy us, Mr. Bagnall !)—a happy thought strikes us —the " title ?"   The title of the book will surely give us some clue to the special want or *desideratum* in our *bibliotheca piscatoria* which it is its writer's intention to supply.   Alas, no! " Piscatorial Rambles" can only mean the rambles of a piscator ; and is not this field already doubly occupied ?—*vide* Mr. Jesse's *Angler's Rambles, Rambles of a Fly-Fisher*, etc.

Evidently, therefore, " to dilate upon the nature of the work " would, as Mr. Bagnall says, " be superfluous."   It has no visible *raison d'être ;* and is consequently obnoxious to the gravest charge which can be urged against any book.   The one solitary ray which its author does vouchsafe to guide us in our chimerian search after first principles, is that it has been his aim to " say nothing which may not, directly or indirectly, be of *practical* utility ; " and for this practical utility **we** are referred to the contents of the **book,** where it **" will be clearly** seen " . . .

Very **well ; we will** take Mr. Bagnall on his own terms **; and in** endeavouring to answer our second critical query—Is the book, as a book, a good one or **a bad** one ?—judge him by the test he himself proposes. We can, at least, trust to merit the acknowledgments which he promises to all who may succeed in pointing out any little defects or deficiencies, **so as** to render future **editions** *" still more worthy* of public approbation."

With **the** utmost diffidence, we **think** then, Mr. Bagnall, that you say nothing **in your** book **which** has not been said a dozen times before; and that what you **have** said **is** as badly expressed as possible. Here **is,** for example—and it may be taken as a fair specimen of the whole—an illustration of the " practical " instruction which it is his ambition to impart :—

" Floating thence **[from Brayweir] on the** bosom **of the** majestic Thames, the **reader may come to an** anchor **and a luncheon** also, at Monkey Island, **which is a good half-way** house from **his** starting-point and Windsor ; and if tired **of** his piscatory amusement, **he may** for an hour indulge his curiosity and **love of** the antique by inspecting relics of ages long since **passed** away. Dropping slowly down, the Waltonian disciple will find some fine stretches of water between this island and his destination ; and trusting that his sport will be commensurate **with his** expectations, I will do the

jackal's duty on this occasion, and hasten forward to order
the dinner he must so urgently require." . . .

Can any human being derive anything "practical"
from such a sentence as this—unless indeed it be a
practical warning against the habit of saying something upon a subject on which the author obviously
feels that he has nothing to say?

We fear, however, that Mr. Bagnall's difficulty
is akin to that of the zoologist who, having under-
taken to produce a treatise on Norwegian serpents,
had to begin and end it by the admission, "There are
no serpents in Norway." Verily, there is no practice
in Bagnall!

But we are doing our author injustice. There is
one point on which he is practical in the highest degree, and that is in eating and drinking, or, as he
would call it, the liquid and viand department. His
appreciation of all that relates to the comforts of the
inward man is most remarkable; and his information
on this subject appears to be the only thing that is
not borrowed in the book. The quotation above was
taken from page **11**; five pages further on, and the
" local and historical allusions " which are promised
by Mr. Bagnall as enliveners of the angler's progress
again show a decided hankering after the flesh-
pots. " Presuming that we have arrived at our destination " . . . he " pleads guilty to being sufficiently mundane *in his* **attributes** (whatever they may

be) to propose **and** seriously recommend a substantial breakfast, qualified**"** . . . **and so on.** A substantial breakfast is clearly the foundation **for a good solid lunch ; and,** accordingly, **in the** very next chapter (p. **22),** where the historical reminiscences of **the river Lea are due,** he returns to the **charge.—"** Well," he **cries,** " could I here expatiate upon **the** venerable remnants **of** former ages **which the various** buildings belonging to the old **Rye House** present **to the observer ;** but " — the **only remnant he can call to mind is** " the **huge** banqueting-room wherein," **etc. etc. etc.,** and the " signboards which **direct the** *piscatorian* **(?)** to public-houses **in** the **neighbourhood (O blessed** sight !)"

Three meals in twelve pages—O insatiable Bagnall ! Not even yet, however, are his cravings appeased. On passing through Enfield he " must stop **at** the well-known establishment kept by host Jarvis, **and** proceeds at once **to recruit his** constitution with **the** liquids and viands **which he** can pronounce always A 1." Thence, " **invigorated by the pleasing process,"** we come to **Edmonton, and the famous old "Bell,"** of John Gilpin renown, the signboard **of** which still represents him in the act of starting on his involuntary ride—

> " Away went Gilpin, neck **or nought,**
> Away went hat and **wig !"**

But all this is, **of course, comparatively nothing**

to Mr. Bagnall, provided he **can** but satisfactorily achieve his everlasting pot of beer, in which **to** "pledge the memory," etc. Poor Cowper may hide his diminished head. Nay, we doubt whether the birthplace of Shakespeare himself would evoke more than a passing stare from Mr. Bagnall, unless coupled with the facilities for swallowing malt liquor. Even the anticipation of the grand ruins of Betchworth Castle cannot suggest a more poetical preparation than a "call in at the Old Punch Bowl," and the imbibing of "a portion of the celebrated Reigate ale, to circulate the blood and comfort the stomach." As it was at Betchworth, so was it at the Thatched House, and so it was at Highbury—"Beer, beer, beer!" or, as *Bon Gaultier's* fat old woman would say, "Stout, more stout!" In fine, the vaunted "local and historical allusions" promised by Mr. Bagnall's preface *almost in every instance* resolve themselves into visits to pot-houses or other places connected directly or indirectly with what he **calls** "edible enjoyments."

Yes, the "gentle" craft is certainly becoming plebeian! It is afflicted with a literature as large perhaps as that of all other field sports put together, and of which nine-tenths would appear to have been written for the purpose of showing how silly and offensive vulgar people can become when smitten by the *cacoëthes scribendi.* We had recently occasion to allude to this misfortune *àpropos* of Mr. Robert Blackey's *How to Angle, and Where to Go*—a typical specimen of the genus " paste and scissors" for which we might almost suppose that the aphorism about the " new and the true" in bookmaking had been originally invented ; and now here is already another aspirant for the cap and bells, whose claims are so strong that in our perplexity we are tempted to exclaim with the bard—

> " How happy could we be with either,
> Were t'other dear charmer away."

The foregoing quotations will give a fair idea of the " matter" of the *Piscatorial Rambles*; the " manner" is, if possible, even less felicitous. Here are a few solecisms culled at random from the first dozen pages of the book :—

(P. 8.) " Those who *have*, or may hereafter *take* the trouble " . . .

(P. 12.) " Contemplating the castle, he may wander back to the time when our warrior kings held court there ; and although the joust and the tournament *has* long given place to more peaceful pursuits, yet " . . .

(P. 14.) " All who have studied the nature of the bait, know that *its* natural position is on the bottom, and pike being particularly fond of *them* " . . .

(P. 15.) " To commence operations cast your bait in near shore, . . . then pull it gently towards you, *imitating* as near(ly?) *as possible the natural movement of the bait you are using* " . . .

So far as the last dozen words have any meaning at all, they mean that the angler is to commence a series of piscatory calisthenics in emulation of those of the fish spinning at the end of his line.

But the soul of a Bagnall soars far above such commonplace trivialities as sense and grammar. How can we expect the vulgar restrictions of Lindley Murray to fetter a genius which can evoke from the depths of its inner consciousness such a peroration as the following, suggested by a sight of Pope's house at Richmond :—

" Awaking from the reverie induced by the thought that fickle Nature had given so frail and disfigured a tenement to contain so glorious and sublime a mind, I drop down the gentle stream and view the fairest of England's daughters engaged in the healthy occupation of urging their fairy boats o'er the bosom of the water, the graceful and voluptuous attitudes called into play by the exercise promoting the most passionate and ardent admiration, each elegant movement stamping them as more lithe than the sculls grasped by their tiny hands, and forming in their many-tinted garbs, aided by the drooping branches of the overhanging trees, a scene of beauty rarely surpassed."

Rarely surpassed, indeed, we should suppose ; and rarely equalled, we will venture to assert, the classical and appropriate lines in which it is commemorated. But then, as our author observes elsewhere, "it requires a delicacy of manipulation, ' a touch how exquisitely fine,' to do justice to these sort of themes."

Such commonplace names as the pike, perch, etc., are quite unworthy of Mr. Bagnall's talents; they become the "pirate of the waters"—the "struggling tyrant"—and so on; whilst the "mottled sides" of the former "remind him forcibly of a dappled grey horse." We will not suggest that there *might* be any other quadruped not quite so elevated in the scale of intelligence, and yet bearing possibly an equal resemblance to *Esox lucius.*

Mr. Bagnall is not much more fortunate when he tries his hand at verse. He wilfully alters and misquotes Thomson's beautiful lines, commencing—

—————"But should you lure,
From his dark haunt beneath the tangled roots
Of pendent trees, the monarch of the brook." . . .

and makes them applicable to the pike instead of to the trout. A few of the original lines with which the chapters are headed are more respectable than might have been expected; but for the most part are well mated with their prose congeners: *e.g.*—

".With silvery scale and ruby fin,
Body deep, yet somewhat thin,
Forked tail, arched back, firm flesh and white,
A beauteous picture—pleasing sight!"

A more pleasing sight we should have imagined, at least in an edible point of view, if the fish had been somewhat less "thin" and more "fat." But fish that are "flat and thin" have evidently a morbid fasciuation for Mr. Bagnall. In his lines on the bream he says :—

> " Broad to the view, and long, *yet flat and thin,*
>   With foul exterior, and *with dorsal fin.*"

Does Mr. Bagnall, by his last line, mean to imply that the barbel is singular in the possession of this appendage ? It would certainly appear so. In speaking of the pike (which, by the way, he represents as " alleviating the cravings of hunger by disposing of the flags, reeds, and rushes which compose his lair !") he states that—

> " His cruel eye sur*veys* and spar*eth* not ;"

but in the next page he describes him as possessing " a beautiful eye, more approaching the human than that of any other fish."

To speak Bagnallally, however, we surveys, but cannot spareth any more space for these little peculiarities, as we think we have said enough to give our readers a fair general idea of the *Piscatorial Rambles.* Had we a parting suggestion to make, it would be, that, out of consideration for the other authors who have dealt in angling rambles, Mr. Bagnall should select an early opportunity of changing the name of his book. He might rechristen it, perhaps, *Be-boggled Bagnall,*" or " *The Pothunter's Vade Mecum ;*" or if neither of these titles was considered sufficiently descriptive, we would make him very welcome to the

alliterative designation which heads this notice. **But**
anything, in **fact,** that defined with tolerable accuracy
the contents **of** the work would do. Its author might
then have the pleasure of reflecting **that there was at**
any rate one new feature in his production which **was**
likewise true, and no one can tell **how far such an**
unusual circumstance would **startle into** liberality the
public piscatorial.

The *Rambles* is, **for some reason** or other that
does not transpire, permitted **to** be dedicated to **Lord**
Coventry, for which permission Mr. Bagnall **hopes**
that his Lordship **will be** " partially recompensed "
in its perusal.   We sincerely trust he may be.

H. C. P.

AN ANGLER AT THE ANTIPODES.

ANGLING in Australia, even in clear rivers, has very little either of art or science about it. Time will probably produce some improvement in this respect. The fish will become more educated—even the wide-mouthed Murray cod may learn more discrimination in baits, and if he still continues attached to raw beef, may at least have his favourite cuts. Nay, as it is, I do not doubt that a good trolling-rod, an oiled silk line, such as I used of old when beguiling Thames trout ("ah! woeful when"), and a yard of first-rate salmon-gut, with a middle-sized Kirby neatly lapped, would kill more fish than the rude hand-tackle in use, especially in hot days and low waters. But it is difficult to make people in England conceive the un-developed state of all sporting appliances in this country. I cannot, for the chance of a possible day's sport, carry a complete angling apparatus all over the county with me ; and there is no more hope of find-ing the dweller on the best of rivers well provided with rod and tackle, and able to assist a visitor's sport effectually, than of meeting with strawberry-ices in a bush hotel. I carry with me all that is absolutely

necessary, **and no** more ; to wit, a box of various-
sized hooks, such as are made for sea-fishing, a file,
some rough lead, and a couple of the fine but very
powerful lines which knowing hands use for snapper.
Strength is indispensable where you may have **a dead**
pull against a forty-pounder. These things **take no**
room in a valise, and are ready for service in **three**
minutes. Two turns will bend on a hook immovably,
and the doubling of the line close to the hook which
is occasioned by this mode of fastening, however
shocking to English ideas of neatness, **has the ad-**
vantage of affording some defence against the sharp
teeth of " Gristes." As for bait, it is quite needless to
be particular. A large worm, a frog, a small fish, or
a piece of a larger one, are good baits. Many sorts
of garbage, if tolerably fresh, are taken eagerly. I
have often shot a magpie or other bird on my way to
the water, and used both the breast and the inside
with good success. But my commonest **resource has**
been a good lump of raw beef, which is generally procurable at any considerable station. **This is always**
taken freely by the larger **fish. It is, by-the-by, a**
curious fact that they **never** can be induced to taste
mutton. I have tried the two side by side again and
again, and never have succeeded in getting the latter
bait taken. If other diet runs short, the capture of
a single fish generally ends the difficulty by making
his entrails available against his fellows. All this,

it will be said, seems so rough and crude that it can
hardly be expected to awaken the elegant enthusiasm
of a British angler.   But after all—

> " Quand on n'a pas ce qu'on aime
>   Il faut aimer ce qu'on a."

And a genuine brother of the craft, even if he be
offended by the rudeness of its implements in New
South Wales, will find much to interest him in the
objects with which he becomes acquainted during its
exercise.   He may lack the technical knowledge of
the naturalist, and the artistic dexterity of the painter,
but he ought to have a quick eye to observe, and a
true feeling to appreciate, **the** objects in which **they**
respectively delight.   **And if** indeed thus qualified,
he will find the accessories of his sport scarce less
delightful **here than at home.   For scenery, indeed,
we can** show nothing **like the** "emerald meadows"
of Driffield **or** Leintwardine, or by Itchin side—no
mountain-girt lakes or deep rocky tarns, mirrors for
the wild shore and the changeful sky.   But we have
craggy gorges, through which the flashing waters
thunder; noble rivers, with endless change of pool,
and eddy, and stream; broad lagoons, around whose
margin the wild-fowl paddle among the blue water-
lilies ; while far aloof the stately swan floats lazily
over the still deep, with rosy bill and glossy plumes :

> " Black, but such as in esteem,
>   Prince Memnon's sister might beseem."

And believe **me,** he who has launched his boat from one of the quays of Sydney, with the first streak of a summer **dawn,** and stealing **down the** harbour has marked **the** sun come forth above the eastern sea, **throwing** out in clear relief islet after **islet** and head-**land** behind headland, lighting up the spires and villas of the many-ridged city, and deepening the purple shadows on many a northern creek and **inlet,** has seen a sight of beauty, not unsurpassed perhaps, but in its own kind unrivalled. Nor will the rambles of the Australian angler be wanting in living objects of interest. The common complaint **as to** the scanti-ness of the fauna **of** New Holland applies only to its quadrupeds, which, with **a few** unimportant excep-tions, are all marsupials. Even in these there is greater variety than Englishmen generally suppose. Sometimes on a grassy slope, between hill and stream, you surprise a group **of tall kangaroos,** and perhaps see "Joey" throw **a somerset into the** maternal pouch, before the whole party, **and make off with those amazing bounds which it is scarce a metaphor to** describe as flight. **Sometimes a rock Wallaby, whisk-**ing his bushy tail, **scuttles along** an overhanging cliff. In the bare scrub of **the** uplands, the **nimble** little kangaroo-rat starts up at **your feet. In the** semi-**tropical** brushes which fringe the rivers towards the **coast, you have** the brush Wallaby **and** Paddy-melon **dodging and** doubling among the tangled growth of trees and creepers ; and as for birds, especially in waders and waterfowl, the variety is inexhaustible.

But it is the creel and not the game-bag that is now in question, and I am going forth for an afternoon's fishing on the Clarence. One of my companions is, in Australian phrase, "a new chum," the other a stately old aboriginal, rejoicing in the name of "Billy." "New chum" landed at Sydney from England but a month ago, and left it but five days since by a Grafton steamer. He thus knows no more of the country than he could learn in a forty miles' ride to the scene of our fishing excursion. "Billy" knows every ford and pool of the river, on whose banks he has hunted and fished ever since the days when he was the acknowledged head of a strong tribe, and the most redoubtable warrior among the northern blacks.

Scene—*Open scrub, sloping down to the Clarence.*

Time—*3 p.m., in early Autumn.*

Veteran, New Chum, *and* Billy.

New Chum. This is a noble river. Are we still upon the estuary?

Veteran. Oh, no. There lie 120 miles of river between us and the Heads, and 50, as near as I can guess, between these pools and the highest reach of the tide. But even here the river is, as you say, a noble one, and when flooded absolutely terrific. You

English folks **have no** notion how water can rise. I have seen **the** Clarence here more than 30 feet above its present **level** ; and at Tabulam, 50 miles nearer **its source, it** rose, during the great rains two years **ago, 67 feet** perpendicular.

New Chum. Spare my nerves, I entreat you, **and tell** me rather why **we** don't **turn down to the river** at once. That pool below **looks very inviting.**

Veteran. **Too shallow, I** assure **you.** Besides, I **trust wholly to our** black, and he, **you perceive, is** leading **straight on to meet the river** beyond **the next** swell of **the ground.** He won't walk a yard further **than our sport requires.** I say, Billy, where are we **to stop?**

Billy. **N**ot long bit now ; see rock yonder? good place that one—plenty cod sit down—there we won- garee [stay].

New Chum. Well, here we **are** at last, I suppose. But if that stony island is the rock your **sable friend** means, I shan't get there without coming **to grief.** How is a Christian in neat's leather to **walk over this** wide strip of smooth stones ?

Veteran. Never fear ; our rocks are rarely slip- pery, even when wet. Only beware if you step on **one** under water ; this dry weather has crusted them **with green slime.** Hilloa! are you down ?

New Chum. No—not this time—but I should **have** taken a bath but for " Billy " here. Your hint was just too late. However, I've reached our fishing-place in safety—and now to work. So—that's a convenient seat, though rather warm. My line is all ready; what had I better bait with?

Veteran. It matters very little; put on half one of those little herrings, taking care to fix it firmly on the hook. I shall try a lump of raw beef. There—that will do very well; now, don't stir your bait till you haul it in with or without a fish. It is very easy to get foul among the rocks here. Ah! ah! do that again, will you?

New Chum. Whom are you appealing to so earnestly? Not King Billy, I am sure—no danger of his doing anything just now. Look at the perfect repose of his attitude, stretched on the warm sand, with his head propped against that round stone.

Veteran. I was apostrophising not Billy, but a cod-fish, who has just been mouthing my bait and can't make up his mind to bolt it, or bolt with it. But I suspect Billy's repose is not so perfect as you can imagine. He has the characteristic fondness of his colour for tobacco, the only thing an Australian aboriginal is ever known to hoard, and though I know he has plenty of his own, he will much prefer smoking ours. See—he is moving; now for it. Well, Billy, what is it?

Billy. You got any matches, governor?

Veteran. Yes, plenty; take three or four.

Billy (after peering into a cutty pipe, and fumbling in sundry queer folds of his raiment). You got any 'bacco for smoke, governor?

New Chum. Here's a cheroot for you, Billy.

Billy. Ugh—s'gar—gentlemans smoke—not much good that fellow.* Never fear—that do this time.

Veteran. Clear out, Billy—give me elbow-room; this chap's in earnest. **Ah—he's fast** now, **and not** a bad fish either, to judge by the pull.

New Chum. What a jerk you gave him! I wonder it did not break the **line, or tear** out the hold.

Veteran. I can trust my tackle; and, let me tell you, unless the bait be actually pouched **it** takes a pretty smart tug to fix one of these coarse hooks in the bone and gristle of kabble-jaws' **upper works.** Even when a fish is running heavily the line is never **so** taut as it seems. Now, my friend—this way if you please—past that rock—up the sand-bank. **So** —throw him up, Billy.

New Chum. What a fine **fellow!** **Six pounds, I** suppose.

---

* The Australian blacks, like many other savage tribes, have no idea of *thanks,* and of course no expression for them of their own— nor do they readily adopt ours. They usually content themselves **with expressing** satisfaction—and that carefully measured and often qualified—on the receipt of a present. Their nearest approach to the language **of** gratitude is by speaking of a benefactor as "their brother" or "their father." The writer has the honour of being one of King Billy's white brothers.

Veteran. Eight, if he's an ounce ; these fish are very thick-set, and weigh heavy for their length.

New Chum. Thick-set with a vengeance (*feeling fish*) ; why, I can't grasp him with the utmost span of both hands ! ***Peste !*** I've pricked my fingers.

Veteran. Ah! now you see (or rather feel) why he has been properly styled the cod-perch. His dorsal fin is worth your looking at. In fact he has two confluent dorsals ; the anterior, with eleven spiny rays, like that of our English perch, though sharper, as your fingers can testify ; the other immediately behind it, much lower, with more numerous soft rays. For the rest, his skin you will see is mottled olive and white, like that of our British Gadidæ, and slimy like. . . . Holloa there ! look out—you've got a **fish ; haul in.**

New Chum. Why the line hangs quite **slack.**

Veteran. Ay, because he has turned and run in towards you. But he was running fast enough just now—ten to one he has gorged the bait.

New Chum. **I** have him, sure enough—and here he comes, **a pretty fish, though not so** big as yours ; he **will turn** five pounds I am **sure.** Could we have **him for dinner?** I feel a savage **inclination** to make a **meal of my own captive.**

Veteran. **By all means—we will send both the fish ; there will be** several **guests** at the station to-night, and they rarely taste fish, though living close to a well-stocked river.   Here, Billy, take these fish up to the house, and tell the Chinaman to cook them for dinner.

Billy. Yan [go] station—give cook two fellow fish—all right—come again soon.

New Chum (calling after him). And see how quick **you** can get back again.—He **will come back, I** suppose ?

Veteran. Then you **have a more** robust faith than I.   **No,** we shall have **to find** our own way home. Your black fellow almost invariably tells the truth **as** to matters of fact, but his promise is worth precisely nothing.   **He** does not mean **to** deceive, but he obeys the whim of the minute, and forgets everything else. And now, in with your bait again—we want some more fish, and the days close **in** very fast.

New Chum. Here's another fish at me—but he bites very queerly, just **twitching the** line without running.

Veteran. Better haul **in, and throw out a few** yards further—there's no **fish in the case.**

New Chum. No **fish ?** come, that's **too good.** I feel him **still, and with a little** patience I hope to nail him.   Ah ! he's on **the move at last, though** very slowly.   Now, sir ! so I've hooked you at last What **say you** to that ?

Veteran. Respice finem, respice funem, as Jonathan Oldbuck says. Look to your line, and see **what comes up.**

I

New Chum. Now then—come out, my friend. Eh! what on earth have I got? Gracious Tweezer, it's a turtle!

Veteran. I could have told you that five minutes since. These fellows are often great nuisances, pegging away at the bait till they have sucked it off. I have caught dozens, mostly by the foot, where I see yours is hooked. If they swallow the hook it's a horrid business. Even if you cut their heads off they bite hard, and hold their grip like bulldogs.

New Chum. Well, I've cleared my hook; what shall I do with him? He doesn't look promising for soup.

Veteran. I never tried one, though I believe the blacks eat them. Turn him on his back for the present, and we can let him go when we leave the water. What are you baiting with now?

New Chum. The inside of one of our fish. Billy cleaned them out before starting. I suppose to lighten his load.

Veteran. You'll catch fish with that, though perhaps not cod. What now? you seem to have got a rough customer.

New Chum. Ay; this is something like a fish; but he pulls very queerly—keeps working dead astern, instead of taking a tack of his own. I can tell you he goes near to cut my fingers.

Veteran. Your garbage bait has lured a big eel,

as it often will in **the** Clarence. **He is** coming in **at** last.

New Chum. **An** eel do you call it? Why, it's **the** great sea-serpent! And what a handsome fish too! spotted like a leopard, reddish brown **on a** pale **yellow.**

Veteran. Ay, **he is** of **the handsome** variety. There is another sort in the Clarence by no means lovely to look upon—a dirty olive-green, with not even the belly bright or clear-tinted. I put him at a dozen pounds—**but** I have caught bigger when **the** river has **been thick.** Hit him smartly over the tail, or he'll make a hopeless mess of your line. That's it—now divide the spine just at the head, and he is safe.

New Chum. But how about my hook? It would take me an hour to get it out of his maw.

Veteran. Pooh! cut it off and bend on another, **and** try a whole herring for bait this time. **Ah, ha!** **I've** a run myself now ; no mistake about this chap ; **he is** going away best pace. Come, this will do ; there's *gristes tertius* for you ; a capital fish for the table, though he hardly pulls 4 lbs. It's your turn now ; throw well out toward the tail of the pool, **while** I rest **on** my laurels and take a cigar.

New Chum (*after a pause*). I have a fish now— **there—there he runs.** Now then! fast, for a hundred. Such a fish! **pulls like** the father of all pike.

Veteran. All right—take **your** time, that's **all, and** don't bring him **to the top yet.**

New Chum. **Bring him ?** I can't keep him down. Mercy on us, **what a head** and shoulders ! Steady, can't you ? steady ! Plague take the **ugly** brute ! **gone** after all ! I could **have sworn** he **was** fast.

Veteran. So he was, depend on it—he has bitten through the line, I'll be bound. See—the hook is gone, and he has cut the line **just** below the lead. It was no fault of yours—he had swallowed the bait so far that his teeth met beyond **the** doubled length next the hook.

New Chum. **Doubled** length ? **I** doubled nothing, it **looks so** clumsy. **I only made** your favourite **hitch, and cut off the loose end close** to the hook.

Veteran. **Well—it's a great pity any way.**

New Chum. **Pity !** I should think **it was. I never** felt such a fish—he couldn't be **under 25 lbs.**

Veteran. Five-and-twenty ? That's a large order ; not but what there are plenty such in the river, but I have my doubts as to this particular fish. But here goes on **my own** account—a big hook on strong double cord that might defy the biggest cod **in the rivers, and half a** pound of steak. **So ! I've reached the very** middle **of the pool ; now** for a good **finish.** Hand me your **line ; I'll bend a** fresh hook on ; we've **no** time to spare.

New Chum. Thank you. **I'm** not very sanguine

after losing that **kraken ; but here** goes for **my** chance. And **now** the lines are in, will you take **a** sup of **sherry ?** (*Puts flask to **his** lips and takes a consolatory **pull**.*) Ah-h-h !

Veteran. No sherry, thank you ; one **of your** cheroots, if you please. (They smoke for ten minutes **in** silence.)

New Chum. This is getting slow—I thought **the** fish were going to feed about this **time.**

Veteran. We'll see our cheroots out before we stir at all events. These fish have their sudden **fits** of sulk, like trout, **and** then come on the feed all at once. **I mean** mischief yet. Ay—there he was sure enough ; just lifted my bait and dropped it again.

New Chum. No wonder, when you offered him such a lump—"steak for three" at least. I shall steal a march on you yet—there was a smart jerk—and another—take your time, Miss Lucy—now for it, gristes or grief! **I** have him, safe I hope. Well pulled, my friend! but indeed you must **come in.** Easy there over the shallow.

Veteran. Well hauled! the sooner you land him the better : **there's a** customer for the steak, and I don't think he'll drop it this time. How steadily the rascal walks away—are you all clear?

New Chum. Ay, "there he lies," as we used to **say** when cock-shooting in the old country. And a **bonny fish, too,** much like your first specimen.

Veteran. Well, you may wind up now, for we have but a few minutes to stay, and I shall want all the pool to myself. This is a **fish of** some mettle, I can tell you, and pulls like a dragon, though I don't think **he** can break me. There was a rush ! luckily, we have no sunken timber just here. There again ! he can't last long at this rate, but I'm in no hurry to look him in the face.

New Chum. He must **be** tired out, I'm sure—come, haul him in. How he wallops along the sand ! Ah, this is a fish worth catching—"a delicate monster," truly. But he's a joke to the kraken I lost. If you had only felt *him*.

Veteran. **Ay,** ay—the old story—*ignotum omne pro magnifico.* **Any** how, this fish is 14 or 15 **lbs.** weight, which is not to be sneezed at.

New Chum. **Oh,** I don't object to him as a fish—I only spoke by way of comparison. Altogether, we have had glorious sport, have we not ?

Veteran. Very creditable indeed, though **I have** known much more done in these waters. But holloa, what the deuce is this ? Here's some property of yours.

New Chum. What, my cigar-case ?

Veteran. **No,** you've dropped a hook, and my **fish in** his flurry has picked it up. Surely this can't be your kraken ?

New Chum (glancing at hook, and turning "celes-

tial rosy red"). What, eh? no, surely—a dead **sell**! (*Shows symptoms of bolting.*)

Veteran. Stop, my dear fellow! stop and help me to carry these fish as far as **the** black camp. I'll promise not to chaff you till we get home. Now then, I've strung the victims on a sapling—heave with a will and away we go. (*Exeunt, walking slowly and gingerly over the river-beach.*)

H. R. F.

" SUN-SPEARING."

EVER since I was able to cast a rod single-handed, or read a fly-book without much spelling, I have been **of** opinion that any new pursuit which enlarges **the** sphere of our innocent enjoyments is so much **added** to the stock of human happiness. If the subject **of** our juvenile philosophy brings us into closer communion with nature, **and** opens a wider field for the observation and study of her works, the novelty is **so** much the more worthy of acceptance and encouragement. **Of all the objects** of our restless desires, *her* treasures alone are inexhaustible, never tire, and leave no sting behind. Both mind and body, on the contrary, become invigorated by contact with her wonders, just as the fabled athlete acquired fresh strength as often as he touched his mother earth. All field sports more or less fulfil the conditions of my early postulate ; but none more fully or agreeably than fishing in its various forms. Numerous as these are, **and** well adapted **to all** ages **and** grades of life, I have been long smitten with the ambition of adding another to the **number. It** may not indeed merit the " button" of an angling club to stamp its worth, or win the smiles of the adepts in special departments of our art ; but, after running over the whole " chromatic scale" of the gentle craft, from its highest to its lowest responses, I have arrived **at the bold** conviction that a new *note* may be introduced into the " harmonic circle" of its attractions. To borrow an illustration from the same source, when Guido Aretino and his successors completed the musical scale by the addition of a *seventh*, there were doubtless many persons at the time to whose ears the innovation sounded superfluous and discordant. An attempt to place SUN-SPEARING amongst the resources of the fisherman's art may, I fear, be exposed to a similar reception. But such has ever been the lot of the precursors of progress. First in the ranks, they are sure to receive the arrows of the opposing crowd. I console myself, therefore, by the reflection, that the philanthropist who would shrink from this kind of martyrdom is quite unworthy of his mission.

The popular estimate of eels, **I am sorry to say, is** at par with the prevailing sentiments **respect**ing the barbarous weapon **with** which they are too often tormented. The naturalists, from whom one might expect fair play, are hardly less unjust. They all continue the repulsive name of *Anguilla* in their systems, as if they really believed that eels had anything to do with serpents, or that they were included in the malediction pronounced upon the latter.

When learned men thus perpetuate calumnies, no wonder ignorance follows suit, and dubs, or rather daubs, the poor thing with the slang **synonym** of "snig." His unworthy fate would seem to pursue him to the last. As all the world knows, he is skinned alive, broiled, fried, or stewed, and otherwise maltreated, even before it has been ascertained that the "vital spark" has fled.

'Tis true, I am free to confess, that there is a branch of the eel family which would seem to provoke this cruel treatment. These pariahs of the tribe are generally found in such filthy places as canals, drains, marl-pits ; and even make their way into the squire's pet ponds. The Cæsarean operation, performed upon these outcasts of the eel family, gives birth sometimes to strange results indeed. I have myself seen large frogs, young water-rats, and ducklings that had wandered too far from the maternal wing, brought to light by the process. It is even said that these demoralised members of the family feed on drowned dogs, cats, and other animal impurities found floating on their favourite haunts. But admitting the worst, it does not amount to a valid reason for condemning the whole race. Amongst most animals, individuals will be found "no better than they ought to be." In the south of Europe, hares, which in this country are deemed rigid "vegetarians," are strongly suspected of carnivorous indulgences,

and for this reason are objected to by some squeamish
epicures. In Ireland the same animals are openly
charged with milking cows at night ; or what is
worse, permit their form and fleetness to be assumed
by witches for this reprehensible practice. While I
write, a company of French gourmands may be seated
round a table, and regaling on a *rôti* of horse-flesh !
When once men start to be epicures and philanthro-
pists, there is no telling to what regimen or laws
they may at last subject **us.**

It is time, **however, to** inform a censorious world
that there is a large class of eels which never frequent the vile places, or practise the vices imputed
to other members of the family. Specifically, perhaps, they are identical with their snig relatives ; but
morally and æsthetically speaking they are a totally
different animal. Just as comparative anatomists
have discovered that there is one variety of the
human race which excels all others in beauty and
intelligence, so should I insist upon the existence of
a " Circassian type" amongst eels. To the Great
Lake Eel alone this pre-eminence properly belongs.
The lake itself, to be worthy of such an inhabitant,
must possess some corresponding qualities. Without
availing myself of the technical repertory of the
geologists to describe it, I would say that it should
be at least four or five miles long " as the crow flies ; "
its sides rock and shingle ; and its bottom for the

most part marl, silt, or sand. If a few nice **bits** of bog break the uniformity of the shore, just **to** keep him warm and comfortable during the long **winter** nights, it is all so much the better. I regret **that** when I saw him last the camera had **not** been used for taking subaqueous portraits, it would **be so much** more agreeable to present the reader **with** a *carte* likeness than a verbal description. **Photography** alone, indeed, could do justice to his imposing volume and fine proportions. In its absence, however, it must suffice to say that his back is of **the dark olive** which distinguishes the whole of the race ; **but** that the sides shade off through a pleasant azure **grey into a pure** white on his abdominal regions. **Popular** taste, for once just, **and** taking **the hint from these** colours, has agreed **to give** him **the name of the** "silver eel." I need scarcely say his nose bears **no** resemblance to a duck's bill, a feature which characterises a different variety of the species. **On the** contrary his physiognomy is prepossessing, **and** wholly free from the sinister expression of the snig. His size is generally greater than that of the river kind, growing sometimes to 8 and 9 lbs. But these weights are exceptional, and **not often at-** tained. From 3 to 5 lbs. would give **a more correct** approximation of his general **weight. For his supe-** rior size and beauty he is doubtless indebted to the localities in which **he** is found. There no dearth

of his natural element cramps his development, or
vitiates **his tastes** by impurities. **A** mass of water,
boundless perhaps in extent to eel intelligence, affords
him unlimited scope for exercise, and supplies him
with an inexhaustible store of wholesome nutriment.
Responsive to the dignity and fostering impulse of
local circumstance, he becomes **the** type, the model
representative, of his "order." In this state of perfect
equality with his more highly-prized and organised
companions of the lake, he has left popular notions
of the economy **of** eel life far behind. As he flashes
in brightness and power through the crystal element,
the common observer would scarcely recognise relationship or similitude to the semi-amphibious snigs
of the manor ponds. Like them, however, he hiber-
nates, for in his highest condition he is still true to
the instincts of the race. But what a difference be-
tween the slimy, sulphuretted ooze in which they
hide their diminished heads, and the pure silt and
vegetable fibre beds **in which** their "silver" **relative**
takes up his winter's quarters, with pearly shells **for**
his pillow, and the white surge of the lake breaking
in music over his head! Often has our tiny bark
paused over these winter colonies in the creeks of the
lake to admire the spiracles of the semi-fluid mass
through which he breathed the purest of water.
Sometimes in spring, according to the temperature of
the season, he shakes off his winter lethargy, takes to

roam once more through his wide domain, and to prepare for that sunny phase of his existence in which I shall presently present him to the reader. Lastly, in this brief record of his habits, he essays in some dark and stormy night of November, or thereabouts, to reach that *Mecca* of the ocean to **which** all true-believing and orthodox eels endeavour to make a pilgrimage, once at least in their life. It was in a fruitless attempt of this kind that I recollect having seen fifteen dozen of these intending emigrants taken of a morning from **a** small weir or eel-trap, constructed under the arch of a bridge that spanned a streamlet running out of a large lake, and not more than six to nine inches deep. What struck me on the occasion was not, of course, the number of the captives, but the fact that there was not one in the lot **less** than about three pounds, and many much more. As they undoubtedly bred in the lakes, these annual migrations to the ocean—from which, unlike some members of the salmon family, they seem never to return—present a problem which the fish philosophers have not yet, I believe, solved.

The instrumental requisites for sun-spearing are a small boat and a spear specially constructed for the purpose. Besides skill **in the** use of these agents, a practical knowledge of swimming, or in lieu thereof " a good conscience," is most desirable. Persons who may never have had occasion to test practically the value of the latter gift, may perhaps inquire its connection with sun-spearing. In reply, I am bound to premise, as well for my own peace of mind as to prevent inquests, that drowning in this pursuit is a contingency quite within the capability of an awkward practitioner. In the event of such a *sub*mergency, as Mrs. Malaprop might possibly say, either of the accomplishments indicated would of course be invaluable. The tyro therefore had better look to it —I am not further responsible for untoward results.

In proceeding to describe the sun-spear, it would grieve me to think that any person could confound it with the articles bearing the same name in the limbo of the squire's forfeited engines of poaching. The relation in fact is more nominal than real. The metallic part of the instrument is thus constructed : —Into a small flat bar of best Swedish iron, 12 in. long, $\frac{3}{4}$ in. wide, and $\frac{1}{4}$ in. thick, 12 teeth of best spring or shear steel, 3 in. long, $\frac{1}{4}$ in. diameter in the shank, double barbed, and carefully pointed as the best fish-hook, are welded, riveted, or better screwed, as the latter admits of a new tooth being easily added in the event of one being broken or damaged. To the upper side or edge of the bar carrying the teeth described, a light socket for receiving the handle is attached by one or other of the processes indicated for fixing the " comb " or teeth. The latter should in addition be carefully tempered ; and the whole *blacked*

by one or other of the receipts, of which each work-
man has his own favourite. All this could be **excel-**
lently well done, once upon a time, by our old friend
Longhry, the village Mulciber of Ballinacarrigy,
though he had not had the advantage of graduating
in the forges of Birmingham or Sheffield. The handle
may be formed of any light, stiff, *bearing* wood. Red
deal, free from knots, answers the purpose well. The
length should not be less than 16 or 17 feet ; and the
greatest diameter not more than about $2\frac{1}{2}$ inches. **It**
should be well finished on the bench, and tapered up to
the top to about an inch in thickness, where it is terminated **by a short** bracket or handle turned **on the**
lathe. **A coat or** two of copal varnish will serve **the**
double purpose of keeping out the damp and giving
it a finished appearance. I frequently thought of
rendering the weapon more portable by constructing
the handle in two parts ; but though **I cut a screw**
and fashion brass into all fishing requirements as well
as most "outsiders" of the trade, **I could never de-**
vise a joint sufficiently *light* and *strong* **to** bear the
strains to **which the** instrument is exposed **in** actual
use. I recollect having seen with the **late** Charles
Scarisbrick, **of Scarisbrick Hall, Esq.**—Squirissime
inter Squiros ! *requiescat in pace !*—stems of the bam-
boo, which he used in jumping the drains of North
Moels in his shooting excursions, **and** which would
make admirable **handles for the sun-spears, if they**

could be readily procured. They might also, perhaps,
solve the problem of reducing the specific gravity of
the weapon sufficiently to enable it to float in the event
of its escaping from the hands of the operator. "An ingenious transmogrification of the old salmon-leister," I
fancy I hear some bilious censor exclaim: "Just such
a transmogrification, sweet-tempered angel, as is a nine-
teenth-century salmon-rod of Miss Juliana Berners'
wattle!"

Any small boat (always excepting "punts"), well
up in the bows to enable the spearsman to stand up-
right over the cutwater without sinking it too deep
in the pool, will answer the purpose. Should it be
deficient in this quality, a boulder or two placed
astern will help to right the balance as well as patent
ballast. Though the craft is chiefly impelled by the
spear alone in the act of looking for the game, a pair
of short handy oars are indispensable companions.
The thorough management of a boat is too obvious a
necessity in this amusement to be insisted on here;
for though water be a very pleasant playmate, it is
not always safe to trust too far. Observing that there
may be risk of immersion, the novice may possibly
ask, "What kind of dress would be suited to the occasion?"—the obvious answer to which would of course
be a "bathing-dress." But he must not be put off
with this ambiguous answer. As fashion rules at
present, I would recommend a Garibaldi suit for the

purposes of sun-spearing. The free-and-easy **style of** the dress of the great Guerilla will oppose **the** least possible resistance to **the** use of the "thews and sinews" in air or water.

The time and place for this form of one of the *Wild Sports of the West,* which would seem to have escaped the graphic pen of Maxwell, are all-important. **It** is highly creditable to the good taste of the lake eel **that** he selects **the best month of** the twelve for his Whitsuntide revels. Generally between the **first** of June and the middle of July, days of calm and sunshine occur which faintly remind us of the brilliancy and **serenity of a** southern clime, even in these humid **islands, in which the sun,** alas! **too** often shines

> "**With smiles that might as** well be tears,
> **So faint, so sad their** beaming."

During this month **or six** weeks, however, the eel, like Mr. Curran's emancipated slave, "walks abroad in his own majesty," and displays himself in all his length and strength to the admiring eyes of those who know where to look for him. For this purpose the eel-hunter must be wide-awake and up early. If the tyro lies abed "till the sun burns a hole in the blanket," as Pat has it, or waits the breakfast-bell to chase away the phantoms of an empty stomach, he had better at once forego the pleasures of this amusement. The pursuit is not exactly suited to the "inner man," being strongly opposed to punctual hours of

refection and a careful toilette before venturing into
the morning air. Of such a pupil it may be safely
predicted he will never spear an eel well, much less
make the "terror" of the jungle "bite the dust," on
joining the *Fag an beleachs* in India. There is, I own,
a certain spice of man's primæval instincts, which un-
consciously clings to our skirts in the highest stages of
civilisation, necessary to the success and enjoyment
of this sport. But against this ruder aspect of the
pursuit are to be placed, on the *per contra* side of the
ledger, the humanising influences with which nature
surrounds its practice. I would not, for the best
"monkey-drake" in my flybook, figure before a material age as a sentimental savage, gibbering of humanity
and fine feelings with a spear in my hand. Yet I cannot help thinking there is a principle within us which
finds something to admire in the prime of the year—
wild scenery and the hopeful hour of dawn—quite as
much as in a heavy "balance-sheet" or the highest
quotations of "scrip." If any branch of our art more
than another tends to foster this nobler principle of
our nature, it is that which now engages our attention.
Around none clusters a more poetic combination of
circumstances, scenic and intellectual, than waits on
the exercise of this pursuit. Short indeed must be
the memory, and defective the organisation, of the
youthful *débutant* in this amusement, who, standing
on the heights overhanging the theatre of his imme-

diate operations, will not recall, and feel better for the recollection, the words of Horatio to Bernardo, as the night waned away before the castle of Elsinore, and which so well describe the picture before him :—

> " But look, the morn, in russet mantle clad,
>　　Walks o'er the dew of yond high eastern hill !"

In the heart-awakening light of these lines, reflecting with so much truth and simplicity the beauty of the hour and the scene, the spear brightens into refinement, and the lake below, sleeping in luminous vapour, half-mist half-sunshine, ceases to be the mere hunting-ground of the savage.　Thus viewing the prospect and his own relation to it through the benign teachings of the poet, the spectator feels that barbarism and such an interpreter of nature can no longer co-exist.　Touched by the beams of the morning sun, and warmed into new life by the inspirations of poetry, the youth with his spear on the shore becomes a symbol of the civilisation of man.

But there must be more than poetry, the picturesque, and their genial influences present, to constitute a good day for sun-spearing.　An absolute calm and a cloudless sky must lend their aid to the undertaking.　If the leaves of the aspen (*Populus tremula*), of which we are told, incorrectly, I hope, ." woemen's tongues are made ;" or the purple spikelets of the quaking grass (*Briza media*), from which we brush the dew as we descend to the lake, show the slightest **movement, the water** will scarcely be found in **a** proper state **for our** work. Assuming, however, **that** these natural anemoscopes are true to their delicate functions—that nature, like Narcissus **at** the fountain, hangs her head **in** perfect repose, as **if** absorbed in the contemplation of **her** own works reflected in the watery mirror, we may confidently push forth our little bark from the shore. While this preparatory step is being made, I may observe that the waters which **I** have found best suited for this sport are situated in **the** midland counties **of** Ireland. Resting on the great central plateau of the island, these waters are generally not very deep ; and some of them—as the Inniel, Owel, Lane, Sheelin, and parts of Dereveragh—present shallow shores and extensive flats covered by not more than ten or fifteen feet of water. In these, and doubtless in many other large lakes of the island, the amusement may be practised with success. **Upon one of these we** are now afloat; and as the oldest of the embarkation, I suppose **I** must—

"Shoulder my crutch, and show how *eels* **were won.**"

One of the first things I would point out to the novice, on crossing his oars, taking the spear in his hands, and standing forward in **the** bow of Dingey, **is the** extraordinary distinctness with which all objects are seen at **the** bottom. This is so remarkable that I intend to correct Cavendish's formula for the composition **of** water, and demonstrate in the next number of **the** *Journal of Chemical Science* that it is composed of hydrogen, oxygen, and sunbeams. **The** latter, indeed, in the present instance, appear to be the predominant element in the combination. My " wrinkle" to the tyro would be on the mode of propelling Dingey when searching for eels. This is performed in one of two ways. When a second person is employed for this purpose, he sits with his face instead of his back to the spearsman ; and of course reverses the usual way of using the oars—he pushes the " fins " of the little bark from, instead of drawing them towards **him.** The arrangement, of course, secures a more perfect view of, and a better under-**standing** with, the spearsman in front. If the latter, **on the contrary,** works alone, the spear itself is used as the sole "motive-power." By touching the water alternately with the heel and point, the operator gives sufficient impulse to Dingey, while looking up the game. An expert may thus give **any direc-**tion and speed to the craft that the sport requires. Showmen, I believe, are invariably allowed the privilege of " drawing the strings," when it best suits their object and convenience ; I have now the pleasing duty to sing **out-from** the paddle-box, not exactly an **enemy's** ship ahead, **but an eel** of the " right sort," **which** I hope to take safely into **port as a prize.** In **size it** might bear comparison perhaps with **one of**

Mr. Carlyle's Pythons, though not exactly of the same *mud* species in which that distinguished but rather eccentric writer delights. It lies stretched at full length on the bottom, some dozen of yards in advance **of** Dingey ; and perfectly composed apparently as **if** Dr. Simpson had just applied the cambric and the chloroform to its nose. Now, then, by the lightest and gentlest touches of the spear on the water, lead up Dingey till its stern stands in a perpendicular line with the eel below. All this, remember, must be done as gently and with as little effort as a swan *oars* himself about on Thames or Trent. But before giving instructions for the stroke, it may be necessary to remind the tyro that there are such things as "laws of refraction ;" and that the eel does not exactly occupy the spot which our eye takes it for granted it does. For the same reason, the spear-handle, when let into the water, seems bent or out of line. But I should hope the youthful pupil has got up these little matters sufficiently well for his "Civil Service Examinations" to save me the trouble of further boring him on **the** subject, or airing my optics. Making, therefore, the necessary allowance for distance and refraction, let down the spear gently but rapidly—*non vi sed arte*—to within three or four feet of the prey—he will not stir a peg—and then, invoking St. George and the Dragon, strike home like a Briton ! A peculiar convulsive shock, communicated through the quivering shaft of the spear, tells at once that it has penetrated a living organised being, and that the stroke has been mortal. Possibly the sensation very much resembles what would be given under similar circumstances by another member of the eel tribe, the *Gymnotus electricus;* but never having had the pleasure of fleshing my spear in the sides of one of these floating or swimming galvanic batteries, I cannot pretend to precision as to the fact. Take up the victim, however, gently; all unnecessary cruelty is of course avoided ; and a few taps of the head of the spear against the edge of a seat will disengage it from the prey. And here let no humanitarian turn up his eyes and hint a prosecution ; for has not that eel died the epic death of a hero? a death which a Diomede or a Philoctetes might be proud to inflict or to receive from a worthy foe by the waters of Simois or Scamander? Here, too, is the proper place to explain more fully the dark allusions made to immersion. In his anxiety about striking, the young spearsman is liable to lean too much forward on his spear, and lose his balance. In that case Dingey, like a vicious little hack, "jibs" back from the stroke, and lands the operator all-fours in the pool. If not a good swimmer, he may make up his mind as he obeys the laws of gravitation that the accident can only happen once.

If the morning continues propitious as it began,

the eel-hunter will not have to travel far for sport.
However naturalists may decide his mode of propagation, the eel is a capital breeder ; and numerous
specimens of the larger kind are sure to be met with
on these occasions. They would seem indeed to be
the sole lords and masters of the lakes on fine days of
this kind, scarcely any other fish appearing to dispute
possession. If rarely a large trout or pike looms in
the distance, they instantly get up steam, **on** sighting
Dingey, and shunt into deep water. Our venerable
friend the squire need therefore be under **no appre-**
hension that any improper use of the spear can be
made in lakes under present circumstances. Trout
and pike would seem, on days of this kind at least,
to be perfectly competent to take care of themselves
without the aid of the game-laws. The eel himself
on some days, though apparently favourable in all
respects, evinces the same shyness as trout and pike
in a very remarkable degree. **No sleight of hand will**
bring him to book **while in** this nervous mood. **The**
moment the spear enters **the** water above **him, he**
smells a rat, and in the next instant is " full fathoms
ten" out of sight in the darkest abysses of the pool.

There is one now, however, in our track, whose
steadiness I would venture to endorse. The tyro
will observe that he is in a totally different position
from the last capture ; he is standing right on top of
his head, and describing with his tail, in the most

scientific manner, the periphery of an inverted cone.
The muscles of his back and sides are obviously in a
state of great excitement ; and to all appearance he
seems endeavouring to bore a hole in the bottom of
the lake, as if in pursuit of some invisible object.
No animal eccentricity I ever witnessed puzzled me
more than this spectacle of the eel when I saw it
first. Bright on the " Federals"—Newdegate on
" nunneries"—Spurgeon on " dip-candles"—or Roe-
buck *de omnibus rebus et quibusdam aliis*, could not
surprise me half so much. At first I imagined—what
will not puzzled philosophers imagine to tide over
their difficulties ?—that the process I witnessed was
in some way connected with the generative functions
of the animal ; but **the** thought was no sooner conceived than abandoned, on observing that there was
no partner near to assist in the offices of reproduction.
No vagaries or curiosities of animal generation,
"equivocal" or otherwise, that I read for a diploma
(which was never of the least use to me after) would
exactly meet the case in point. So, like the well-
trained spaniel, I made a second cast, and this time
concluded that the eel was making a comfortable
morning meal **on** little **molluscs,** insects, and larvæ,
that abound on the bottom of lakes ; and not under-
going, like a parish pauper, the penal charity of a
board of guardians, by making holes and stopping
them up again. Our purpose, however, at present is to

make him acquainted **with the** virtues of " cold iron,"
rather than to discuss his sexual or alimentary pecu-
liarities. Of these he is of course himself the competent **judge ;** but being in a direct line with **the**
spear, it is obvious that the stroke must **be** made
obliquely or transversely to take effect. This precaution being observed, I will assume **that the**
tyro has already transferred him amongst the floating cargo of the **dingey. He doubtless** feels **in-**
dignant **at the sudden change of** element ; **but** such
accidents seem **to be the law of** animal **life. All**
creatures prey **on other** organised or sentient **matter ;**
and omnivorous man most of any. An Œdipus **or an**
optimist may solve the dark enigma of the arrangement **to his** own satisfaction ; but how many dreary
volumes of mere guessing would philosophers have
spared us **if** they only possessed the courage to say,
" We don't know," when such questions as the
" writhing" of eels, and **of** animals higher in the scale
too, occupy their ingenious **pens ! The late Dr.**
Whately was only **more candid and daring, though**
not more convincing perhaps, than **his** predecessors,
in declaring that a world without pain was an im-
possibility. -

But the morning, which has been hitherto all that
could be desired, has suddenly undergone a change.
A dark cloud, that has broken away from its companions on the distant horizon, is now passing be-

tween us and the sun ; and in a moment all around the dingey becomes black as a wolf's throat. The little zephyrs too, which reposed so quietly all the morning in the underwood of the islands, by some peculiar sympathy with or signal from the cloud above, come forth, and with inflated cheeks puff the surface of the lake, here and there, into patches of the tiniest ripples. Their playful movements, though refreshing on a hot morning in June, are fatal to the pursuit of sun-spearing while they last. It is one of the advantages of large lakes and their scenery to supply resources of amusement during intervals when eels can't be seen and other fish won't bite. There is Church Island within the length of the spear-shaft from Dingey, in which there is natural history and antiquarianism enough to fill a volume. Or if " in the vein o' it," there are skulls in the old crypt " with mantling ivy clad," one of which may serve to point the moral of a morning homily on the transient glories of men and eels, beginning with, of course, an " Alas, poor Yorick !" The herons, now engaged in the interesting work of incubation in the attics of the tall firs above your head, will stretch forth their long necks in evident admiration of your elocutionary essay ; and the grebes and wild ducks, which make the best of *claquers,* will applaud your hits from their nests upon the benches of the "pit" below. But lo ! there's an interruption of your soliloquy threatened

by the approach **of a new** invader of the solitude of
the island. Far down the lake appears an animal
turning **the** waters aside from his broad chest, and
making towards us with rapid strokes. An otter or
a cormorant? exclaims the inexperienced **tyro, on
sighting the** strange apparition. No; not exactly
either, friend; these animals pursue their prey, and
work the "pool" in quite another fashion. It is only
that incorrigible knave, Diver, who has **slipped his**
collar, and is **playing his old** game of following **us to**
the lake. **At fishing or** fowling, he is equally at
home, **and never** misses **a** chance of being one **of the**
party, when these sports are in hand. He watches
the **splash of a** rising trout with as much zest as the
flash of a fowling-piece; and is quite as eager to take
the water after a hooked fish as to fetch a winged
mallard. Force alone indeed can keep him from being
as soon into the net as a "hooped" **trout.** While
taking a swim, just to give time **to your shirt to dry
on** the island after a thunder-gust, he rows **himself**
alongside, takes your arm most affectionately **in his
mouth,** and imagines no doubt it is his peculiar **pro-**
vince to keep you afloat. **A sort** of canine Flibberty-
gibbet, his quaint tricks are inexhaustible; and he is
sure **to be** always "master of the occasion." The
crafty scamp knows full well now that we *must* take
him into Dingey, though he puts on a look of peni-
tence and compassion as if he were sinking. There!

his paws are already on the stern-board, which **he** knows of old to be the safe point of access to Dingey's interior. His addition to the crew will only subject us to a momentary shower-bath, as he shakes the protoxide of hydrogen and sunbeams from his glossy side. During the **rest** of the voyage he will take charge of the eels, reproving their impatience to scale Dingey's gunwale by an occasional pat of his paw. If there be a place of rest for dogs—and what monopolist of ultramundane beatitude *knows* that there is not in their own " bright particular star" of Sirius?— I would fondly hope that dear Diver is enjoying the rewards of the many pleasant hours we spent together on land and **in** water.   .   .   .

The cloud which interrupted our proceedings **has passed away,** and **once** more "dancing sunbeams on the water play." **Just** push• Dingey on about 100 yards on the submerged flat that connects the pair of islands before us. There, that will suffice for the present. Observe attentively the group of tall plants rising sparsely from the bottom, and showing their inconspicuous flowers alone above the surface. They stand in 10 or 12 feet of water at least, and are each **as** straight and tough as a plumb-line. The botanists, **who I am** sorry to say are famous for hard names, call the plant *Potomogeton lucens.* **The** loach-troller designates it by a less respectful synonym, as it often costs him a portion of his tackle. Around one of its stems there is **at present an eel of** great beauty and volume coiled **in a way which an** eel alone, or perhaps a **tree** serpent, could accomplish. Most persons, **I presume,** will have seen the conventional repre- **sentation of** Mercury's wand, with a snake twined **round** it. I can recollect no better emblem of the appearance of the eel in his present condition. If asked what he is doing there, I must candidly own I am not certain on that point. I can only answer for **the** fact of having met him frequently in the same position, and taken him off **his perch with my spear.** If conjecture is admissible **in** the case, I **would be** inclined to say that he is simply feeding on small water-shells and insects that adhere to the under surface of the leaves of these plants ; and also perhaps on a gelatinous member of the algæ family found attached to these and other acquatic vegetables, and which the rustic botanists call "eel-bite." I must, however, leave the **subject an open question for future** investigation, and request the young spearsman, who **has now** had sufficient elementary instruction for the purpose, to place, by a careful stroke, the object of discussion amongst the goods and chattels of our cargo. Diver will be happy to lend a *tooth* in disen- gaging him from the spear.

E. N. M.

HEY FOR COQUET!

Awa' frae the smoke an' the smother!
 Awa' frae the crush o' the thrang!
Awa' frae the labour an' pother,
 That hae fettered our freedom sae lang!
For the May's i' fu' bloom i' the hedges,
 An' the laverock's aloft i' the blue,
An' the south-wind sings low i' the sedges,
 By haughs that are silvery wi' dew.
  Up, angler, off wi' each shackle!
   Up, gad an' gaff, an' awa'!
   Cry—Hurrah! for the canny "red heckle,
    The heckle that tackled them a'!"

Off, off to the bonnie brown Norland!—
 It haunts me for aye i' my dreams—
To torrent, an' mountain, an' muirland,
 An' to Coquet, the queen o' the streams!
To Coquet, the beautifu' river,
 Beloved by the bards that sae lang
Upheld her the foremost for ever,
 An' hallowed her banks wi' their sang!
  Up, angler, off wi' each shackle, etc.

O Sharperton streams, we are comin'!
　O Halystane, greet us wi' glee!
O Rothbury, deep i' **the** gloamin'
　We'll bring our first creelfu' to thee!
An' Alwinton, Harbottle, Hepple,—
　If the great trout, the glorious an' strang,
Still sport i' your current's quick ripple,
　We'll measure their **inches ere lang**!
　　Up, angler, off wi' each shackle, **etc.**

From Blind-burn, **'midst** crag an' hill-hollow,
　To Warkworth, anear the **salt main,**
Each turn o' fair Coquet we'll follow,
　Each haunt o' our childhood regain!
At Thropton we winna dissemble
　Fu' hearts, nor at Harbottle-hold,—
An' at Weldon, wi' voices a-tremble,
　We'll pledge THE GREAT FISHERS O' AULD!
　　Up, angler, **off wi' each** shackle, **etc.**

We'll see if the Sharperton lasses
　Are winsome, as in our young days—
If they'll rin to the ringin' o' glasses,
　Or the lilt o' the auld merry lays.
Oh! we'll shake off the years wi' our laughter,
　We'll wash out our wrinkles wi' dew,—
An' reckless o' what may come after,
　We'll revel in boyhood anew:
　　Up, angler, off wi' each shackle, etc.

Then back to the smoke an' the smother !
The uproar an' crush o' the thrang !
An' back to the labour an' pother—
But happy an' hearty an' strang—
Wi' a braw light o' mountain an' muirland
Out-flashing frae forehead an' e'e,
Wi' a blessing flung back to the Norland,
An' a thousand, dear Coquet, to thee !
As again we resume the auld shackle,
Our gad an' our gaff stowed awa'—
An'——good-bye to the canny " red-heckle,
The heckle that tackled them a'!"

T. W.

A TORPEDO AT ONE END OF THE LINE.

To the fisherman—whether belonging to the genus *angler* proper, or to the successors of those who once let down their nets into the Lake of Gennesereth—there can be little doubt that *sport* is one of the principal attractions of his craft, and his sport may be pronounced of the most harmless as well as the most amusing kind ; but whether the following can be termed harmless to those who were engaged in it, is left to the judgment of the reader, to whom also will probably be confined the amusement to be obtained in the adventure itself which I have to **relate.** The fishermen concerned in it had too **little enjoyment in** what they met with to be desirous **of** experiencing a repetition of it, although when **all is** past the story **may be** related with some degree of glee.

It is to be supposed that the general habits and also the special faculties of the more common species of the Torpedo, emphatically called in English the Cramp Ray, are well known ; as they were in very ancient times in the Mediterranean, **where** this fish

is more often met with than with us, and where its
remarkable powers attracted the attention of the most
eminent philosophers, whose utter ignorance of the
nature of the phenomena characteristic of the fish
could only lead them to the belief that they were to
be ascribed to the then usual cover for what they
could not understand—the supposition of a magical
quality. With this obscure theory to act upon, phy-
sicians were accustomed to advise the application of
the living fish to the head of a patient for the cure of
pain in that part, and also to other parts of the body
for diseases of relaxation ; but where the living fish
could not be obtained, they expected to obtain the
same benefit from the application of the lifeless body ;
and even the cooked flesh was prescribed for the cure
of some diseases. But even in a living state, from
the manner in which it was used we judge that the
strength of the influence which this fish is capable of
exerting must at the times referred to have been un-
derrated, as it also seems to have been in the experi-
ments made at a more modern date, of which an
account has been given in our *Natural History of the
Fishes of the British Islands ;* and which deficiency
may be explained by the length of time during which
the fishes employed had been under unnatural circumstances ; and it is on this account the narrative
that follows may possess no small amount of interest
even to the natural historian.

The better to understand the story I have to relate, it is proper to remark that in fishing with a ground-sean in the sea, the operation must be conducted late in the evening or at night ; as, indeed, to be eminently successful, must be every kind of fishing in the ocean ; **and** when, instead of drawing this sweep-net or sean to land, it is to be received into a boat, a purse, or what is technically termed a bunt, is formed in the body of it, within which the captive fish become collected, that they may be the more easily secured and taken on board. On the south coast of Cornwall ten men proceeded together on such an expedition, and were successful in getting a good quantity of fish into their net, and which, while the bunt of the net remained in the water, they prepared to take with their hands into the boat. But while thus engaged, the man employed in handling the fish was heard to utter what his comrade described as a most unearthly yell, and then he fell backward to the bottom of the boat, so that his associates supposed that he had **been at the** least seized with **sudden** illness. **Several** minutes passed before he was able to utter a word, and consequently to relieve the anxiety **of** his friends, how it **was he had** been smitten ; but one of his companions, who manifested less sympathy with the terror under which he laboured than the rest, ascribed it to his being what he termed nervous ; but as in answer to this the sufferer ascribed what he had **felt to some-**

thing contained in the net, this individual exclaimed
that if the devil were there he would fetch him out,
and then, turning upward his shirt-sleeves, he proceeded to grasp in good earnest the fish that were in
the purse. But this formidable ray was a match for
all this bluster, and presently this man uttered a yell
to the full as loud as the scream of his comrade, on
hearing which all was consternation on board the
boat. The cause evidently was a fish, but of what
sort no one seemed to imagine. It was clear that
something must be done, and by some means yet
untried ; and after **some** consideration, one of the
company procured **a** pole, and with it he made a
thrust at the fish, **in the** supposition that at a safe
distance he might do so **with** impunity. In this,
however, he found himself mistaken ; and, as in the
instance of the case mentioned by the Greek poet
Oppian, where the shock passed through the line, a
shock was sent through his limbs, and, like his com-
rades, he fell down to the bottom of the boat. Fortunately it happened that among these fishermen
there was one who possessed some knowledge of the
nature of **a** fish able to exert powers which might
produce the effects witnessed, and all the crew **were**
resolute in their determination **not to be overcome.**
Various then were the contrivances they were prepared
to adopt to get their formidable assailant on board ;
and yet it so happened that before they succeeded,

every one of them was made to experience the powers
of their antagonist. It may be supposed that after so
many discharges of the torporific or galvanic influence,
the powers of this fish had become greatly exhausted,
but their experience had taught them not to trust in
this, and therefore a quantity of seaweed was procured, on which the bag or purse was laid, with the
fish still remaining in it, and in this way the whole
was brought safely to land.

J. C.

Polperro, *August* 18, 1865.

CARP-GOSSIP.

IN the *Whole Art of Fishing*, published in 1719, we
are informed that " the carp is a stately and very
subtle fish, called the fresh-water fox, and queen of
rivers." And the renowned Randle Holme, in his
very scarce and extraordinary work the *Accademiè of
Armory*, tells us that in heraldry " a carp is the
emblem of hospitality, and denotes food and nourishment from the bearer to those in need." This last-
mentioned book is probably one of the most curious
productions in our language, being a kind of panto-
logia, or encyclopædia written and arranged in a
heraldic form. Nothing is too high, nothing is too
low, for our author's comprehensive mind. Every
real and imaginary being, corporeal or spiritual, every
science and pseudo-science, every gradation of rank,
from the emperor with his ensigns of authority and
the ceremonies of his coronation, down to the butcher
and barber with the implements of their respective
trades, find a place in it. In this compendious
omnium gatherum we may find architecture and the
seven cardinal virtues maintaining their position
beside palmistry and the seven deadly sins ; cock-

fighting, quite unabashed, jostles with chronology ; while grammar and gambling, if so inclined, may pair off together. Bricklaying, glass-painting, and wrestling, philology and surgery, tennis and theology, are all **there**, and all represented by very **proper cuts in copper.** Nor are the technical terms used by hunters and fishers forgotten, among **which** last **we** may find a chapter explaining—"How every sort of fish are named after their age and growth," where we learn that a **carp is first** "**a** seizling, then **a sprole or sprale**," before it arrives at the full growth **and dignity** of carphood.

The well-known Horatian motto, *Carpe diem*, might, without any great violence to the original, be rendered, Catch your carp to-day, if you can, for the cunning customer may not be inclined to give you a chance **on the** morrow. Its suspicious carefulness is almost proverbial among fishers, and **it** even contrives **to** elude the fatal sweep of the net, **as described in** the *Prœdium Rusticum* **by Vaniere, who has not** inappropriately **been termed the French Virgil, and** is thus translated by **Duncombe** :—

> " Of all the fish that **swim** the watery mead,
> Not one in cunning can the carp exceed.
> Sometimes, when nets enclose the stream, she flies
> To hollow rocks, and there in secret lies ;
> Sometimes the surface of the waters skims,
> And springing o'er the net undaunted swims ;
> Now motionless she lies beneath the flood,

> Holds by a weed, or deep into the mud
> Plunges her head, for fear against her will
> The nets should drag her and elude her skill ;
> Nay, not content with this, she oft will dive
> Beneath the net, and not alone contrive
> Means for her own escape, but pity take
> On all her hapless brethren of the lake ;
> For rising, with her back she lifts the snares,
> And frees the captive, with officious cares ;
> The little fry in safety swim away,
> **And** disappoint the nets of their expected prey."

Hidden under a mountain of antiquarian lore, in one of the ten volumes* of the *Censura Literaria*, there is an amusing song commemorating the crafty character of the carp. It was written by the late Chief-Justice Abbott at Denton, in Kent, the seat of the late well-known literary antiquary, Sir Egerton Brydges, who is celebrated in it as the Knight of the Lake. Sir Egerton, though the House of Lords refused his claim, always alleged himself to be, *per legem terræ*, Baron Chandos of Ludeley, and a lineal descendant of that hero of romance, Sir Launcelot du Lac. The musical Lord of Penbury's board, mentioned in the *jeu d'esprit*, cannot be now identified. As the song is completely buried from the notice of the general public, in the only place in which it appears in print, no apology can be required for introducing it here :—

* Vol. ix. p. 369.

"THE CUNNING CARP AND THE CONTENTED KNIGHT.

*(**To** the Tune of St. George and the Dragon.)*

" Within the wood a virgin **ash**
   Had twenty summers seen ;
The elves and fairies marked **it oft**'
   As they tripped on the green ;
But the woodman **cut it** with his **axe,**
   He cruelly **fell'd it down,**
A rod to make for the Knight of the Lake,
   A knight of no renown.
Turn and taper round, turner,
   Turn and taper round,
For my line is of the grey palfrey's tail,
   And it is slender and sound.
     St. George he was for England,
   St. Denis he was for France,
     St. Patrick taught the Irishman
       To tune the merry harp.
     At the bottom of this slimy pool,
       There lurks a crafty carp,
    Were he at the bottom of my line,
How merrily he would dance.

" **In the Pacific Ocean**
   There dwelt a mighty whale,
And o'er the waves from London town,
   There went a noble sail,
With hooks and crooks, and ropes and boats,
   'Twas furnished in and out,
Boat-steerers and bold harpooneers,
   With sailors brave and stout :

The dart flew true and the monster slew,
  The seamen blessed the day,
All from his fin, a bone so thin,
  At the top of my rod doth play.
    St. George, etc.

" Moulded and mixed is the magic mass,
  The sun is below the hill,
O'er the dark water flits the bat,
  Hoarse sounds the murmuring rill,
Slowly bends the willow's bough,
  To the beetle's sullen tune,
And grim and red is the angry head
  Of the archer in the moon.
Softly, softly, spread the spell,
  Softly spread it around,
But name not the magic mixture
  To mortal that breathes on ground.
    St. George, etc.

" The squire has tapped at the bower window,
  The day is one hour old,
Thine armour assume, the work of the loom,
  To defend thee from the cold.
The Knight arose, and donned his clothes,
  For one hour old was the day,
His armour he took, his rod and his hook,
  And his line of the palfrey grey.
He has brushed the dew from off the lawn,
  He has taken the depth by the rule ;
Here is gentle to eat, come partake of the treat,
  Sly tenant of the pool.
    St. George, etc.

" The carp peeped out from his reedy bed,
    And forth he slyly crept,
  But he liked not the look, for he saw the black hook,
    So he turned his tail and slept.
  There is a flower grows in the field,
    Some call it a marigold-a,
  And that which one fish would **not take,**
    Another surely wold-a !
  And the Knight had read **in the** books of the **dead,**
    So **the** Knight **did** not **repine,**
  For they that cannot get **carp, sir,**
    Upon tench may very well dine.
        St. George, etc.

" **He has brushed the dew from the lawn** again,
    He hath taken the depth by the rule :
  Here is boiled bean and pea, come breakfast with me,
    Sly tenant of the pool.
  The carp peeped forth from his reedy bed,
    The carp peeped forth in time ;
  But he liked not the smell, so he cried Fare you well,
    And he stuck his nose in the slime.
  But the Knight had read in the books of the dead,
    And the Knight **did not repine,**
  For they that cannot get carp, sir,
    Upon tench may very well dine.
        St. George, etc.

" Then up spoke the Lord of Penbury's board,
    Well skilled in musical lore,
  And he swore by himself, though cunning the elf,
    He would charm him and draw him ashore.
  The middle of day he chose for the play,
    And he fiddled as in went the line ;

But the carp kept his head in the reedy bed,
  He chose not to dance, nor to dine.
I prithee, come dance me a reel, carp,
  I prithee, come dance me a reel—
I thank you, my Lord, I've no taste for your board,
  You'd much better play to the eel.
    St. George he was for England,
  St. Denis he was for France,
    St. Patrick taught the Irishman,
      To tune **the** merry harp.
    At the bottom of this slimy pool,
      There lurks a crafty **carp,**
    Were he **at the** bottom of my line,
How merrily **he would** dance."

In a **very** remarkable old work, written **nobody knows when, by** nobody **knows who, but first published in 1480, under the** title of *Dialogus Creaturam Moralizatus,* the **carp does not** figure to such **great** advantage as **a prudent and cunning fish.** It appears, according to the moraliser, that at a great fish festival, the carp and grayling quarrelled, as their betters have often done, on the rather delicate point of precedency. "I bask in the favour of the great and powerful," said the carp; "**even man** condescends to take care of me, and make **ponds for my special use and** protection." "**But,**" retorted the grayling, "**look** at my elegant **form and glittering scales;** I am much handsomer than **you are.** The other fishes commencing to side with **the** contending parties, a scene of general strife seemed **imminent, when** the wily old trout restored peace to the company by saying—"Why should we all be disturbed by this ridiculous quarrel? Let the disputants go to Judge Dolphin, he is a wise and just fish, and will soon decide the question." Accordingly the carp and grayling went to the dolphin, and, having laid the case before him, he said—"My children, you place me in a very awkward position. I am bound to do you justice, but how can I, having never seen either of you before? While you have been residing in fresh waters, I have all my life been rolling about in the restless waves of the ocean. Consequently, I cannot give a conscientious opinion as to which is the best fish, without I first taste you." So the dolphin incontinently snapped up the carp and grayling, and swallowing them down his gullet, said :—

> " No one ought himself to commend
> Above all others, lest he offend."

The carp is the only one of our fresh-water fishes that has attained to mythical honours. Its extreme cunning, so well characterised in the preceding quotations, and its peculiar colour, may have contributed to this elevation. **Pope,** in his *Windsor Forest,* speaks of

> " The yellow carp in scales bedropped with gold. "

And Vaniere gives the myth connected with that peculiar feature in the following lines :—

> " **The** carp, which in the Italian seas was bred,
> With shining scraps of yellow gold is fed ;

> Though changed his form, his avarice remains,
> And in his breast the love of lucre reigns,
> For Saturn, flying from victorious Jove,
> Compelled of old in banishment to rove
> Along th' Italian shore, a vessel found
> Beyond the lake of wide Benachus bound.
> He for his passage at a price agreed,
> And with large gifts of gold the master fee'd ;
> But he, the master, Carpus was he named,
> With thirst of gain and love of gold inflamed,
> Prepared in chains the passenger to bind.
> But to the God his face betrayed his mind,
> And from the vessel, in revenge, he threw,
> Into the waves the pilot and his crew ;
> Then into fish the traitors he transformed ;
> The traitors, still with love of lucre warmed,
> The sailing ships for golden fragments trace,
> And prove themselves derived from human race."

Taking into consideration the difficulty of catching a carp by ordinary means, this avariciously-inclined fish may be an emblem of the typical golden hook, with which the followers of the gentle art are not unfrequently taunted.

A fish, nearly allied to, if not perfectly identical with, our English carp, is found in several Indian rivers, where it is called Rohita, a name given by Cuvier as a generic appellation to several of the Indian Cyprinidæ. This fish has a sort of semi-sacred character, among both the Hindoo and Mussulman population of the East. In the Hindoo mythology, it is said to be the form of this carp which Vishnu assumed in his second *avatar*, for the purpose of recovering the Vedas or sacred books, that had been carried away by a demon during the devastation caused by a deluge. The Mahometans respect the Rohita for a very different reason, as they allege. There is an Oriental legend recorded in the Koran, to the effect that Abraham, after sacrificing a goat instead of his son Isaac, threw the sacred knife away, which falling into water miraculously struck this fish, thereby intimating that it was suitable for human food; and, consequently, a fish is the only animal that can be eaten by a Mussulman without previously having its throat cut. The Rohita is one of the most valuable fishes found in the rivers of the Gangetic provinces, and its beauty both in form and colour fully equals its excellence for the table. It need scarcely surprise us, then, to find that a fish of such value, having so high and ancient a mythical history, should be selected as the appropriate emblem or badge of a peculiar honour, styled in Persian, the diplomatic and court language of the East, Mahi Maratib—the Order or dignity of the fish. Those admitted to the Order receive the high-sounding titles of " Victorious in War, Saviour of the State, and Hero of the Land ;" and are distinguished by a representation of this carp, formed of gilt metal and partly enveloped in a mantle of green embroidered cloth, the sacred colour of the

Prophet—being carried on a pole before them, by an officer seated on an elephant.

The Order originated with the Mogul Dynasty in India, having been founded by Zenghis Khan, the conqueror of Asia, in the year 1206. One Englishman has received this decoration. In 1803, when the late General **Lake** visited Delhi, immediately after his brilliant **successes** in the Mahratta war, Shah Aulum conferred **this honour** upon **him.** Subsequently the General was created Lord Lake by George the Third, **and a few years later was** advanced to the title of Viscount Lake of **Delhi,** with an augmentation to his paternal arms, indicative **of** his Asiatic honours, described **by the** heralds as "**the** Fish of Mogul surmounting **the Goog and Ullum.**"

The Hindoos, **too,** commemorate the mythical **connection of** their religion with the Rohita or carp by a curious **device** frequently found in the sculptures and paintings of their temples. It represents three carps, forming a tri-corporated fish under one head, while between each are depicted stems and flowers of the sacred Indian plant, the Lotus—the *Nilumbium speciosum* of botanists.

The county of Surrey was, **in** the olden time, famed for producing the largest carp found in our English waters, and modern experience has not conduced to lessen its reputation in that respect. In 1836, the late Mr. Yarrell exhibited, at a meeting of the Zoological Society, a carp that had been netted in a piece of water called the Mere, at Pain's-hill, in Surrey. This specimen weighed 22 lbs., and was **in** length 30 inches, being in girth, taken at **the** commencement of the dorsal fin, 24 inches. **It** belonged to the well-known naturalist and angler Edward Jesse, Esq., by whose permission **it was** exhibited. Mr. Yarrell observed to **the** meeting, that " he could find no record of any carp **so large** having before **been** taken in this country." [*]

A curious **purpose for a carp to be** applied **to is** mentioned **in the manuscript** diary **of one** Bonnivert, a French **Protestant** officer **in** the service of King William III., that the writer once edited for an Irish archæological **journal.** Bonnivert was one of a detachment of dragoons employed in guarding treasure on its way from London to Ireland, in 1690 ; and he says :—

" Within three miles of **Namptwich is a very fine** house belonging to Sir Thomas Delft, with a very fine pool **full of** all wild fowls. You may take notice of a carp, that was **taken** here, three-quarters of a yard and odd inches long, which is set up as a weather-cock at the **top of** the house."

The writer was one of a party who disposed of a carp of about the same size in a much more sensible manner—at least, as they thought—by cooking it according **to the directions** given by the venerable Izaak Walton. Knowing well that culinary instructions

[*] *Proceedings of the Zoological Society of London,* Nov. 22, 1836.

are seldom carried out to the letter, they superintended the operation themselves. One of the party
proposed that some or all of the onions might be
omitted, and that the claret should be qualified with
an equal part of Madeira ; but these amendments were
overruled by the more enthusiastic Waltonians, though
subsequently at dinner it was unanimously acknowledged that they might have been passed with advantage.   Premising that it is not without some trouble
or charge, but will recompense both, **Walton** gives
his recipe thus :—

"Take a carp, alive if possible, scour him, and rub him
clean with water and salt, but scale him not ; then open him,
and put him, with his blood and his liver, which you must
save when you open him, into a small pot or kettle ; then take
sweet marjoram, thyme, and parsley, of each half a handful, a
sprig of rosemary, and another of savory ; bind them into two
or three small bundles, and put them to your carp with four
or five whole onions, twenty pickled oysters, and three anchovies.
Then pour upon your carp as much claret wine as will only
cover him, and season your claret well with salt, cloves, and
mace, and the rinds of oranges and lemons ; that done, cover
your pot and set it on a quick fire, till it be sufficiently boiled ;
then take out the carp, and lay it with the broth into the
dish, and pour upon it a quarter of a pound of the best fresh
butter, melted and beaten with half-a-dozen spoonfuls of the
broth, the yolks of two or three eggs, and some of the herbs
shred ; garnish your dish with lemons, and so serve it up, and
much good do you.—Dr. T."

None of the many able and inquisitive Waltonian

commentators, **not** even Sir Harris Nicholas himself, has ventured an **opinion as to who this "Dr. T." was,** thus quoted **by the renowned Izaak.** But, in the writer's humble opinion, there can be no doubt that he **was** Dr. Theodore Turquet de Mayerne, **a** well-known contemporary of Walton, having been **physician to** James I., Charles I., and Charles **II. He was** equally as famous as a **cook as** a physician, **and** the **best** work on cookery, published **in the** seventeenth century, under the grandiloquent **title** of *Archimagirus Anglo-Gallicus,* **was written by him ; and it contains a very similar recipe for cooking carp to that given** in the *Compleat Angler.* **It is most probable that** Turquet was, at least, an acquaintance **of** Walton, having an equally genial happy temperament. Though a noted *bon vivant,* he attained the advanced age of eighty-two years, and then ascribed the immediate cause of his death to drinking bad wine at a convivial meeting in a tavern in the Strand. **"Good wine,"** he used to say, "is slow poison ; I have been drinking it all my lifetime, and it has not killed me yet; **but** bad wine is sudden death."

W. P.

THE SILURUS GLANIS.

In the autumn of 1852 I started with a fellow-collegian from the University of Tübingen on an excursion into the "Upper Country," as the level tract is called which lies between the upper Rhine and the upper Danube. It is intersected by the watershed of these rivers, some of the streams falling into the Lake of Constance, and abounds with smaller and larger pools, much frequented by aquatic and grallatorial birds, which are rarely met with in the more densely-peopled districts of the "Lower Country." Our intention was to make ourselves acquainted with the living representatives of the species, the zoological characters of which we had diligently studied during the course of dry lectures from stuffed or prepared examples, and to shoot and collect wherever we should find opportunity.

The pools vary much in size, most of them not being larger than a mill-pond. We first visited the largest of them, a round lake of about a mile in diameter, called the *Feder-see*, literally *lake of feathers*, from the quantity of birds frequenting it. As it is one of the head-quarters of the fish of which I am going to give an account, and as its physical features are most remarkable, it will not be out of place to enter into a short description of it. The soil in its neighbourhood is composed of peat, and the ground becomes more and more boggy at a distance of a quarter of a mile from the margin of the lake. As we got nearer to it, we perceived that we were no longer on *terra firma*, the ground sinking and undulating under our feet at every step, and soon becoming perfectly impracticable without the aid of a pair of long planks or oars, upon which to step, and which, by offering a greater surface of resistance, prevent one's sinking into, or rather completely breaking through, a yard-thick crust of vegetable matter and soil, covered with a very luxuriant crop of grass and reeds, and resting on the surface of the water. A little farther on, perhaps a hundred yards from the visible margin of the lake, the crust, which to the very brink has the appearance of a meadow, is so thin that it bears only the weight of the ducks and snipes which rise in every direction.

Finding the walking over this treacherous ground —which, moreover, is frequently interrupted by regular holes and channels—inconsistent with our terrestrial habits, we went to a landing-place and took one of the boats, a very clumsy kind of punt, with a flat bottom and vertical sides ; it was propelled by a pole about twelve feet long, dilated into a blade at one end, which did not reach to the bottom of the lake, but enabled **us to** steer our course by means of the dense masses of weeds growing out of the mud, or suspended in the water. Sometimes a floating island of several yards in diameter offered a *punctum majoris resistentiæ*, but soon disappeared beneath the pressure of the oar. Nothing can be more singular than to see the grassy margin of the lake, just as the boat seems on the point of landing there, disappear beneath its weight, and continue yielding before its advance, which **it** does to such an extent that in some places one may push the boat for sixty or seventy yards over this floating meadow.

The lake is cheerful enough on a bright day, its surface being dotted **over** with water-lilies, the pure white colour of which beautifully contrasts with the brown, non-transparent water, and with the black coots swimming and diving in hundreds between them. But on a stormy day it has a very different and a most desolate aspect. Venturing out in bad weather, we found the wind blowing so hard .against us, that we could not reach the landing-place with **our** unmanageable boat, and so were obliged to cross the lake, which was covered with white foam, and to work our way through **a narrow** channel cut in the **crust** for such emergencies ; **the** latter, meantime, by **its continued and** regular **heaving,** showed clearly that it rested on deep water.

Now, this lake forms the western extremity of
the geographical range of the European species of
siluroid, which is known in most parts of Germany
under the name of *Wels** or *Weller* ; in Austria it is
named *schad,* in Hungary *harcsa,* in Sweden *mal.*
It belongs to a family which is entirely composed of
fresh-water fish, only a few entering brackish water,
and always keeping close to the **shore.** They are
found in great numbers **all over** Asia and Africa,
South and North America, and Australia, there being
not less than 675 species known.† **They** are distinguished from the cyprinoids, salmonoids, pikes, etc.,
by the total absence of true scales, and by the great
development of barbels round the mouth. The
species peculiar to Europe belongs more to its
eastern and central than to its western portions ; it
is not found in Italy, Greece, the Pyrencan Peninsula,
southern Switzerland, France, and those parts of
Germany which are drained by the Rhine and its

---

* This name is derived from the German *wälzen,* **English** *wal-
low.* *Wels* is a fish **wallowing in the** mud ; as the name **is less**
foreign to the English language than the Greek *silurus,* I have not
hesitated to adopt it ; the German name of *huchen* has been simi-
larly introduced into English, although no Saxon root is known
whence it may have been derived. The name "sheat-fish" cannot
be recommended, as it is more commonly applied to a marine fish ;
and that of "cat-fish" is better reserved for the American silur-
oids.

† A complete account of them may be found in the fifth
volume of my *Catalogue of Fishes.*

affluents.   There is no evidence, either geological or historical, that it ever existed in Great Britain or Ireland, and its reception **into** several works on British fauna is rather indicative of a wish that so remarkable a species should not be missing from the list of British fishes.   It is said to be found occasionally in the Lake of Neuchatel, but the most western locality for it, where it thrives, and is of value as an article of food, is, as I have stated, the country north of the Lake of Constance.   In speaking of rivers as *habitats* of the wels, or *Silurus glanis*, I must add that it is a lake rather than a river fish, avoiding even gentle currents, and retreating to those parts which **are almost dead water.**   In such spots it is found throughout the system **of the** Danube, and as far south as Constantinople.   The sluggish rivers of Northern Germany, and the numerous lakes of Mecklenburg and Northern Prussia abound with the wels ; in Scandinavia it appears to be limited to a few localities, being more numerous in the eastern than the western parts ; it is found in the systems of all the rivers running into the Black and Caspian Seas, and probably it extends further eastwards into Central Asia, but in China and Japan we find it replaced by other, although closely allied species.

It is a historical fact, worthy **of** the notice of those who would attempt the acclimatisation of the wels, that it has naturally extended its geographical

range within the last century; it is now of not un-
common occurrence in the Lake of Constance, into
which it was accidentally introduced by inundations;
and several instances are known of its capture in
Holland, although it is evidently not indigenous to
that country.

THE SILURUS GLANIS OR WELS.

The wels in general appearance has some similarity to the burbot; the head is large, broad, and
depressed, as long as the trunk, which ordinarily is
subcylindrical, but appears also very broad when the
fish has filled its capacious stomach, or when the
female is full of roe; the tail is compressed, and
longer than the head and trunk together. The entire
fish is destitute of scales, and covered with a smooth
slippery skin like the eel. The snout is truncated,
the mouth not cleft far backwards, but broad, with
the lower jaw longest and very extensible. There are
six barbels round the mouth, two of which, situated

on either side of the upper jaw before the eye, are
very long, nearly extending to the tail ; the other four
are much shorter, and arranged in pairs on the chin.
Both jaws and palate are armed with broad bands of
small, closely-set teeth, which give to the bones a
rasp-like appearance. **The eyes are** very small, and
a thin, more or less transparent skin passes over **them,**
so that the perception of light must be very limited.

When we recollect **that the** water of the rivers
and lakes inhabited by the wels **is** generally coloured,
it is evident that only a few rays of light can pene-
trate to the depth where the fish chooses its lurking-
place. **Now in fishes** which inhabit dark places or
great depths, we find the organ either extremely **large,
as in nocturnal animals, in order to collect as many
rays of light as possible, or quite rudimentary. The
latter is the case with the wels, but this** fish is provided with a compensatory organ in the barbels surrounding its mouth, especially those of the upper
jaw, which can be moved voluntarily in every direction ; and anybody who has had the opportunity of
observing one of these fishes in an aquarium, must
have been struck by the constant and peculiar motion
of these barbels, **which is** very **similar** to that of the
common aquatic **worms known by** the name of
Sœnuris. When the **fish** moves about leisurely, it
uses them constantly, feeling its way with them.
Therefore **these** barbels have the double purpose of

attracting other fish, which mistake them for worms, and of serving as feelers.*   When the wels perceives its prey close enough to be seized, it makes a dart, which, considering the width of its gape, and the nature of the armature of its mouth, can rarely fail to be successful.

To return to our description of the head, we have only to mention that the gill-openings are very wide, and extend forwards to behind the chin. No other European fish has the fins developed in so peculiar a manner as the wels ; the dorsal fin is very small and short, placed at no great distance from the head, whilst the anal fin is very long, composed of about ninety rays, and occupies the entire lower surface of the tail, running to the caudal fin, with which it is joined ; the caudal fin itself is rounded. The pectoral and ventral fins are rather small, compared with the size of the fish, and the former is provided with a short bony spine, which, however, is too feeble to be used as a weapon of defence. Tropical species have this spine powerfully developed, inflicting with it serious, and sometimes fatal, wounds. The structure and arrange-

---

* I much regret having omitted to make the following experiment, which never occurred to me till this moment, and which I recommend to those who may have the opportunity of watching a wels in an aquarium. I fed my little welses with young breams, but I have no doubt that they would take also roe or pieces of raw meat. In this case it would be interesting to see whether the wels feels the food offered with the barbels before seizing it.

ment of the fins of the wels are entirely in accordance with its mode of life ; being a bottom-fish it does **not** require a development of those fins by which the body is balanced and kept suspended in the water ; therefore pectorals, ventrals, and dorsal are small. The only motion necessary for its subsistence is to dart after the fish which approach it ; to enable it **to do** this with rapidity, either forwards or sideways, its long flexible tail is admirably adapted, the anal fin increasing the surface of the organ, and rendering the stroke more powerful. For the same purpose the pike has the dorsal and anal fins placed far backwards, close to the caudal.

All the upper parts and the fins are bluish-black, passing into blackish-green **on the** sides ; the lower parts whitish, marbled with black.

The wels is the largest species of fresh-water fish **in** Europe, the sturgeons belonging as much **to the** marine as to the fresh-water fauna ; specimens from 4 to 5 feet long, and from 50 to 80 lbs. in weight, are of common occurrence, and single individuals of 4 or 5 cwt. are caught almost every year ; their increase **with age is proportionately** much **more** in girth than **in length, and they sometimes attain** such a size in **the body as to exceed** the compass **of a man's arms. The wels is** very sedentary **in its habits, lying in a** hole or behind some **projecting** object **during the day, and** moving **slowly about in the** night, **but never to a**

great distance from its chosen retreat. If disturbed,
it darts away, throwing up clouds of mud raised by
the sweeping motions of its tail. When its place of
retreat is known it may be easily caught by means of
a hook baited with a lively fish, and sunk sufficiently
deep ; the coarsest tackle may be used, and the fishermen generally haul it up bodily, like a codfish.
When once out of the water, the wels seems to become almost torpid ; and I recollect especially one
occasion when, requiring the head of a large example
for examination, I was witness to the decapitation by
one of the Berlin fisherwomen of a perfectly healthy
wels **of 40 or 50 lbs.** weight, the fish, from the moment it was placed on the block, making no further
struggle than by a slight vibration of the muscles of
the tail,—the headless body afterwards disgorging a
fresh roach which had served as breakfast during the
time the fish was in the tub.

Night-lines, spears, wicker-baskets, and nets, are
generally used in its capture. As we might anticipate from its habits, the wels principally preys on
bottom-feeding fish : roach, red-eyes, carp, tench, eels ;
but it will take any other moving creature, frogs and
all sorts of diving birds being frequently found in its
stomach. Salmonoids have little to fear, because
they rarely inhabit the same locality with the wels,
and even should that sometimes be the case, their
habits of feeding are so different from those of the

bottom-feeders, that a wels must have but rarely a
chance of catching them.   Under favourable circumstances the wels grows quickly in the earlier part of
its life, attaining a weight of $\frac{1}{2}$ lb. in the first year,
and 3 lbs. in the second ; it is very probably a long-
lived fish, growing, like many others, during the whole
of its existence.   Different opinions exist as to the
flavour of its flesh.   That of young individuals is
certainly not inferior to the flesh of the pike ; and
that of old ones appeared to me to taste exactly like
the flesh of a sturgeon.   In districts where it is
found in some quantity, the air-bladder is preserved
and used as isinglass.

At one of the first meetings of the Acclimatisation
Society of Great Britain, to which I had been invited
in order to give my opinion as to the feasibility of the
introduction of the pike-perch (*Lucioperca*), I opposed
the plan, for reasons which I then detailed, and directed
the attention of the meeting to the wels, stating that
it was the only species which could be recommended
for acclimatisation at present.   The acclimatisation of
tropical fish, no matter whether from lowland waters
or from mountain-streams, is a thing as impossible as
that of palm-trees ; yet it has been proposed, talked
of, and even written about.   In a climate like that of
Great Britain, only those species can thrive which are
taken from a temperate zone ; therefore, the idea of
transporting a valuable species from the temperate

parts of Australia to Europe, would not have been so chimerical, if the persons who entertained it had only been able to fix upon such a fish. But the ichthyology of Australia is at present in its infancy, only a small proportion of the species being known, much less their habits. Not less than five different kinds of fish, as distinct as perch, burbot, and pike, were brought over under the name of "*Murray Cod.*" The promoters of the experiment of introducing the salmon into Australia do not appear to be aware **that** they have there already salmonoids as **nearly akin to** the European kinds as we can expect in two countries so remote from each **other.** As long as our knowledge of Australian fish is so incomplete, I cannot believe that the time has arrived when we may look for successful additions to our fauna from the Southern Hemisphere.

Thus we ought to limit ourselves to the freshwater fish of temperate Europe and America, but it is surprising how small is the number **of** such **kinds** which are not naturally indigenous to Great Britain. For leaving aside valueless fish, we find that **all the** genera occurring **in** Europe and **North America—** salmons, salmon-trouts, trouts, chars, vendaces (Coregoni, whitings), perches, **burbots,** eels, etc.—are represented in Great Britain, so that the forms found on the Continent and in North America can be considered as merely local races, which, if they could be transplanted, might deteriorate, **or** at all events yield no greater advantage than the native ones. There are, however, two genera, to which this similarity of the fish fauna of Great Britain with that of the Continent and America does not extend—viz. river charrs and silures. There is a magnificent kind of the former genus in the Danube, a fish well known to all the readers of the *Field*, under the name of *huchen*.* If the efforts to restore the Thames to the number of salmon rivers should fail, it would be an attempt worthy of the Acclimatisation Society to introduce the *huchen* into it, as it does not go down to the sea, and would of itself fairly compensate for the gudgeons and roach which form its principal food. Moreover, its introduction by means of artificial hatching would be the best way of convincing those who with *Von Baer* † contend that artificial impregnation produces sickly fry with the blood-vessels incompletely developed.

The silures are represented in America by several species, but none of them attain to the size of the wels, nor are they esteemed in their own country as an

---

* The question has been discussed whether there exist charrs passing all their life in rivers ; the *huchen* is an instance of such a fish, as it is proved by its zoological characters to belong to that group ; other examples could be mentioned from Canada and the rivers west of the Rocky Mountains.

† The great natural philosopher of St. Petersburg, who may be called the inventor of artificial inpregnation of fish-eggs, and whose observations on this subject are invaluable.

article of food. On the other hand, the wels recommends itself for acclimatisation in more than one respect. It may be procured in large numbers from the numerous lakes in Mecklenburg and Northern Prussia, at the place indicated in the beginning of this paper; the price of 1000 young fish would not exceed £15. Its tenacity of life insures an easy transport during the two or three days' journey, without any considerable loss, if young examples, not above 10 inches in length, be selected, and the transport be made during the cooler part of the year. The place for its reception must be judiciously chosen, but there are numerous lakes in the north of England, Wales, Scotland, and Ireland, whose physical features are in accordance with those of its native place; and we sincerely hope that the few specimens which are now in possession of the Society of Acclimatisation may be the forerunners of a more extensive immigration, which might draw yet another presumption in favour of success from the fact that all the immigrations of animals which are known to have taken place in a state of nature have proceeded from east to west.

A. G.

FLY-FISHING BY NIGHTLIGHT.

" Non fumum ex fulgore, sed ex fumo **dare lucem.***"—Horace.*

IF it **be** sometimes difficult to understand the ways
of nature, it is often more difficult to understand the
ways of philosophers. Their explanations, indeed,
are more perplexing **than** the problems they propose
to solve. In subjecting the operations of matter and
mind to theory, some fact, condition, or circumstance
is generally omitted, **which** vitiates the result. **New-**
ton himself, I am told, **for I** have not myself **verified**
the statement, is only digestible with a sauce **of ex-**
ceptions ; and Locke has notoriously failed **to enable**
us to comprehend the " human understanding." **But**
the greatest defaulters in this respect are undoubtedly
Gall and Spurzheim. Those " Davenport Brothers,"
professing to untie the " knot metaphysical " of
thought, mapped out the **brain** into little molehills,
in which **were to** be found explanations of all the
passions, powers, and subtleties of mind, down to the
psychological **curiosities of** a " sensation novel," or
the ministerial reply **to an inquisitive** member of the
" Opposition." **But in** their craniological chart, the

site of the "organ of angling" is actually omitted.
No elevation appears there to mark the seat of the
"gentle craft." Now, of the existence of such a
"bump," in some corner or other of the human brain,
no reasonable doubt can be entertained. To the
numerous votaries of the craft no appeal on the subject need be made. Though unconscious perhaps of
carrying this particular cerebral development under
their fishing beaver, they have all felt its excite-
ments. Otherwise, how indeed should we be able to
account for that spasmodic twitching of the flexor
muscles of the hand and forearm to grasp a rod, which
we have all experienced, when lakes or rivers cross
our path at home or abroad? The amiable weakness
too is often most forcibly felt in out-of-the-way places,
where we are least prepared to indulge its promptings.
But the "organ" throbs notwithstanding, in unavailing pulsations. As it has occurred doubtless
to many others, so has it happened many times to
ourselves. Amongst the far-off affluents of the
Tagus, and the little brook of Balsain flowing down
from the snows of the Guadarama through the green-
est of pine-forests to the pleasant summer retreats
of San Ildefonso, I have often experienced this
Angleomania in full force. The latter rivulet, indeed, was well calculated to test the activity of the
latent "bump," as it gave ocular demonstration of
containing the largest number of small trout I re-

member to have seen sporting in so diminutive a
stream. Wordsworth's description, which so much
amused Byron and his friends in former days, would
exactly suit it :—

> " I measured it from side to side,
> 'Twas two feet deep and three feet wide."

Boulders and fragments of rock were considerately
thrown across its bed at short intervals, to increase
its volume and give a wider playground to its tiny
inmates. In the *churros* or merry little pools caused
by these obstructions, almost any number of small
trout might be caught of a morning with a grub or
worm. A stone causeway ran along its margin for
the accommodation of royal feet, when it so pleased
them to go a-fishing. A diplomatic friend amused
himself in the regal way ; but it was dull work after
all to pull up a troutling at every other cast. Fly-
fishing was impracticable from the extreme brightness
of the water and clearness of the atmosphere. I had,
therefore, only to look on in compassionate silence at
this specimen of royal angling, and think of a bounding
skiff, a stiff breeze, and the drake just released from
his *pupal* prison starting on his first flight from the
crest of a swelling wave on the Inniel or the Sheeling.
Larger trout, I was informed, were to be found in
the reservoir which fed the famous fountain of *La
Granja*, hard by. This was a pretty tarn called *El
Mar*, in the grandiloquence of the Castilian, remark-

able for the purity of its waters and the charming
frame of mountain and pine forest, in which, like a
huge mirror, dark in its own lustre, it was partially
set. As the shortest way to test the accuracy of the
information, I cross-lined an angle of it with some
old river-flies supplied by my friend ; but the evening
was too calm, and the "mount" too imperfect, for a
satisfactory experiment. So I returned to the gardens,
to witness half the hierarchy of Olympus playing at
"aquatics" through all the curious devices of
hydraulic engineering, amongst which Fame, perched
on her lofty column in front of the palace, shot a
dazzling jet of purest crystal high above the neighbouring elms, on which it returned in copious showers
of prismatic spray, as many-hued and evanescent as
the fallacious voices of her own trump.

If the indulgent reader who has followed me
through this rather devious introduction to the immediate object of this paper be not wearied with my
discursive flights, I would respectfully invite **him to**
join me in a night excursion to **a** locality at home,
where better sport was to be had in former days than
in the royal preserves of San Ildefonso. It is only
a stone's-throw (or a " good shout," as our imaginative
boatman awaiting us measures space) beyond the
green hills in the distance. The glories of a summer
sunset will illumine, the dews of evening refresh us
on the way. By night-angling, however, I would

beg to premise, that poking in the dark at the tail of a weir or mill-dam, with a "blue-bottle" or "down-looker" wriggling *in articulo mortis*, is not exactly meant. No ; that was not the vulgar desecration of the angling rites of old Nox which was practised in other days on the waters of the Lane or Bawn. The first-named of these Irish lakes will serve as well as any the purposes of illustration. I select it not for its great extent, for there are many larger ; nor for its beauty, for there are many fairer ; but for the fact of my having acquired there my first knowledge of night-angling. It presented, however, all the requisites for this description of fishing in perfection ; and many of the local and traditional characteristics which give to its practice a colouring **and zest.** Every description of fishing-ground was represented by extensive sharps, winding shores, wooded islets, and reaches of water fringed with the purple bloom of the reed and bullrush. Of fairy lore and feats of enchantment, there was an abundant garnish to this, the romance, as it might be called, of angling. The waters themselves were but the traditional evidence of the punishment of one of seven royal sisters submerged in the waves for the old offence of female curiosity. They were tenanted besides by many anomalous beings, which, under various forms, sometimes unceremoniously surprised maids that "loved the moon" and a twilight bath. Popular belief had also attributed to the waters of this lake the, to anglers, curious and interesting property of communicating to those who washed their hands in it the power of being ever after able to unravel with ease the perplexing tangles of their tackle. Instead of referring to the pages of an almanac, there seems to be no valid reason why I should not mark the proper date for commencing this description of angling, by drawing on the calendar used in the locality of the lake itself for the division of time. **It** usually began, then, to be practised about the festival of St. John, contemporaneous with the summer solstice, when the fires of Baal, at the time **I** chronicle, might yet be seen blazing at midnight on the surrounding hills ; and the hierophants, in the mixed rites of paganism and Christianity, scattering the last embers of the expiring piles amongst the corn-fields to secure them against blight and barrenness. Over the superstition of the usage let no brother of the angle shed a tear of sentimental horror. The actors indeed in these festive scenes were, I can assure him, much more alive to the lively **music of** the piper or the fiddler who ministered to the dance on those occasions, than to the worship of the pagan deity or the Christian saint to whose feast-day the unholy fires were said to have been transferred by the early missionaries. Neither would I recommend him to waste his indignation on the barbarous *coina*, or

funereal dirge, which might at this **period be still**
heard to dwell in wild and mournful cadence over the
waters of the lake, as some lost member of the old
race was borne to his last home in the grey abbey-
grounds at the back of the hills. The strain itself
indeed is not to be despised. The antiquarian
musician, interested in such matters, will find it in
Bunting's last collection of Irish airs, and may judge
for himself. The *motif* at least forms a noble chant;
and I can aver that though having wound up *de pro-*
fundis many fine trout to the tune, I never once
smelt the whisky **by** which it has been said to have
been accompanied, nor witnessed the faction fights in
which, if we are to credit some recent writers, it
usually terminated over the grave.

But the sun is within a few strides of the sum-
mits of Ben and Carrick hills, which another heave
of the old Titans might have elevated to the dignity
of mountains, just as intelligibly as the "geological
forces" employed for such heavy work nowadays.
The "lucid interval" may be usefully employed,
before we descend to the lake, in describing the tackle
employed in night-angling with the fly and the mode
in which it was used. Any sound lake-rod sufficed
for this purpose; the amateur might please himself
in minor details of "fashion," but his choice in length
was limited to fourteen feet, and under. The line
and reel were identical with those employed in day-

angling.   The pole or handle of the landing-net, the indispensable companion of **the rod,** was from six to seven feet in length, and spiked at the lower end. The hoop, ovate or circular, but always of wood, measured about twenty inches in its greatest diameter.   The net part of the article, I may here observe, has the disagreeable property of becoming rotten without the leave or knowledge of the owner. Large trout sometimes took advantage of this idiopathic **infirmity of hemp, and** at the critical moment of life or death, **shot through it as** if so much **gossamer.**   The accident **is** about as awkward as **any** incidental to angling.   The absence of a recognised standard-gauge amongst hook-makers, some using numerical, others alphabetical symbols, renders precision in the description of the flies employed somewhat difficult.   To state that they were of the usual lake-fly size would, at least to some anglers, convey an erroneous impression of their magnitude.   The fisher of Welsh **lakes would assume probably that** river-flies were meant.   **Not a few of the anglers** even of **the great Scottish** lakes would **be** likely **to** commit **a** similar mistake.   But more extraordinary still, I have seen a certain class of sedate, middle-aged votaries of the "gentle craft," starting on an excursion **to** the Irish lakes, with their fly-books (fly-dictionaries would be a more appropriate name), stuffed with these small **river-flies for** presentation to

the six and "seven pounders" of Kiltoomb! I will
not assert that large trout *never* rise to this kind of
fly in Irish lakes, for I know that they have done so.
But the instances are so few and accidental that the
exception in such cases proves the rule to the contrary. The size, then, of the fly here intended for
night-angling, is one or two sizes less than the ordinary salmon-fly, with which I presume all anglers are
acquainted. The selection of the species or varieties
of flies to be employed, though of much importance,
is not so readily disposed of. Indeed a jury of Irish
anglers themselves would, I fear, have to stand a
long siege in the jury-room before giving a unani-
mous verdict on the subject. A general instruction
must certainly suffice, where certainty is impracticable. As a rule, the flies found to kill best by
day will answer best by night. To describe the
materials, the style of dressing, and other *minutiæ*
of manipulation of even half-a-dozen of flies for this
purpose, as such duty should be performed, would
occupy more space than could be well devoted to the
task in this place. I must therefore assume that the
angler is sufficiently acquainted with the water he
fishes, and the flies suitable to it, to make his own selection. His next step will be to mount the flies chosen
on two foot-lines, one of which he attaches to his
line ; the other, as a reserve cast, he winds round his
hat. If an accident should occur, or a change of flies

become necessary, a foot-line on his "beaver" is more accessible in the dark than deposited in a fly-book. Those flies were almost universally used on the foot-line, and about three feet apart, in fishing the Irish lakes. The same rule was observed in night-angling. I need scarcely add that the foot-line was of single gut, which should be of the strongest salmon kind. If the angler resided near the lake, he generally mounted his rod before starting. It saved time and the trouble of manipulating a number of small things in imperfect light. As the rod which **is** now equipped for action is not very heavy, and may be worked occasionally by one hand, there is no objection to adding a few "Havanas" to the contents of the fly-case. The faculty of smell in fish is, I believe, confined to their own element.

All these minute details and preparations, which doubtless for many anglers are superfluous, centre in the use of a light handy boat, without which night-angling on lakes would be a bootless occupation. Through its agency alone could the haunts **of the** fish sought for be reached, and adequately angled. A rower who can propel his craft over the water as silently and efficiently as an otter can regulate his movements in that fluid is desirable. The little craft should be perfectly under his command. "A land-lubber" is bad enough by day ; but at night would be intolerable. Two persons accustomed to these nocturnal excursions may conveniently practise this **kind of** angling in the same boat. They are seated respectively, **one at the stem,** the other at the stern, the rower occupying the middle seat. The fishing is conducted partly by trolling the flies, partly by casting. That is, while the boat is being taken up to the head of the wind and of the reach of water to be angled, the flies are trolled with about twenty or thirty yards of line out, and the rods lowered to the gunwale of the boat ; but the above points being gained, the craft is **allowed to** drift parallel with the **waves and by the action** of the wind alone. It is the duty **of the rower to keep** the boat perfectly in a line **with the** wave, so that one of the anglers is not advanced **before the other.** If the craft is properly **constructed for** lake-angling, with stem and stern **alike,** it will keep its proper place on the drift without assistance of oar or helm. The rods are now taken up, the lines reeled in to the proper length, which will be about that of the rod used, and the process of casting commenced; the casting is of course performed alternately by the anglers in the direction **of the** wind, care being taken that the process is **well** timed, and that the flies fall lightly on the **water, and are drawn in a** line somewhat diagonal **to the** trough of the waves. When the reach of fishing - ground selected is exhausted, another is chosen, and so on.

One essential precaution remains to be noticed. When the boat is being rowed up for another fall, it should not pass over the ground intended to be fished by casting only.   It is obvious that by such a mistake the fish would be scared from their feeding haunts. From what has been stated, it may be inferred that this kind of angling is entirely different from that practised on the Tay in salmon-fishing from a boat.

Though large trout will rise to flies freely at night in trolling, **night angling** in the Irish lakes was considered, by those who practised it, a **work** purely of *casting*, **and in** this indeed consisted one of its chief charms.   As in all other kinds of fly-fishing, a certain amount of wind is advantageous ; it should not however be inconveniently high.   A light breeze will best fulfil the requirements of the occasion.   An overcast sky has its uses, not on account of diminishing the quantity of light, but for intercepting shadows, which, if the moon "ruled the night," would be troublesome accessories.   The low muttering of distant thunder and vivid flashes of lightning, which often prevail at this season, though adding much to the beauty and solemnity of lake scenery at night, are inauspicious omens.   I have observed that fish, though some of the family are expert electricians, are not in general partial to electricity.   It seems neither to sharpen their appetites, nor to enliven their movements.   **As** it does not therefore add to the chances

of success, and a flash might cut the line too closely
for personal comfort, as happened once upon a time,
the angler had better not select what my Cheshire
friends call a "thunnery evening" for a night-angling
experiment.

The hour, however, has at length arrived to descend, rods and net in hand, to the lake. The moment
is accurately and gracefully defined by old Sam
Rogers. It is just **when**—

> " Twilight's soft dews steal o'er the village green,
>   With magic tints to harmonise the scene,"

that this step in advance is to be taken. Our boat
awaits us in a little creek on the shore, and is simply
made fast to a submerged pine stump, which Pat, our
native "skipper" for the night, declares "must have
been growing long before Adam was a *gossoon*," a cor-
ruption probably of the French *garçon*. Now, whether
Adam really passed through that interesting stage of
humanity referred to in Pat's remark may of course
be doubted, though Dr. Colenso's high authority is on
his side of the argument.

But we **are** spared the necessity of philosophising
further " on our stump," for Pat has unloosed the
chain, and sent us and himself afloat amongst the
rustling reeds, whose gentle murmurs, so familiar to
the fisherman's ear, are certainly more agreeable to
listen to than the appalling discords of geology.

They still indeed make good their claims to mytho-
logical origin, and make us almost fancy that Pan
and Syrinx are whispering their loves amongst **the**
leaves. But the pleasant music of the Pandean
orchestra is soon interrupted by an outburst of angry
voices from the aquatic birds, which love, feed, and
flap about in these reedy coverts by night. The poor
things are obviously angry at our untimely intrusion.
If their strength and unanimity were indeed equal to
their indignation **and numbers,** they might jeopardise
our further progress to the fishing-ground. The simple
peasant, impressed by the stillness **and** darkness of
night, might be almost excused for confounding the
wild variety of their cries, colours, and movements
with those of the enchanted beings which he believes
to inhabit the depths of the lake. Pat is not at all
convinced·that these nocturnal sounds are emitted
by the gentle social tribes of waterfowl that hover
over, or make their toilet on, the glassy surface of **the**
lake during the day. For the peculiar habits of one
section of the family it is not so easy to account. **The**
group consists of a number of small gulls, which
hover overhead in the wake of the boat, and pursue
it for miles in whatever direction it takes. Whether
actuated by love, fear, or hope of prey, the voices of
the aërial choir produce one of the wildest and most
mournful of " Notturnos." It might well serve as a
dirge for one of Ossian's heroes. Pat solves the prob-

O

lem of its supernatural character by supposing it to
emanate from certain "troubled spirits," **condemned**
for some unknown offences committed in the flesh
thus to wander in the **air** by night till **the** term of
their punishment has expired.   He is not, however, in
the least terrified, but rather amused, by the screams
of these "troubled spirits" during *the day*, when,
gracefully flitting amongst the waves, they contend
with each other **in** picking up the May-fly, of which
they appear as fond as the trout themselves.

Amongst these local accompaniments of a night
excursion on **the water, we** proceed to the fishing-
ground.   Upon the selection of this important **part**
of the subject of night-angling, a word or two may be
interpolated between the pauses in Pat's *yarn* on the
feats of the " Great White Horse" of the lake, whose
nocturnal visits to the neighbouring farmers' brood
mares and corn-fields were then a popular "Irish
grievance," though **never,** I believe, brought before
Parliament.   **It will** have been observed, however,
that the flies **have not** yet been wetted or the rods
lowered **to their proper** places, though **we have** been
some time afloat.   **As we** were pursuing a course
through the centre and deepest parts of the lake, it
would have been superfluous to do so.   Trout do not
generally rise to flies from great depths at night—sel-
dom even by day.   **Their** favourite haunts for feeding
at this hour **are** extensive sharps, the margins of

reed-ponds, and the wooded shores of creeks and islands. **Lakes** which do **not** possess these local characteristics will seldom be found suitable for this kind of angling. The large fish are doubtless attracted to the localities indicated by the small fry of various kinds which frequent them, and the abundance of insect life amongst woods and shady places. The proofs indeed of this idiosyncracy of large trout, if not visible to the eye, are often made sensibly audible to the ear of the night angler, by the frequent plunges after small fish, and the hollow gulps **of** juicy moths or caterpillars, heard amongst the reeds or under the shade of trees.

But the conclusion of our remarks upon local fitness for this kind of angling, and of Pat's *yarn* about the enchanted horse of the lake, has brought us to a favourable . specimen of fishing-ground along the reedy and wooded shore of an island of considerable extent. **Pat** instinctively and silently **crosses** the oars, the boat's side **is given to the breeze, and as it** drifts evenly and slowly before the wind, **the** anglers alternately drop their flies on the waves. Expectation, not unfrequently mixed perhaps with rivalry about a first rise, supersedes precept and lake lore. The angling virtue of patience, however, so necessary on all occasions, is pre-eminently required here. The larger description of trout I have never found so numerous in any water that I have fished,

as they are supposed to be by most anglers. Many
feasible arguments might be adduced in favour of
this experience. Rapid "rising" of such fish, by
which I mean trout of 6 or 7 lbs. weight, is not
to be looked for in this or indeed in any other kind
of lake-angling with flies, with which I am acquainted, except under some peculiar circumstances.
The majority of trout caught were of the same species,
and in the best waters are always considerably below
the weights named ; the larger specimens being only
the *rari nantes in gurgite vasto,* whose size and weight
compensate the angler for their paucity of numbers.
Such captures indeed are but the great prizes in the
lottery of angling. The night fisher must therefore
not be impatient. His pursuit is more likely to
secure the higher class of fish than any other kind of
angling with flies. Success will reward his perseverance when he least perhaps expects it. A cast over
a favourable haunt may make all the difference between doubt and certainty. "The froth outside the
reeds, sirr," exclaimed Pat, after a long and reluctant
silence ; " jist tickle its edge with the bees"—a generic
name applied by him to all artificial flies—" and you'll
find maybe something under it"—pointing at the
same time with dilated pupils to a broad stripe of
foam stretching down the lake. As he spoke and the
flies fell on the favourite locality, a loud splash followed, the divided froth disclosing in the hazy light

the black arched back of a full-grown *laker*, as he plunged to the bottom with one of Pat's "bees" fast in his larynx to keep him company.

"Hould fast, sirr, and keep him from takin' a dance among the reeds;" and in pursuance of the exigency of the case he turned the boat's head to deep water.

Having gained the latitude which he thought safe for a fair fight, he resumed his commentary on passing events. "The ould schaming sinner," he continued, "it's an advantage he'd be takin', shure enough, of thim innicent bits ov corncrake's feathers and the wool of Monaghan's brown cow, thinkin' they wor the fat *plum perlauns* (moths and beetles) he used to waylay among the reeds and the froth, when he ought to be asleep in his own cabin like other honest people;" and with a satisfied shrug of his shoulders, and a humorous leer at the line, as it cut through the waves in unison with the movements of the "ould sinner," he crossed his oars once more and took the landing-net in his hand. With large trout, such as has been assumed as the subject of illustration, the acts in the tragic drama might be extended to the legitimate number; for the hero of the piece has quite sufficient strength and vitality to protract the *dénouement* to that extent. But at night, when the performance cannot be so satisfactorily witnessed, the clear indication is to terminate it as soon as possible.

For this purpose, the *onus* must be thrown on the rod and tackle, which require to be managed with a stiff **hand, and** subjected to the severest test. The first time therefore that the truant can be brought to the efficient distance of the net, that useful implement should at once transfer him to the safe-keeping of the locker. **Pat** may be safely intrusted with this important duty; and is anxious no doubt to smoke a pipe at the captive's " wake."

The capture of one of these large fish is in most cases **so** like another, that further description would be superfluous. **After** twelve too the sport need not **be prolonged. The** fish themselves appear to feel the **drowsy influence of that** hour ; and to slacken in **their raids on the moths** and other insect lovers of **the night.** Our noisy **little** companions, the gulls, **have ceased their scolding** in the air, and folded their heads under their **downy** wings. The bittern, the last of which **was** shot in this district some 45 years ago, has suspended his hollow booming in the marsh. The **hawk and** the heron—those mortal **enemies, which nature** by some inscrutable **arrangement** ordains **to** build their nests in neighbouring trees—have discontinued their nocturnal combat, into **which they were** roused by our approach to the island. **The** owl, the otter, and the fox—those stealthy apparitions of the night, which so often crossed my path in **these lonely** regions—are no **longer** heard or seen to pursue their loves or their prey. **All** nature would appear disposed to rest, as if to gather fresh strength for the coming day. To witness such scenes, and to enjoy the pleasures they impart, few plans or pursuits are more appropriate than night-angling on **a** large lake. The picture attempted of both, and the practical hints introduced, **derive little** or no aid from art or the imagination. The impressions sought to be **conveyed are simply** those of reality, often experienced in early life. In taking leave of the scene in which they were realised, and **when** my last cast **has** been made in **its** waters, **the lines of** Moore **rise** unsought to my **pen :—**

"Sweet Innisfallen, fare thee well,
    May calm and sunshine long be thine ;
How fair thou art let others tell,
    To *feel* how fair shall long be mine !"

E. N. M.

A LAY OF THE LEA.

I'M an old man now,
Stiff limb and frosty pow,
But stooping o'er my flickering fire, in the winter
weather,
I behold a vision
Of a time elysian,
And I cast my crutch away, and I snap my tether!

Up i' the early morning,
Sleepy pleasures scorning,
Rod in hand and creel on back, I'm away, away!
Not a care to vex me—
Nor a fear perplex me—
Blithe as any bird that pipes in the merry May.

O the Enfield meadows,
Dappled with soft shadows!
O the leafy Enfield lanes, odorous of May blossom!
O the lapsing river,
Lea, beloved for ever,
With the rosy morning light mirrored on its bosom!

Out come reel and tackle—
Out come midge and hackle—
Length of gut like gossamer, on the south wind
    streaming—
      And brace of palmers fine,
      As ever decked a line,
Dubbed with herl, and ribbed with gold, in the sun-
    light gleaming.

      Bobbing 'neath the bushes,
      Crouched among the rushes,
On the rights of crown and state, I'm, alas! encroach-
    ing—
      What of that? I know
      My creel will soon o'erflow,
If a certain Cerberus * do not spoil my poaching.

---

* Does any one of my readers happen to remember the Cerberus in question, Tim Bates, the guardian of the Crown waters, at Waltham Abbey, some five-and-twenty years ago — the omnipresent, the incorruptible Tim Bates, whom no expostulation could move, no entreaty melt, and who was even impervious to half-crowns? This unwinking worthy, one of the *bêtes noires* of my angling boyhood, spoiled me many a day's sport by his untimely apparition; and I confess to a feeling of heathenish satisfaction, on hearing of the Lea's ingratitude, and how, unlike Tiber in the case of Horatius, it did *not* "bear up" Tim Bates's "chin," when he slipped into its depth, with mortal result, one foggy night or morning.

Chatto mentions him in his *Angler's Souvenir*, and celebrates his "lynx eyes."

As I throw my flies,
Fish on fish doth rise,
Roach and dace by dozens, on the bank they flounder.
Presently a splash,
And a furious dash,
Lo! a logger-headed chub, and a fat two-pounder!

Shade of Isaak, say
Did you not one day,
Fish for logger-headed chub, by this very weir?
'Neath these very trees,
Down these shady leas,—
Where's the nightingale that ought to be singing
here?

Now, in noontide heat,
Here I take my seat;
Izaak's book beguiles the time—of Izaak's book I say,
Never dearer page
Gladdened youth or age,
Never sweeter soul than his blessed the merry May.

For the while I read,
'Tis as if indeed,
Peace and joy and gentle thoughts from each line
were welling;
As if earth and sky
Took a tenderer dye,
And as if within my heart fifty larks were trilling.

Ne'er should angler stroll,
Ledger, dap, or troll,
Without Izaak in his pouch, on the banks of Lea ;—
Ne'er with worm **or fly,**
Trap the finny fry,
Without loving thoughts of him, and—*Benedicite !*

So to sport again,
With my palmers twain—
Ha! a lovely speckled trout—where's its peer, I
wonder?
And there's a dace—you ne'er
Saw finer, I declare—
There's—by all that's cruel, yes—there's my Cerberus
yonder!

Up go rod and tackle!
Up go midge and hackle!
Hurry scurry, down the path, fast my foe approaches—
Wheel the line in steady !
Now all's right and ready—
Izaak makes a sudden plunge 'mongst the bleak and
roaches.

Hollo, hollo, hollo !
Will he dare to follow?
Over dykes, with flying leaps—over gates and hedges !

> Hollo, hollo, hollo !
> Will he dare to follow ?
> No ! I look behind and see nought but stream and
>   sedges.

*   *   *   *

> O the pleasant roaming
> Homeward thro' the gloaming !
> O the heavy creel, alack ! O the joyful greeting !
> O the jokes and laughter,
> And the sound sleep after,
> And the happy, happy dreams, all the sport repeating !

> I'm an old man now,
> Stiff limb and frosty pow,
> But stooping o'er my flickering fire, in the winter
>   weather,
> Oft I see this vision
> Of a time elysian—
> And I cast my crutch away, and escape my tether !

T. W.

THE PUFF PISCATORIAL.

WHAT an excellent article might be written on puffing!—puffing in all its hydra-headed forms! First, there are the more refined categories of puff, such as the "puff **preliminary,**" the "**puff** oblique," and **the** "puff reflective ;" **then we have** the puff direct—as **when the critic assures his** unfledged poetaster that **the bays of Homer,** the spirit of Goethe, and **the** mantle of Shakespeare, have descended upon him in a heap ; the "sensational puff," the "puff political," "preliminary," "poetic," "alliterative," "epigrammatic ;" **and winding** up with the class of advertising puffs which are designed, we can only suppose, **to appeal to** the unmitigatedly gullable **of** this **world**—**the** Moses Primroses, **Verdant** Greens, and **Young-men-**from-the-country strata **of society**—**and which might** perhaps be classified roughly as the "puff hyperbolical," the "puff mendacious," and the "puff utterly preposterous."

What **an** excellent article, **as we** have said, might be **written on** these manifold developments of the art of puffing !—but then again **it might not** : and at any rate we don't intend **to write it.** So we will leave it as a legacy to some of our more gifted or cosmopolitan contemporaries, and confine ourselves here to a branch of the art of puff falling strictly within our own scope, and which we will denominate the "puff piscatorial."

Mr. FREDERICK ALLIES, of the good and ancient town of Worcester, who, besides being a vendor of fishing rods and tackle, is, as he describes himself, "Pisciculturist," and "Inventor and Maker" (whatever these titles may signify), has issued to his friends and admirers in general a hand-bill—or, as it were, manifesto —setting forth the various merits of the Artificial Grasshopper, in the manufacture of which, it seems, he considers he has a sort of pre-eminence or monopoly, though on what grounds we confess we do not quite understand, as we happen to know that the invention was first introduced to the Teme graylingfishers, by Mr. Jones of Ludlow, some five-and-forty years ago, and as Mr. Allies' insects appear to be in all respects very much like those sold by many other fishing-tackle dealers. As we are always ready, however, to lend a helping hand to modest merit when we meet with it, we will give Mr. Allies the benefit of our pages gratis, and circulate his hand-bill for him, capitals, italics, and all—

"Not wholly free, and yet as 'twere for nought "—

only (as Mr. Allies would say) begging our readers on no account to read it, because it *is* so *very* funny!

"THE ARTIFICIAL GRASSHOPPER.

"**THE** SEASON for the Grasshopper Fishing **is** ARRIVED for TROUT, and **the** Grayling will **follow** in quick succession.

" This Artificial Bait, not generally known, has been **in use for** Forty or Fifty Years, and anglers on the rivers Lugg and **Teme,** *in this locality,* are well acquainted with its deadly attractiveness when used for Grayling.

" The bait was originally made for Grayling **ONLY ; and** its work was considered to end there, but in using it **for up-** wards of **twenty years, I have found** that nearly all fresh- water fish can **be taken with it, when made of** different sizes and shades **of colour.**

" The fish **do not nibble, but rush at the** bait **as a** grey- hound **would throw at a hare, or like fish** generally run **at** any other Trolling bait. I have taken with it Trout, Gray- ling, **Perch** (any quantity), Pike, Chub, **Shad,** Twaite, Dace, Roach, Ruffs, Gudgeons, and Flounders.

" The **Artificial** Grasshopper is a sink-and-draw bait, **equally** good **in** PONDS as in Rivers, used near the bottom, in **the usual** haunts of the FISH you REQUIRE. Sinking and **drawing** UP and DOWN, **at** the rate of about **25 ups and 25** downs **per** minute, about 15 inches EACH DRAW **OR LESS.** Anglers generally **use a small bit of worm on the point of the** hook, or a Cadiz Grub **for Trout. The natural Grasshopper for** Grayling, or a **bit of Worm, or** a gentle, they serve **just to** hide the BIG HOOK which **is** intended to take the fish ; but when the fish are well on their feed there requires no disguise **to this** Artificial bait. Anglers that use the Artificial Grass- hopper consider it a mountain or a mouse, *i.e.* one day every fish seems eager to be the first to take it, and another day no fish will **look at it.** Although essentially a Grayling bait, it should only be **used in** EXTREME CASES. All that can be said in its favour is, that the Angler will take a much greater proportion of large fish and such Grayling as seldom rise at a fly, **viz. 2 lbs. to 3** lbs. weight **each.** I have sent out a **much greater number** of these **baits this** year and last season, **than usual.**

"**I** trust Gentlemen will NOT ENCOURAGE these Deadly baits **in their GRAYLING Streams,** or there will be a sad falling off **in the** fly-fishing, which **is the** most legitimate bait.

" Last year a Club of Anglers **met** for three days' Artificial Grasshopper fishing in a **Grayling** stream, *in part of our* RIVER, *the* TEME RIVER. **They took** upwards of 5 cwt. of Grayling by fishing with this deadly contrivance. The season for using this **bait** is all the year, but best in the Autumn and Winter for Grayling. **For** other FISH, when the FISH are **best** in season.

*　　　　　*　　　　　*　　　　　*

"**Prices, 6s. the half-dozen, with 6** feet of gut complete for use.

" **Apply to FREDERICK ALLIES,** Pisciculturist, etc."

This is very funny, is'nt it?

Well, but this is not all. Mr. Allies is by no means **content** with **the fame to be** acquired for his grasshoppers by the limited circulation of a hand-bill amongst mere private acquaintances ; his light must be more widely diffused—as **it** were from a candlestick,—so **he republishes the** substance of this Epistle **to the Gentiles in the** form of a letter to the *Field* newspaper—mice, mountains, and all.

It might have been imagined that this double publicity would have satisfied the vanity even of " an **Inventor** and Maker," **and** that the soul of an Allies would have found rest. It would not, perhaps, have

been so unreasonable to suppose that some good-
natured friend might have mildly suggested to him
the possibility of a connection in the mind of the
irreverent vulgar between Worcester grasshoppers
and Jerusalem ponies. But not a bit of it ! **Mr.
Allies** speedily returns to the charge, only refreshed
apparently by his previous efforts, and for the space
of two years scatters his 'hoppers' broadcast over the
verdant of the *Field.* Here is an example :—

"My caution in your columns of last season as **to** not
using the artificial grasshopper for taking grayling does **not**
seem to be **of any avail.** Gentlemen anglers are **even now, in**
the extreme lowness of our parched-up streams, taking grayling
wholesale with these destructive baits, and thereby spoiling
the choicest of all fly-fishers' autumn and winter sport. I
know, from the quantities of country orders for these baits,
that mischief is brewing. *Gentlemen, once more, let the grayling be left for the fly-fisher, and don't tear these beautiful sport-
ive fish from their native element neck and crop with these rough
anglers' contrivances."*—*Field*, 27th August **1864.**

Now *is* it not **funny?** Here is **poor Mr. Allies,
who** has got to **get his** grasshoppers, like so many
unmarriageable daughters, off his hands, and at the
same time to maintain an elevated and pure standard
of sporting morals in the midst of the first grayling
county in the world.

Well, grasshoppers are deadly things, no doubt,
and Mr. Allies makes them ; so far it is all plain
sailing: but if the clubs won't have them—forbid

them, in fact, except on certain days—what is to be done?   So Mr. Allies, poor man, finds himself between **Scylla** and Charybdis—the " carpet-bag on one side, and the tongs on the other "—and in his agony he cries **aloud,** " Don't! oh, let me beseech you, don't, kind anglers, buy my grasshoppers,—they are only 6s. the half-dozen, trace and all, and they *are* so deadly ! Do not encourage them, dear gentlemen, I say do *not !*"

Unfortunate but noble Allies !   Can any one for the life of him help recalling that immortal scene in " Pickwick " where the persecuted Mr. Winkle is endeavouring to touch the obtuse feelings of his about-**to-be second,** Mr. Snodgrass ?—" Snodgrass," said Mr. **Winkle,** stopping suddenly, " Snodgrass, do *not* let **me be** baulked in this matter—do *not* give information to the local authorities—do *not* obtain the assistance of several peace officers, to take either me or Dr. Slammer, of the 97th Regiment, at present quartered in Chatham Barracks, into custódy, and thus prevent this duel ;—I say, do *not !* . . . ."

What a sell it would be for the grasshoppers if the angling Snodgrasses, like their prototype, meta-phorically seizing the hand of the wretched Allies, were to reply to his adjuration—" Not for worlds !"

We will not indulge ourselves by criticising *in-limine* **Mr.** Allies' rhetorical effort ; nay, so self-denying are we, that though sorely tempted, we will not even pick out a few of the plums for our own

private delectation. If the Teme grayling *will* rush
at the bait like greyhounds, or any other hounds—or
whales, if they like—in heaven's name let them ; let
Mr. Allies work his BIG HOOK as many times up, and
as many times down, per minute, " more or less," as he
pleases ; yea, and let the anglers "who consider the artificial grasshopper to be either a mountain or a mouse,"
still remain in that somewhat peculiar zoological belief ;
—we will not, even by our affectionate solicitude, run
any risk of damaging the symmetry of the structure.
Mr. Allies' circular shall remain in its " integrity for
us ; one perfect whole, inimitable, *impayable.*"

So much for the puff direct.

Another branch of piscatorial puffing, and one
which is rapidly assuming most obnoxious proportions, is exemplified every week in the advertising
columns of our sporting literature. This is the " puff
hyperbolical," wherein certain unscrupulous owners
and lessees of hotels, fishing-quarters, and rivers of
unpronounceable orthography in various outskirts of
the three kingdoms, **endeavour to** delude the guileless
into their nets, or more correctly " man-traps." **Woe**
betide the fisherman who commits himself to the Night
Mail North, or, still worse, the Irish Express, on the
faith of such tempting allurements. The chances are
two to one that the confiding wretch so beguiled finds
himself landed at " a well-appointed family hotel,"
(consisting of a couple of roofless attics over a floor-

less kitchen) "picturesquely situate in the midst of"
—(a howling wilderness), "traversed by a well-stocked
salmon river" (which being regularly netted three
times a-day)—of course "presents to the lover of the
gentle craft truly magnificent," etc. etc.

Verily the tender mercies of such advertisers as
these are cruelty!

The following flowery effusion, of which the original is in our possession, if coming strictly perhaps
somewhat under the category of the puff hyperbolical,
has at least the merit of being comparatively harmless,
and with the exception of the "fishing" (which we rather
think, considering the locality, must have been the
addition of some wag), is no doubt honest enough,—

"Why Go to Brighton?

Pay 3s.—travel over 100 miles to throw stones into
the sea—no dinner—1s. for the boat for sea-
sickness, and get home tired and weary?

Why Go to Salisbury

To see a lot of old rubbishing stones—travel 200
miles—waste your time and pay your money—
tired and weary again?

Why Go to Hastings?

Who knows you there? Nobody, and nobody cares
for you—you pay your money, and they say,
'There goes another Cockney.'

WHY DON'T YOU GO TO THE SWAN INN, FULHAM?

(FERRY HOUSE, PUTNEY BRIDGE).

Sunday dinner, half-past one, 1s.—tea, 9d.—London articles at London prices—civility gratis.

Boats, fishing, lovely walks. Omnibuses every **ten** minutes from London **to Putney** Bridge. Home easy, comfortable **and happy,** *and* **cost** *less money.*

You will then exclaim—

' Now is the winter of our discontent made glorious summer.'

EDWIN JOHN PAGE, *Proprietor."*

We shall certainly devote our first vacant Sunday afternoon to a trial visit **to** Mr. Page's establishment of many attractions, and, as this will probably not be before December, **we** shall at **least** have an opportunity **of testing the efficacy of that** portion of **the** *carte* which **relates to a** desirable modification in the programme of **the** clerk of **the weather.**

We have elsewhere referred to the " puff oblique," which, **if** somewhat less open and flagrant than its two congeners, is, as a system, proportionately more reprehensible and disingenuous. The system we allude to is that of fishing-tackle manufacturers publishing angling books, which, whilst nominally appealing to fishermen as books of guidance or instruction, are practically little more than elaborate catalogues designed to puff off their writer's wares. The offensiveness of this practice is increased when *noms de plume* are assumed which mislead the public as to the real authorship of the books. Our attention has been called to this particular description of puff by reading *The Modern Angler*, etc. etc., by "Otter," which is published by Alfred and Son, Moorgate Street,—Alfred and Son being, as we understand, also the authors of the same. This *Modern Angler*, which it is hardly necessary to say has no claim to be considered as in any sense a literary production, is merely a *réchauffé* of the most trite and catchpenny of the common angling manuals, illustrated by neat diagrams of quill-floats and other equally mysterious paraphernalia of the angling craft. But to this of course we have no right to object. Everyone is at perfect liberty to believe that his mission is to write a book—or two if he likes—and to publish them, if he so pleases, even if his title to do so be no better than that to which *Hudibras* refers when he says—

> "Tho' he that has but impudence
> To all things has a fair pretence."

Nay, he may even do so on the self-sacrificing principle which, so far as we know, was not found strong enough to induce Job's contemporaries to comply with *his* requests in that particular—

" O that mine enemy would **write a book !**"

But when people buy a work on fishing, bearing the name of one person, and find afterwards that **it is** written by another, and that other the fishing-tackle maker whose wares are therein recommended, and who is moreover the publisher **as well,** they certainly have a very considerable right to be dissatisfied; and such a duality **as is here referred to** has, unless our memory plays **us false, been** carefully kept **up by** **" Otter," or** Alfred, or Alfred and Son, whichever **he** or they may be—in their occasional letters to the sporting papers. As Pat O'Flaherty says : " Tother is so remarkably like both, that you can't tell neither from which."

Otter's **Modern** *Angler* begins, for instance, with four pages of " Angling Requisites," and **ends with six** of the prices which should **be paid for them**—these requisites and prices **not being inserted openly as au** advertisement, **but forming a** part and parcel of **the** book itself. After **this it** is needless **to** say that " Alfred's Sensation Silver Baits," " Alfred's Pectoral Baits," " Alfred's Improved Spinning Rods," his "Japanned Tin Cases," his " Celebrated 'Wellington' and 'Emperor' Trout-Flies," and a host of other rods, baits, and insects—which, if not quite so celebrated

as the persons after whom they are christened, are evidently of much greater interest to their vendors— are **recommended by** "Otter" **as** amongst the essentials of the angler's equipment. All this, too, when, as we have said before, the actual fishing-matter of the book, and for the sake of which it is purchased, is utterly contemptible. This is the second book which Messrs. Alfred, **Otter, and** Son have thus given **to the world; the first,** *Otter's Complete Guide to Spinning and Trolling*, being, if possible, even worse than the **present—or, as we** once heard it expressed, **the** " **wonderful wusser!**" It is to be observed also that **the tendency of this** "oblique" method of advertising appears **to** be to produce a corresponding obliquity in **the moral vision of the** producers, as, unless we are **greatly** mistaken, we have more than once seen letters **in the** *Field* signed by "Otter," referring, in certainly not *un*complimentary terms, **to** "Alfred," and *vice versâ*—a sort **of** "pea-and-thimble trick" **by** which we cannot believe that the interests of the angling public are advanced.

If the sporting papers are willing to allow their columns to be used **as a** vehicle for about a hundred and fifty letters puffing **off** "Fagg's Wading Boots," **or** "Allies' Grasshoppers," or any other wares of **known** tradesmen, it is their own business and not ours—(and as, after a short time, nobody reads them, **they** are of less consequence)—but we do protest most strongly against fishing-tackle makers writing books under aliases, and making use **of their** synonyms to play into their own hands. "Good wine **needs no** bush;" **and** fishing-tackle, like all other commodities, may very safely be left to the discrimination of the public, who seldom **fail** in the end in discovering what are the best things, and who sells them.

H. C. P.

DEESIDE JOTTINGS.

THE influence of habit is so powerful in reconciling us to the **evils of** social arrangements, that it requires no small effort to break the **spell.** The process is never agreeable ; **and** often exposes the best motives **to be misunderstood.** It demands us to reconsider customs consecrated by time ; to call in **doubt the wisdom** of those who preceded us ; and **to** measure **the utility of** their acts by **a** comparison of the good produced with the evils intended to be removed. **If** man had not counteracted the intentions of nature by **the** excess of his greed and **the** nullity of his laws, there can be little doubt the Dee **would be a pleasant** and prolific river to fish. But the savages who once roamed the neighbouring woods probably drew more food from its bed than do now the civilised communities dwelling **on its** banks. This is merely to say, in other words, that each successive link in the chain of protective legislation yielded in time to the pressure **of the** circumstances which it was framed to amend.

Nor is it very difficult to understand how sterility has totally blighted some of our streams, and reduced all perhaps below their natural standard of productiveness. Public **and** private rights were, in the first instance, established without sufficient counter-checks to secure the objects for which the rights themselves were granted. As sometimes happens in mechanics, an excess of power operating uncontrolled destroyed the working equilibrium of the machinery, and defeated the very purposes for which it was contrived. The effects of such power, without a " governor " to moderate its action, were felt all the more fatally as they fell upon animal life, the laws of which are never violated with impunity. The bounties of Nature are freely and liberally dispensed ; but are not inexhaustible, or proof against outrage. **If** drawn upon beyond *her* reproductive capacities, she soon avenges the infraction of her code, and ceases to bestow her treasures on savage or civilised man.

The course of the fine river which suggests these remarks is estimated in round numbers at a hundred miles. The variety and extent **of** its feeding and breeding ground are **patent to** the humblest connoisseur in pisciculture ; and unlike most of our rivers of the same volume, its lower reaches are undisturbed by navigation, with the exception of light fishing **and** passage boats, and an occasional " flat " at tide-time.

At no point of the stream are its waters, I believe,

polluted **by** mining and manufacturing impurities. Mills are not, to say, numerous ; the weirs must be within the compass of salmon muscle to overcome as the fish ascend to the entrance of Bala Lake. The scenery throughout its whole length makes agreeable companionship to the wanderings of the angler, and fair accommodation is provided for him at moderate distances along its **banks.** To these natural and social advantages, the accidental one of running through the properties of some of the largest and wealthiest proprietors of the island — Grosvenors, Wynns, Vaughans, *cum multis aliis*—might be added. But in my observations as a " bird of passage," I have not found that these " magnates " have taken much interest in the prosperity of the salmon-fishery, in return for the beauty and celebrity which the stream confers on their wide domains. As an ill omen for the existence of such **a** disposition, it may be stated, *en passant,* that the unsavoury dens of the fishing colony which devastates the lower Dee almost abut on the principal entrance to the princely mansion of Eaton Hall !

Of the number of salmon that now enter the Dee from the sea it would be difficult to form a conjecture near the truth. With the exception of the rental of what is called the " **cage** " on the causeway **at the** old bridge of Chester, there are no trustworthy statistics upon which to found an accurate opinion.

In the absence, however, of the requisite data for such an inquiry, I should be inclined to rate the produce of the river at a very moderate figure. Though highly prized by the civic epicure, Dee salmon is a comparative rarity in the Chester market. I am aware that much of the produce of legal and all the results of illegal fishing are disposed of by private hand, and never consequently find their way to the dealer's stalls. But making every allowance for this fact, it is highly improbable **that** if any considerable quantity of fish were taken, a greater proportion of it would not be exposed for public sale. One conclusion at least is certain, that the scarcity of fish caught is not the result of any lack of zeal or the number of the fishers ; and that of the salmon which venture to enter the river, few, large or small, return to warn their companions of the dangers that await them between the shores of Flint and Chester Causeway.

The chances of successful fly-fishing for salmon **in** the upper waters of the Dee may be inferred .from what has been stated respecting the practices in **the** lower part of the river. The prospect is certainly not encouraging. Yet it is extraordinary to find that so many fish pass the *atri janua Ditis* of the lower Dee, and make their ascent to the upper parts of the stream. Some fortunate accident of the natural state of the bed of the river,

I presume, combined with the imperfection of the gear employed for their capture, enables a considerable number to perform this heroic exploit. There are certain points of the river where this agreeable fact is made visible to the angler by the salmon themselves. One of these places is the weir of Erbistock Mill at Overton Bridge, distant some fifteen or sixteen miles road measurement from Chester, but many more by the numerous and graceful windings of the stream through this charming pastoral district. Here, on favourable occasions of weather and the state of the stream, the angler may enjoy **the** interesting spectacle of fresh-run fish "fencing" the opposing weir like so many trained hunters. The great majority of the fish, however, which gambol in the troubled waters of this fine pool are probably smolts that have not yet ventured to pass the complicated webs spread for their reception by the merciless "water-spiders" of Hambridge, in the passage of the lower Dee. Poor things! should they succeed in reaching the sea, fortunate indeed will be their lot if they ever return as grilse or salmon to the home of their youth, and show what fine fellows they have become since they grazed in those unknown pastures of the deep, whose anti-Banting properties are still a puzzle to ichthyologists. But even in this delightful locality, which might be supposed the abode of rural innocence and simplicity,

the " rising generation " of the Salmonidæ are not safe
from the wiles and ingenuity of the rustic poacher.
At a point commanding the pool below the weir
stands a suspicious-looking customer, apparently fishing with flies. On more minute inspection, however,
his rod will be found to be rather longer and stiffer
than usual. On looking to his line, it will be observed, that instead of being terminated by one of
more salmon-flies, it is armed by a large number or
naked dangling fish-hooks, with a small leaden
plummet at the end. Amongst the thickest of the
ruck of fish sporting in the pool, this demi-savage
ever and anon casts his infernal machine, in which
the barbarity of the spear is multiplied by the number
of the hooks and length of line, in the hope of course
that as he pulls it to him rapidly through the water,
some of the hooks may take effect, and drag one of
the fish ashore ! Whether the miscreant often succeeds in his dodge, I am unable to say ; but that he
puts it in practice at all is a certain index of the
large number of fish that must occasionally meet in
this pool. Fly-fishing for salmon and trout would
naturally commence here on the Dee ; but though
there are many fine reaches for the purpose to within
a mile or two of Llangollen, this part of the stream is
so haunted by the neighbouring miners and their
coracles, that it is not much frequented by the regular
angler.

The salmon " meet " at Llangollen, to borrow the
familiar phraseology of another department of the
sporting world, is the next on the river. The turn-
out of pink and white on the field is not quite so
large as at Overton ; but the barrier being more perpendicular, and better adjusted to the muscular forces
of the gymnasts, the practice is perhaps superior.
While admiring the play of the performers, preparatory to the final jump, I thought of Dick Milliken's
bit of natural history in the famous " Groves of
Blarney," in which he introduces—

> " The trout and salmon,
>   Playing at backgammon ; "

and concluded that the parody of the Dublin "Droll"
was not after all more extravagant, in making the
" finsters " of Blarney engage in a " twopenny hit "
at backgammon, than the antics attributed to Irish
characters by a certain class of novelists for the
amusement of the public. Milliken's was at least the
racy genuine specimen of what Moore nicely defines
as the " back-water of Irish wit ; " theirs the vulgar
pinchbeck imitation, fabricated out of materials
gleaned within the " Circular Road " of the Irish
metropolis. But whether intoxicated by the sparkling
champagne of the pool, flowing down cool and fresh
from the mountain-springs, or intent upon higher
purposes up stream, it is certain salmon are seldom
tempted by the **angler's** lures on occasions of public

display of this kind. There are two or three "greenhorns" in the art on the opposite bank, cutting and carving the pool into as many lines as intersect a Highland plaid ; but the fish eschew their labour as officious, ill-timed, and out of place. They make no sign whatever of acquiescence in the polite attentions of their juvenile friends, who ply their task with a diligence worthy of a better reception. Neither do these capricious epicures, when embarked in long runs to some favourite haunts, seem much inclined to turn aside from their purpose, and indulge in the luxury of flies.

In the Dee there are many such special resorts **of** salmon, as have been alluded to, from a mile or two below Llangollen to Corwen, and all as well known to the *habitués* of the river as the contents of their own fly-books. In the pools between the places just named, most of the salmon taken by the fly-angler in the upper Dee are caught. One or two fish are considered a successful day's sport ; and, all things con- . sidered, should satisfy the expectations of the angler acquainted with the economic arrangements of the lower portions of the stream. Such occasional success attracts a considerable number of competitors for such prizes as the river affords ; and serves to retain the name **of** the Dee in the catalogue of salmon-fisheries. Anglers of more sanguine, or I should rather say sanguinary, temperaments, content only with salmon *battues*, would of course look upon the moderate fishing of the Dee as " stale, flat, and unprofitable." For minds so diseased, the costly, though not always productive preserves of Scotland, or the yet unexhausted fjords of Northern Europe, can alone administer the suitable remedy. Failing these, there is yet balm in Gilead for heroic Waltonians—a berth in the next whaler from Peterhead or Aberdeen, and a run amongst the virgin streams flowing into the Polar basin. Happy the angler, who, deaf to the seductions of ambition and the despotism of fashion, can **betake** himself **to** some unhackneyed stream **amongst the** hills, or modestly flowing between ranks of meadow-sweet and flag-iris in the plain, and make **his own** skill and the manipulation of his tackle the sources of pleasure, not surpassed in the more aspiring walks of the art.

The salmon-flies in general use on the Dee claim that especial adaptation to the locality demanded by almost all other rivers. If we are to receive implicitly the theories of local fly-dressers, there can be no doubt of a distinct centre of creation of flies for every salmon stream in these islands. Huxley and Owen may dispute the problem in the case of man and other animals as long as they like, but in those curious compounds of pigs'-wool, feathers, and fish-hooks, called by courtesy or poetic licence salmon-flies, a separate *genesis* must be assumed as an established fact. According to the new philosophy the subject has passed the metaphysical method of investigation, and taken rank amongst the proved items of M. Comte's Positivism. By the advocates of this doctrine we are assured that salmon would commit suicide by inanition sooner than they would rise to a fly that was not **born** and bred on the banks of their own river. It must be of the true local *sui generis* description to suit the tastes and habits of these scrupulous Brahmins of the stream. I have often in my angling peregrinations sought to trace the origin of the **favourite lures** of **most rivers,** but cannot **add that I** have been successful. **When** I inquired who the daring Prometheus was that stole fire from heaven and animated these monsters into an ephemeral popularity, I was generally referred for their paternity to the priest, the parson, the doctor, **the** half-pay captain, and the Waterloo pensioner of the village, who had only two real legs and an eye **and** a half between **them.** The fact **was the latter,** poor fellow! had just **been** *couched* for *cataract* by the salmon doctor, who left half the membrane still floating in the aqueous chamber of the **one eye he** had, and thus sadly reduced his patient's optical resources as a "judge of colours." Sometimes I found it was **the** village barber, cobbler, but above all a certain mysterious tinker, who "like a shadow came and so departed," that bequeathed to posterity the invaluable secret of some of these infallible lures.

Looking merely to the high qualifications **of** the inventors, the most prudent course would be, perhaps, **to** bow at once to their infallibility, and ask no questions. Yet, mixed up with empiricism as the question is, it is one well worthy of the investigations **of the** scientific angler. It would surely be worth knowing how it happens that salmon rise to artificial flies of which there are confessedly no natural originals; how far the allegation is true or false that fish take certain flies, and in particular rivers **only**; and **lastly, by** what intuitive guidance the fly-milliner invents these nondescript products of his brain. The **models to** which they bear the most distant resemblance are **few** indeed, being confined to the limited family of the dragon-flies, and an inconsiderable number of the larger Ephemeridæ found on British waters. But it would appear that, just in proportion as nature has been sparing of her originals, art has stepped in with spurious creations to supply the deficiency. To such an extent has this practice been carried that it would be impossible to form a collection upon any rational principle of selection. As fancy or caprice alone presides at the mint, there can of course be no limit to the issue of the counterfeit coinage. **Most** readers of current angling literature will doubtless have met one of these ingenious artificers who can strike off any number of these pseudo-imitations at a heat. Most of the class would seem **to** have taken Tom Moore's

receipt for brewing nectar as their formula. As many
may not recollect the original, it is here given, with
the substitution of a few words only :—

> " 'Twas insects fed,
>   Of old 'tis said,
> Our salmon, trout, and grayling ;
>   And man may brew
>   His insects too,
> The rich receipt's unfailing—
>   Take wool of pig,
>   Jay's wing a sprig,
> With these and twist be blended
>   A golden **fleck**
>   From pheasant's neck,
> And there's your " clipper " splendid !"

Of the value of productions conceived in such a
spirit and executed on such principles it would be
out of all reason to doubt. The Dee salmon-flies,
however, though originating in similar formulæ, lack
the meretricious finery which fascinates the fish of
other rivers. They are modest, unassuming creations,
which, like " beauty unadorned," please most. A cin-
namon-coloured body, wings from the tail-feather of
a gled or kite, a furnace hackle, tail, a few fibres from
the larger neck-feathers of the darkest red domestic
cock, and ribbing of fine gold twist or thread, may
serve to give an idea of a simple and favourite lure
of one of the best salmon-fishers I know on the Dee.
The body of another equally successful fly by the

same dresser is formed of peacock herl, wings of turkey-tail, or the feather of the wing of the hen-pheasant, a black hackle extending from the vent to the head, and a few turns of black ostrich harl and twist or gold tinsel at the tail. The whole resembles a good deal a palmer to which wings were added. As exemplifying the caprice of salmon, or of those who profess to know exactly their **tastes,** it may be remarked that the flies used on a neighbouring river—the Conway—and rising in the same mountain range as the Dee, often combine the brightest tints of the silk-dyer with the richest **colours of** tropical plumage. Possibly **the mystery which now** envelopes the question may yet **be reduced to narrow limits.** Problems of equal or **greater** difficulty in other departments of natural **science** have yielded to perseverance, research, and well-directed experiment.

For the information of anglers unacquainted with the topography and arrangements of the Dee fishery, it may be necessary to observe here, that what is called the Glendwyr Preserve, embracing the finest part of the river for salmon-fishing, extends from the village of Llansaintffraid, about three miles below Corwen, **to** the chain bridge near Valle Crucis Abbey. The distance between these points is about seven miles, road measurement, but twice that length perhaps, following the sinuous windings of the stream. In this space are included the four most celebrated salmon-pools of the Dee. The railway station of Carrog, on the continuation of the new line between Llangollen and Corwen, gives easy access to this part of the river. For four miles below this station the Dee may be fished from the bank with occasional wading; but to fish any part of the Glendwyr Preserve in the best way, the use of a coracle is indispensable. The employment of such a craft, however, and the regulations of the Preserve, impose rather serious restrictions on the freedom and pursuits of the angler. To many the restrictions arising from both causes amount to a positive prohibition of fishing the best casts of the stream. In the first place, none but subscribers of three guineas per annum to the Preserve are allowed to fish it with a coracle at all. In the next place, there being not more than three coracle-owners on the river, to whom a person unaccustomed to this primitive style of navigation could prudently confide his safety, one of these men and his frail bark must he engaged by the intending angler several days in advance, as the demand for their services is very considerable. Nor can this be wondered at, when we recollect that the fishing-ground of which we are writing is within a few hours' run of all parts of the wealthy and populous district of Lancashire. After poisoning every stream and river within their reach, the lords of the shuttle and vat issue forth at stated times, like clouds of locusts,

to devastate the game and fish of their neighbours'
fields and waters. The resources of nature herself
would seem no longer adequate to meet the demands
of the summer swarms of pleasure-seekers. Like the
Roman matrons, she sinks beneath a plethora of gold
and the number of her invaders.

E. N. M.

SPRING FISHING IN LOCH ARD.

WHEN a man makes inquiry **what** sort of angling **is** to be had at this or that place, or this or that time, he is apt or almost **certain to be misled.** He will be told of **" good fishing " or of** " poor fishing ;" but these phrases **have no fixed meaning, and express the most** different state of **things in** the mouths of different people. What would be reckoned wretched as a day's " take " in one district, is regarded as a magnificent spoil in another. For instance, " a good day's fishing " means quite a different thing in the south-eastern from what it means in the south-western counties of Scotland—the former districts being the best, and the latter pretty nearly the worst in the kingdom **for** river-fishing for yellow trout. Never shall **we** forget being induced to perform a day's severe bogtrotting and hill-climbing in Galloway, on the assurance of " splendid fishing " in a certain elevated region, and finding, after careful and laborious experiment, that nothing was to be had but abortions blacker than **your hat,** and smaller than your little finger. Not certain—as no angler in strange waters ever ought to be certain—but that the fault might be in the fisher, and not in the fish, we returned towards the place whence, on false pretences, we had been taken, weighed down by a sense of humiliation, and by that heaviest of all burdens—a light basket; but our grief was turned, not quite to joy, but to astonishment, by finding that everybody who had impudence and importunity enough to overcome our reluctance to exhibiting our capture regarded us, not with the contempt we thought we merited, but with admiration and envy. "Sic a grand basket!"—"the like o' that hasna been seen here for a dizen years"—were among the exclamations which greeted the display of two or three dozen of ill-thriven, ill-coloured dwarfs. The fact was that, from the want of a proper standard, having never in their lives seen " a good basket," the people in that district did not know what a fair day's fishing meant, in the signification which that phrase bears in the happier regions of Tweed and her tributaries. And here let it be said in passing, that the violent differences between the number and condition of the trouts in the waters of different districts, between which no material difference—atmospheric, aquatic, or geologic, —is to be detected, is a matter regarding which less is known, and, which does not necessarily follow, less has been said, than on almost any other point connected with angling. A similar confusion of tongues often arises in speaking of angling at different seasons : what is properly enough called good fishing in and *for* March, April, or early May, being perhaps **75** per cent below anything that **ought to** be called good fishing in **genial and** abounding **June. Let it** be considered, too, that what some people not quite correctly term " excessively moderate" fishing, at **a time** when **the** appetite for the sport has been whetted **by** the long winter's abstinence, really gives as much **pleasure** as does much better or more productive fishing at a later season, when greater things are naturally to be looked for. Therefore, when we **say** that good fishing is to be had in March **and April, and** that the best place in Scotland to get that fishing is Loch Ard, **on** the borders between Perthshire and Stirlingshire, we mean that the fishing is good for these early months, and for that particular district, which—witness the black and barren waters of the Lennox—is on the whole no angling paradise. The extent of commendation meant to be bestowed on Loch Ard is simply this—that there you may get, on an average day, a dozen, a dozen and a half, and occasionally two **dozen** trout, of very fine quality, and weighing nearly three quarters of a pound each, at that early period when it is spring in the almanack and nowhere else, and when trout-fishing in almost all other districts of Scotland is a depressing and desperate enterprise.

It is by no means clear, and indeed nothing in that department is clear, why Loch Ard should fish earlier than almost any other loch and than any river in Scotland. It used to be an accepted belief that lochs fished earlier than rivers, but the exceptions to the rule are too numerous and important to leave it much value: for instance, there is Loch Leven, where the fishing can scarcely be said to begin till the latter end of May. There may be a great deal in the fact that Loch Ard, though really in the Highlands, lies on a low level. But there is Loch Leven, on about as low a level, and with a rich marly and grassy bottom, and in a flat and warm country, **whose fishing** does not begin till that of Loch Ard is nearly over ; and **there** is St. Mary's Loch, in Selkirkshire, 600 feet above the sea, with a hard bottom and amid cold hills, where the fishing (barring frosts) begins as early as in **Loch Ard. Be** the causes what **they may,** Loch Ard **begins to yield** very fair fishing in March, and continues to do so up till the end of May, and sometimes a little later. A good deal, of course, depends on the weather, and especially on whether winter has lingered long, and has been " open " **or " hard." The** winter **of** 1863-4 was open and early—that of 1864-5 **was hard and late ;** so that the fishing in Loch Ard was **a month later** last year than in the year preceding, **and is still later this** year, when winter may be **said not to have begun till** March—the trouts being **in April of** these two **years scarcely** in such good condition or such good **taking temper as** they generally **are** in March.

The size of fly in most successful use is remarkably large for a loch so much fished, and where the fish do not run large—what is known as the full-sized Loch Leven fly, or even, when the surface is rough, the still larger size in use on Loch Tummel. The colours in favour, at least in the early season, are reds and purples for body, and "white tops" and drakes for the wings. Trolling with minnow, either natural or artificial, is not much in use till the fly-fishing season begins to wane—it seems, indeed, a fixed idea of the boatmen that there is **no** use in trying minnow till May ; but that that rule **may be too** much relied upon we have had evidence—and even in the earliest part of the season a phantom minnow sometimes beats the fly.

The best portions of the loch in the early season are towards the upper end, which "lies better to the sun," and is shallower, and with a warmer and richer bottom than the lower end, which, however, gives good fishing in June. The best winds are those between south **and west;** the nearer south the better, as a straight west wind is apt to be rather hard in both senses ; an east wind is bad if dry, but good if moist ; and the north is, as almost everywhere else, the worst of all. What is ordinarily called " a coarse day" is generally the most productive. The prevailing winds are those from the west and the south of west ; and on a day when the wind has set in from that direction,

the best plan is to pull almost straight across from
the pier at which the boats are kept on the north
side ; coast up the south side to the top, keeping inside and going round an island where there is a house,
with table, seats, and fireplace for the convenience of
visitors ; and then, after reaching the top, drift down
the north shore, which, at least up to the middle of
May, we should say is the best. There are some
beautiful bays on the south side, running far up
among the birch-clad knolls—two of them called, we
think, Upper and Lower Poolygarten, and another with
a name which we have always failed to pronounce,
and cannot hope to spell. These bays fish better in
the middle than the beginning of the season, and
better in the late than in the early part of the day.

The ordinary way of reaching Loch Ard is from
the Bucklyvie or the Port of Monteath station on the
Forth and Clyde Railway, to the hotel at Aberfoyle.
Bucklyvie station is the nearest to Aberfoyle, and by
a better road, so that the Port of Monteath route is
not used, excepting by pedestrians, and for the sake
of variety. There is a near cut for foot-passengers
from Bucklyvie over Gartmore Hill, making the distance to Aberfoyle only five miles ; but the driving,
or at least the *hiring*, distance is seven. The nearest
road from Port of Monteath is seven or eight miles,
and in wet weather there are formidable difficulties.
Return tickets, extending from Friday till Monday,

can be had at Edinburgh or Glasgow for Stirling, and
thence for Bucklyvie or any other station on the Forth
and Clyde line. Mr. Mitchell, the hotel-keeper at
Aberfoyle, can have a conveyance waiting any train,
if notified by a letter posted at Edinburgh before
3.30 the day previous, or in London in time **for the**
evening mails two days before.

The liberty of fishing in Loch Ard is **to** be had
by moderate payment, and **under fair** arrangements.
The fishing of the loch is **rented by Mr.** Dick, formerly
of Glasgow, who **has had a house and shootings** in
the district for more **than thirty years, and was the
first man** that ever paid sporting-rent to the dukes
of Montrose ; and Mr. Dick, instead of restricting
angling leave **to** his friends or to importunate visitors,
very properly and liberally throws the loch open to
the public at a charge merely covering expenses. He
keeps seven or eight **smart** boats, for the use of one of
which, leave to angle, **and the services of a boatman,**
the charge is 6s. **a-day. Mr. Dick's boats are under**
charge of a family **named** Cleland, very intelligent **and**
obliging young **men, on whose advice the** stranger
angler will do **well to rest and** be thankful. At times
—**especially when** the Glasgow **and** Stirling Angling
Clubs have their annual competitions—boats are apt
to be scarce ; and it is prudent to try to engage a boat
by writing, beforehand, with **time** for an answer, to
Mr. D. Cleland, Loch Ard, Aberfoyle, by Stirling.

Besides fish—and no true angler thinks only of fish—there is much interest of scenery and of romance at Loch Ard and on the road to it. The loch is in the real "Rob Roy's country," and the genius of Scott, in his great novel bearing the name of the famous outlaw, has given charm and consecration to almost every spot around. Even the flat and ugly bogs of the Lennox, which you cross on your way from the station to **the** inn, become picturesque when you remember that you are passing across the same ground as **Frank** Osbaldistone, and Bailie **Nicol Jarvie, and Andrew** Fairservice rode across that **day when they** left behind "the comforts of the **Saut Market," and set** forth on their immortal expedition. **That** region looks now **much as Scott** described it to **have been** a century and a half **ago :—**

"**I shall never forget the** delightful sensation with **which** I exchanged the dark, smoky, smothering atmosphere of the Highland hut, in which we had passed the night so uncomfortably, for the refreshing fragrance of the morning air, and the glorious beams of the **rising** sun, which, from **a** tabernacle of purple and golden **clouds, were** darted full on such **a scene of** natural **romance** and **beauty as** had never before **greeted my eyes. To the left lay the** valley, down **which the Forth wandered on** its easterly course, surrounding the beautiful detached **hill, with all** its garland of **woods.** On the right, amid a pro-**fusion of** thickets, knolls, **and crags, lay the bed** of a broad **mountain** lake, lightly curled **into tiny** waves by the breath **of the** morning **breeze, each** glittering in its course under the **influence** of **the sunbeams.** High hills, rocks, and banks,

waving with natural forests of birch and oak, formed the
borders of this enchanting sheet of water ; and, as their leaves
rustled to the wind and twinkled in the sun, gave to the depth
of solitude a **sort of life** and vivacity.   .   .   .

"Our route, though leading towards the lake, had hitherto
been so much shaded by wood, that we only from time to time
obtained a glimpse of that beautiful sheet of **water. But** the
road now suddenly emerged from the forest ground, and, winding
close by the margin of the loch, afforded **us a** full **view of its**
spacious mirror, which now, the breeze having totally subsided,
reflected in still magnificence the **high** dark heathy mountains,
huge grey rocks, **and shaggy banks by** which it is encircled.

And **that same night the travellers rested, in a** fashion,
at **"the Clachan o' Aberfoyle," and** there **had** that
famous **encounter in** which the Bailie distinguished
himself by his deeds with the red-hot culter. Why,
there is the identical culter that made Inverashalloch's
plaid smell "like a singit sheep's head," pendent from
an iron ring in the tree before the hotel door ; and it
is another fact, remarkable also, but not more remark-
able, that the **culter has in former times been** often
sold to English and foreign tourists, and carried away
to grace private museums **in** far countries. Farther
up towards the loch, **too, you** shall have pointed out
to you the very tree (looking rather young for its age)
from which Bailie Nicol Jarvie hung suspended by
his coat-tails during the fight between the caterans
and the red-coats. On the other side of the hills, to
the north, **we find** the story of Scott's "Lady of the
Lake" in **like manner** more than half consolidated

R

into a tradition of actual events, having some undoubting believers and many unhesitating narrators. When the angler leaves the hotel in the morning to go to the loch, he goes through the same scene, and ought to experience the same sensations, as Francis Osbaldistone, when, as a prisoner to Captain Thornton, he passed the Highland line and entered Rob Roy's country :—

"Our road continued to be, if possible, more waste and wild than that we had travelled in the forenoon. The few miserable hovels that shewed some marks of human habitation, were now of still rarer occurrence ; and at length, as we began to ascend an uninterrupted swell of moorland, they totally disappeared. The only exercise which my imagination received was, when some particular turn of the road gave us a partial view, to the left, of a large assemblage of dark-blue mountains stretching to the north and north-west, which promised to include within their recesses a country as wild perhaps, but certainly differing greatly in point of interest from that in which we now travelled. The peaks of this screen of mountains were as widely varied and distinguished as the hills which we had seen on the right were tame and lumpish ; and while I gazed on this alpine region, I felt a longing to explore its recesses, though accompanied with toil and danger, similar to that which a sailor feels, when he wishes for the risks and animation of a battle or a gale, in exchange for the unsupportable monotony of a protracted calm. I made various inquiries of my friend Mr. Jarvie, respecting the names and positions of these remarkable mountains ; but it was a subject on which he had no information, or did not choose to be communicative. ' They're the Hieland hills— the Hieland hills—Ye'll see and hear eneugh about them before ye see Glasgow Cross again.' "

Two miles further up is the lovely waterfall of Ledeard, of which Scott gives a charming description in Waverley :

" At a short turning, the path, which had for some furlongs lost sight of the brook, suddenly placed Waverley in front of a romantic waterfall. It was not so remarkable either for great height or quantity of water, as for the beautiful accompaniments which made the spot interesting. After a broken cataract of about twenty feet, the stream was received in a large natural basin filled to the brim with water, which, when the bubbles of the fall subsided, was so exquisitely clear, that although it was of great depth, the eye could discern each pebble at the bottom. Eddying round this reservoir, the brook found its way over a broken part of the ledge, and formed a second fall, which seemed to seek the very abyss ; then, wheeling out beneath from among the smooth dark rocks, which it had polished for ages, it wandered murmuring down the glen, forming the stream up which Waverley had just ascended. The borders of this romantic reservoir corresponded in beauty ; but it was beauty of a stern and commanding cast, as if in the act of expanding into grandeur."

It is to some extent unlucky that at the time when the fishing in Loch Ard is about its best the scenery is pretty nearly at its worst. That region shows but little verdure in April—the trees, if not bare, are dirty brown, and the mountains do somewhat suggest the idea of elephants in the mange. But the season has also its compensations—the air is vocal all the day with songs of birds, and the heart of man, when winter is over and gone, and spring and summer are

felt to be coming, is better attuned to hope and joy.
And, whatever be the season, is it not something to
float all day beneath the shadows of Ben Venue and
Ben Lomond, forgetting until eve, though then you
are pleased to remember, that in three hours you may
be back in Edinburgh or Glasgow, a better man in
soul, body, and mind?   "I shall never think on Loch
Ard but the thought will gar me grew [shudder] again,"
said Bailie Nicol Jarvie, thinking of the indignity he
had suffered and the murder he had seen.   "I shall
never think on Loch Ard but the thought will soothe
and cheer me," will be the exclamation of every true
angler or lover of nature that has dreamed away a
day in that lovely scene, where, if his fish happened
to be few, his thoughts ought to have been the more
abundant.

A. R.

CURIOSITIES OF ANGLING
LITERATURE.

As we explore retrogressively, and dive deep into the mysteries of old books upon Natural History, so do we find how the flood of light which is now poured by the **lamp of scientific research upon all** things animate and inanimate dwindles gradually to a more minute spark : and curious it is to reflect that that little ray, penetrating in times past through only a narrow crevice, or peeping modestly out of the chamber of literature through its well-nigh closed shutters, was the parent of the great living TRUTH, which in these latter days finds nothing too low and nothing too high for its shining, and which by the aid of the telescope **and the** microscope **has** left **but** little unrevealed, **or at** least unexamined, whether **of** things on the earth, **or things** under the **earth, or** things over the earth. **The** books we have been recently plodding through **date** from 1600 to 1740, and **these show** how, for the most part, truth and error were unwittingly, and as we might almost say conscientiously, **woven** together.

In the course of our search we have chanced upon

a few curious illustrations of the jumbling-up of fact and fiction in matters piscine or piscatorial, which may not perhaps be altogether uninteresting, or at least unamusing, as examples of the sort of science current within the last couple of centuries. A belief, for instance, in igneous waters, underground streams, haunted wells and fountains, and generally in preposterous or non-existing eccentricities of river administration, appears to have been very common. Here are a few authentic specimens of *quasi*

"Waters Bewitched."

G. Nelson, Rector of Oakley, in Suffolk, in an old work by Dr. Grew, says, " I would not embellish this book with fiction, because I intend to serve the Truth. And yet in the next page we find :

" The water of the river Thames is very remarkable, being tempered with **some** kind of acid, which it licks from its banks. . . . The mariners are forced to hold their noses when they drink it, yet it does not make them sick ; and after a third or fourth fermentation, it becomes very sweet ; whereas other water is irrecoverable, and dangerous after its stinking. This water in eight months' time acquires so spirituous and active a quality, that upon opening a cask and holding a candle near the bung its steams **have** taken fire like the spirits of wine, and sometimes endangered the ship."

After this the problem of setting the Thames on fire may be considered as solved.

The water of the Nile, as might perhaps be expected from the mystery of its source, is also exceedingly peculiar in some respects. According to Ludolphus—"It is muddy and thick, and not wholesome of itself, but they have a way to cure it. They have large earthen vessels, which being filled, they rub the inside with three or four almonds, and in the space of a **quarter of an hour the water becomes very** clear. Being thus **purged, it** is very wholesome, **so** that it never does any man harm ; because running so long a course, and through so hot a country as Æthropiars is, the sun corrects and cleanseth it from all crudities. Those that bring the water to the houses have always a paste of almonds to rub the vessels with."

We find the name of Harris (probably Mrs.) attached to the following highly-credible **story :—** "There is a wonderful water-tree in **one of the** Canaries whose leaves continually distil pure **water :** it is a single tree as big as a middle-sized oak. In the night a thick cloud or mist always hangs about **it, and** the water drops very fast and in great quantities. There are lead pipes laid from it to a great **pond which is** paved with stone and holds 20,000 **tons of water, yet is** filled in one night. There are

7 or 8000 people, and many more thousands of cattle, all supplied from this fountain. The great pond communicates its water to several lesser ones, which disperse it through the whole island."

" Plenty of fish is an indication of good air and wholesome water. . . . Tibiscus, now called Tyssa, a river in Hungary, is so replenished with fish, that in summer, when the river is low, the people say the river smells of fish. The river Bodrock is said to consist of two parts water and one fish ; on this river is Tockay, famous for its wine. The fecundity of rivers is ascribed to the various salts, which are to be found in the bottom of a river, or washed from its banks." . . .

" Agricola observes that the water of Steurewald comes forth of a marble quarry, and that such as drink it fasting discover shortly a smell like rotten eggs, and also an odour of brayed marble. . . . Vitriol is a smart acid, and nauseous of itself, yet it is corrected by a well-concocted sulphur ; so that some springs, although impregnated with acids, yet taste like milk." Assuredly, then, it is not from Agricola's springs that the London dairies draw their water supplies.

" Lough Loman is famous for its floating island, for fish without fins, and for being frequently tempestuous in calm weather ; thereabouts is the merlin, a kind of hawk of small size ; it hath very tender feet, which cannot endure cold ; wherefore nature hath provided that it hunts a bird in the evening, sits upon it all night to keep its feet warm, lets it go in the morning without hurt, and hunts another bird to prey upon." Making a warming-pan of a fag **at** school must sink in the scale of inventions after this.

Surely in the following we have the original of Tennyson's " violent sea ?"—" Huntingdonshire hath its share of fens, and there are several violent meers, which have **plenty** of fish, but the waters are often furiously disturbed in the calmest weather to the great danger and terror of the fishermen, supposed to be occasioned by eruptions of wind underneath. **Wittlesey** Meer, six miles long and three broad, is clear water and full of fish, yet like the rest it is troubled much with wind ; the air about is foggy and stinking, fatal to strangers, but the natives bear it well and live long."

As the witty Curran sought **to** soothe sleep-dispelling Boreas by an offering of a box of peppermint lozenges cast from his bedroom window, may **not** the modern growth of the peppermint plant upon the banks of these once *windy*-meers have had an even more successful effect in smoothing **their** agitated beds ?

Rivers that take it into their heads to run dry when they might naturally be expected to be overflowing, and *vice versa*, are very common.

"**Chichester** is watered by the river Lavant, whose course is entirely unaccountable, being sometimes quite dry, and at other times runs with a violent stream even in the middle of summer."

But this eccentricity of behaviour is attributed to many rivers—as in the case of the Lambourne, for instance, a tributary of the Kennet, which has been handed down, even to the present day, as being a stream "almost **dry in winter** and most full in summers of great drought." We are accustomed to judge for ourselves where it is possible in such cases, and regret to have to dispel the poetry of history, by stating that after carefully watching this and other **rivers for** a series of years, we have not been able to detect the slightest evidence **in** favour of the fact in **any one instance.**

Then we come to waters which, like the hero of Thackeray's Revolution ballad, seem to fulfil only one, and that a somewhat abnormal purpose in life—viz. *drumming ;* thus—

"Oundle, on the river Nyne, in Northampton-shire, is noted for its drumming well, generally thought **to** foretell war, or the death of some eminent person, as appears by a late printed account of this **prodigy.**" Taking, we presume, a hint from the boy who cut open the drum to see where the sound came **from ;**—" It has been once emptied to find out the cause of the noise ; but the man that went down to the bottom could perceive nothing, but only heard a noise above him. It is not unlike the beating of a march ; uncertain in its continuance, sometimes **lasting** but a short time, at other times **a** week or longer, nor is it always heard at the same distance." What a fortune this well would be in the hands of spiritualists ! would it not be well—nay better—if we could get them all down there, and then put the **lid on** ?

It is satisfactory to **find,** however, **that** in describing **this as a well of** " one idea," we have done it injustice. **In a** subsequent passage we are told that " it supplies four families with water, which is good **at all times,** whether drumming or not."

Northamptonshire, it appears, enjoys by no means a monopoly of " sounding waters."

" At Kilgarring, in South Wales, there is a cataract in the river, called the Salmon's Leap, because they take their tail **in** their teeth, and spring over **the cataract. On which** coast also is **Bosharston-Meer,** so deep **it** could never be sounded. It bubbles, foams, and makes a **noise** against a storm, that is heard ten miles off."

A most obstreperous mere this, certainly ! Then again :—

" **In a** cliff, off Caerdiff Point, is an island called **Barry,** from Baruch, a holy man buried there. In a **rock hereof,** by the seaside, there is **a** small chink,

to which if **you** lay your ear, you **shall hear, as it**
were, the noise of smiths at **work, one-while** blowing
the bellows, another-while striking **of sledge and**
hammer ; sometimes the sound of **a grindstone and**
iron tools rubbing against it, also the hissing sparks
of goads from **the furnace."** Can this be Vulcan
forging the bolts of Jove, with which tradition states
that Neptune once armed Britannia's hand **for a**
highly patriotic **purpose?**

Endless are the springs we meet with that "freeze
in the hottest weather and are hot in winter," **and**
lakes which seem to possess some irritable Genius **who**
does not like the throwing of stones, for we read of
two or three, "the which, if a pebble is cast into
them, they **raise** storms of hail, lightning, and
thunder." Waters, "which **have** the most marvellous
and rapid effect in petrifying **all** that **they** come in
contact with," are also to be found—at least in books.
Collier mentions that "Chatri Columbe, a tailor's wife
in Burgundy, accidentally drank of some of these
waters after she was married, the result of which
was, that her first child, a daughter, when **born, was**
discovered to **be a** perfectly-formed petrifaction. She
lived in the time of Henry III. of England."

Of waters which, for some **occult reason** or other,
prefer a subterranean channel, the examples also are
very numerous if we are to believe these old his-
torians :—

"**In Surrey is** a place called 'the Swallow,' under White Hill, and where the river Mole, called the English Anas, runs under ground for about two miles, so that the inhabitants may boast, as the Spaniards do of their Guadiana, that they have a bridge which feeds several flocks of sheep."

White Hill, so marked upon old maps, but now known as Box Hill, has nothing whatever to do with hiding the Mole, nor is its course for **a** single foot hidden from the sight of those who, like ourselves, have followed its every inch from the many streamlets of its source down to the Thames. Camden, however, generally pretty accurate; Izaak Walton, devoted to **truth**; Chamberlayn, in *Present State of Great Britain*, 1743; Milton, "Sullen Mole that runneth underneath;" Pope, Drayton, and others, have all "**swallowed**" this apocryphal text.

"Bishop Tunstal first discovered that the fathomless Hell-Kettles, near Darlington, had passages under ground. He marked a goose **for a trial, and** then put him down, and afterwards found him in the river Tees."

"The snow lies eight months," Tournford tells us, "on the mountains Ararat and Caucasus, and breeds white worms as big as one's little finger, which being crushed, there issues out a moisture colder than snow itself."

"**The ordinary** water at Gourron **breeds** worms in

the feet and legs, which are very dangerous, if not pulled out whole; therefore when a worm begins to appear out of the flesh, they tie the end of it to a roller, and wrap it round gently by degrees. If it break, the remaining part in the flesh often proves fatal; the whole would be a yard or more in length."

But we fancy we have given sufficient examples of superstitions affecting water. We could easily multiply them almost *ad infinitum*, even down to rivers which, like "the Avon, near St. Vincent's Rock, Cornwall," are "so full of diamonds, that a man may fill whole baskets with them;" we will spare the recapitulation, however, and hasten on to another genus which may perhaps be classed in some future catalogue of the British Museum as—

"Odd Fish."

Let us take Mermaids to begin with :—

Dr Meyer assures us, "that in 1403 a mermaid was cast ashore near Haerlem, who was brought to feed upon bread and milk, taught to spin, and lived many years. John Gerard of Leyden adds, that she would frequently pull off her clothes, and run towards the water; and that she imitated speech, but it was so confused a noise as not to be understood by anybody; she was buried in the churchyard because she had learnt to make the sign of the cross." He

" speaks this upon the credit of several persons that had seen her."

From her frequently attempting to "*run* towards the water," it is evident that this young lady belonged to a very high class of mermaid indeed, and rose superior to the disabilities under which her sex have been usually supposed to labour, as regards the organs of locomotion.

We soon come, however, to one with the orthodox termination :—

"In the seas of **Newfoundland is the** mermaid which was **seen by** Captain Waithburn. **At** St. John's Harbour, A.D. 1610, he spied a creature coming towards him, which in all the upper parts was like a woman, the hair excepted, but instead of that there were blue streaks very like hair round about the head, and as it were hung down to the neck. **She** seemed to wish to make acquaintance, but the captain retired from her. She came afterwards to the side of the boat, and attempted to come **into it,** but one of the men struck **her with an oar, and made** her tumble into the water ; another was seen by two of Hudson's men, who saw her tail, it was like the tail of a porpoise."

So much for mermaids. Then "there is the **manati in** Jamaica, having a head like an ox, his body long like an otter, and who has two feet like an elephant's : some are about twelve yards long and four broad. A certain Indian king kept and fed one of them **with** bread twenty-six years in a lake near his house, which grew tame beyond all that the ancients have written of dolphins. He would sometimes carry a few people on his back across the lake with ease. There is the head of one in Gresham College."

"In the Mauritius there is a fish called Man-atee, **which** useth both elements ; **its** fins serve for stilts at land as they **do** for oars at sea. It delights at beholding **a** man's face, and is valuable for a stone found in the head, which being pounded and drank in wine, fasting, cures **the** cholick."

Apropos of dolphins, **we** light once more upon our **friend** Harris. Appion tells us that "he was an eyewitness, besides many more that flocked from **afar** off to see, of a dolphin which a boy on his way to school on the Lake Lucrin used to feed, and in return for this kindness, the dolphin would carry the **boy** across on its back over the bay from Bara to Puzzoli." But we have not done with Harris ; he is evidently strong upon dolphins. "Sir Thomas Herbert tells him, Harris, that they much affect the company of men, **and** are nourished like men ; they are always constant to their mates, so tenderly affected to their parents that when they are 300 years old, they feed and defend them against hungry fishes ; and when **they die, carry** them ashore and bury them."

"**In China,**" says Thevenot, " there is a fish that

cries like a child when taken ; its fat is of that nature that when it once burns, neither water nor anything else can quench it. There is a fish called the swimming cow, which comes sometimes on land and fights with other cows; but when it stays any considerable time out of water, its horns soften, and it is obliged to return to the water to recover their hardness."

"There is a sort of waterfowl about as **big as a** crow in Tubut Island, called Lugan. They slip **into** the mouths of whales, which swallow them alive, **and** have their hearts eaten up by **the bird, by which** means **many of them are killed, and** the bird found alive in the carcase."

In Linschotten we are told that "the crew of a ship, sailing from Mozambique into India, found themselves, for a whole fortnight, instead of sailing forwards, **still** going back, although against the wind ; **until at** last the boatswain spied a great broad tail **of a** fish that had winded itself round **the** head of **the ship,** the body being under the **keel, and** the **head of it** under the rudder, **swimming in** that manner, **and** drawing the ship contrary to the wind and their right course ; which they with much ado struck off with staves, and then the ship went right again."

"About here (the Moluscos) are serpents thirty feet long, which eat a certain herb, then get upon **trees by the bank** of the sea, or rivers, and vomit up the herbs ; **to** which the fish gather and are intoxicated ; which makes them float on the water, and **become** the serpent's prey."

Is it possible that this tree, up which the serpents climb and make beasts of themselves, is " the toddy-tree which yields that famous liquor so called ? It is as thick as a man may clasp with his arms, straight and tall, without boughs to the very top ; but hath a rough bark, which gives assistance to the climber, and **the natives mount** them with incredible celerity. **The liquor distils from** the branches upon making an incision. **It is a** delicious **wine,** as smooth **as new white wine, but much** more **fine and** clear." There was **a canine animal once** yclept " Negus." Upon a parity **of** reasoning this toddy-tree might be called **as** appropriately the dog-tree, **being** all whine and **bark.**

" In the rivers of Terra Firma is a small fish, about the bigness of a smelt, which hath four eyes, two on **each side, one** above another ; and in swimming, it is observed to keep the uppermost two above, and this **other two** under water."

Can the following be our old acquaintance the sea-serpent ? " There is a water-snake of so strange **a quality, that** whatsoever touches it sticks fast to it, and **by that** means it gets its living. It is of a vast **length, but** can contract itself wonderfully. So he comes ashore, lays himself down close, and whatsoever stumbles upon him is catched by his glewy skin; then he whips away with it to sea, and returns to **his** natural length, which is equal to a large cable. One of them was found dead with two wild boars in his belly."

Thus much as to a few zoological curiosities of fish literature. Another kindred subject upon which the inventive faculties of anglers and naturalists have delighted to exhaust themselves in theories, possible and impossible, is that of—

Oils and Scented Baits,

and **their** attractive influences **upon the** piscine appetite. This *vexata quæstio* **has been a** prolific source of controversy and gross exaggeration on the part **of** angling authors in times past; and even now the **web of fact** and fiction which they **have** ingeniously **woven** can hardly be considered **as** fairly disentangled.

The question is—Have fish the sense of smell, and if so, to what extent? It is conceded that almost all animals have **this power, more or less, and that in** some the gift takes the characteristics of the marvellous; and until it is proved to the contrary it would certainly seem, according to all the accepted laws of logic, that creatures with nostrils should be admitted into the category of smellers. We might, indeed, thus easily settle the question, and say, in

approved parliamentary language, that **the "noes"
have it.** But against this prominent feature of the
argument we get the somewhat sophistical blow, that
there **exist** individuals **who, like** the blind deprived
of sight, the deaf of hearing, and, it may be added,
the unfeeling of the sense of touch, are equally
bereaved of the olfactory attribute. Man, as a general
rule, possesses a greater perceptive sagacity in this
facial organ **for** the detection of coarse and objectionable odours **than the** gentler **sex, while the latter,
apparently** ignorant of the presence of much **that is
offensive to the** ruder nature of man, **can** analyse
shades of difference in the essential odours arising
from a flower almost **to the extent** of determining
thereby the exact period **of the day.** There are few
of us but are acquainted **with some one or** other of
our fellows **who will faint at the smell of a rose,** be-
come pale and sick in too close proximity **to a melon,
who cannot sit down to table if** there **be** vinegar at
the board ; **and, on the** other hand, have **a** vigorous
relish for **exhalations** unbearable to **the rest of the**
community. **We knew a** young lady **once,** whose
delight (when **in** the country) was to **lean** over the
balustrades and blow out the lamps, the fumes from
the viscous gases of which she thought exquisite, as
reminding her of the opera ! Again, with us, a passing "sniff" will recall the minute details of some
scenes of interest long past, or remind **us of circum-**

stances which we neither cared for at the period of their occurrence nor ever after. All these, and endless other instances to which we could refer, tend to prove that where there exist noses, there the absence of the sense of smell must be taken as the exception, and not as the rule. Davies quaintly tells us of that—

" Next, in the nostrils she doth use the smell,
    As God the breath of life in them did give ;
So makes he now this power in them to dwell,
    To judge all airs whereby we breathe and live."

If then, in other words, we accept the general conclusion that the nose is the sentinel of the stomach, and we find by proper examination that fish possess the organ with its due proportion of muscles and nerves, we cannot conscientiously deny that they likewise are probably endowed to some extent with the power of discriminating by smell what is good or bad for them. Most anglers are aware that the fresh bait of to-day eagerly seized and pouched by the **salmon** or the pike, and to-morrow rejected by both, will **be** greedily devoured by the less fastidious eel, which yet, after a greater degree of staleness in the bait, would turn up its nose at it, whether blunt or pointed ; thus giving the still greater scavenger of the water— the craw-fish—the chance of making an acceptable meal. Call this an exercise of *taste*, or by what name **you will**, it is too intimately connected with smelling

—which in some persons means the same thing—to be rejected in the question.　Our forefathers certainly, one and all, as anglers, gave fish the credit of possessing the faculty to so refined a degree that even the apparently infinitesimal distinction between the fat of the kidney of a lamb and that of a sheep is insisted upon for the proper admixture of certain descriptions of pastes.

We have shown that a stale bait will be rejected by different descriptions of fish ; it will be as easy for us to get an affirmative to the assertion that mouldy bread or bran is equally repugnant to the delicate palates of trout, chub, roach, etc., either used as ground-bait or in the form of paste.　The same objection to a dead or putrid worm may be noticed in reference to trout and perch.　It may be urged that this aversion is arrived at by a close ocular inspection on the fish's part.　But if such be the case, we should probably find fish in the morning upon the hooks of night-lines, whether the worms were fresh or otherwise, and this is not the case.　Smell, in fact, is less fallible than sight, for there are a great many things that look repulsive which are good to eat, and there are few things, if any, that smell objectionable which the palate or stomach will tolerate.　When fish take to eating stale or corrupt baits, either by day or night, it will be so much the worse for the water-rat and the moor-hen, and that immense minor

world of life—the insect classes—the wise ordering
of which keeps our rivers free from organic matter,
and which is never ceasing **in its** beneficial conver-
sion of what is *effcte* into fresh combinations and vital
material.

The Rev. C. D. Badham, in his *Prose Halieutics,*
says that the Izaak Waltons of antiquity employed
divers pastes, equal to (and it would be hard to **sur-
pass**) our own, for complicity of composition, and the
truly surprising effects resulting from the different
ingredients introduced.

That some fish **were attracted** by strong scents,
and would take a whole pharmacopœia of " fœtids,"
prescribed by a scientific practitioner, was indeed as
well known to the poacher of early days as now.
Oppian speaks of myrrh dissolved in wine-lees, and
again of certain drugs familiar to the sons of Æscu-
lapius as well as fishermen, and turned to account by
the latter in impregnating **their nets, as** expedients
that never failed. These substances entered into **the**
composition of many fishing pastes, the recipes **for**
which have come down **to us. They were of two**
classes, intoxicating **and** poisonous. **Pliny** records
that all aristolochias yield an aromatic smell, but
that one, called popularly "the earth's poison," is
successfully used by Campanian fishermen for the
purposes of their craft.

" I have seen them use the plaut," says he, " incorporating it with lime, and throwing detached pellets into the sea, one of which was no sooner swallowed than the fish, immediately turning over, floated up dead." But the most interesting of these poisons is unquestionably prepared from the cyclamen, or sow-bread, two species of which possess the property of drugging fish in a remarkable degree, the *C. Hederæ-folium* and the *C. Neapolitanum.* The lazzaroni, from whom we first learned the qualities of this plant, stated that they were in the habit of mixing it with other ingredients, in a paste they called *lateragna,* which is either thrown in lumps from a boat, or enclosed in a bag, and thrust by means of a long pole among the rocks, when, if any fish are within smell, the crew are sure of a good haul; it was found, they said, particularly successful in the capture of Cephali, and generally of low-swimming fish, whose nostrils come in more immediate contact with it on the ground.

A paragraph in Cavaliere Tenore's *Neapolitan Flora* quite confirms the correctness of the above statements.

The ancient anglers never appeared to entertain a doubt but that fish were as particular in their diet, and would be as much charmed by its variety, as any other class of animated nature. One of the oldest works upon the subject of angling has this passage— a passage for its atmosphere of *goût* equal to anything

in Ude, Francatelli, or Soyer :—" Pastes are a species
of artificial baits, to be angled with at ground, or
within the water. *There are, or may be, as many
distinct sorts of them as the luxuriancy of every fancy
will suggest.*" Lucullian—is it not ? Could a Bel-
gravian Gunter, throwing open his doors to the
aristocratic lovers of all that is gustatory, have expressed himself in a more comprehensive or enticing
manner? Then follows the query—Did the fish of
the period appreciate this "luxuriance of fancy?"
—and have they, just in an inverse ratio to the
civilisation **of** man, eschewed the high feeding of a
past age to content themselves with the simple fare
of plain bread and water in this? It would seem so,
if we are to believe the modern fisherman, who may
be here inclined to deny that these piscatorial desires
ever had an existence, excepting in the imagination
of men living in a benighted age—insinuating that
even modern cooks **have** been known to ask for
champagne, as an addendum to stewed kidneys,
which never reached beyond the neck of the bottle
(unless it was to run down the throat of the *chef*),
and hint at a *cuisine* whose **sauce** was encouraged
by burnt brandies obtained under the excuse of
requirements of mince-pies and plum-puddings.
Those cynics who are inclined to take this view
of the great masters of *pisciculture*, must be pre-
pared to back their slanders with something better

than mere assertion, because, if they would insinuate that the variety of preparations of " rabbit, roasted bacon, white bread, mutton-kidney, butter and cheese," followed with a constitutional nip of " aniseed," was but to serve as a sly dinner for the biped and not for the fish, they must be prepared to show that men in that time were equally disposed to refect upon " the flesh of whelps," turmeric mixed with bean or wheat flour, or a dash of assafœtida, and the whole washed down with a full draught of Venice turpentine, instead of Barclay and Perkins or Ind Coope.

"I make but little boast," writes one who fished in the fifteenth century, " of my unguents, for there are those about who would steal of my secrets and lie in wait, abounding like a robber for that which I use, that they the whereof could take to the man of cunning, and set aside each of its components, and thus become master of that which is none of theirs ; but this I will venture, for none such purloiners of man's goods is there even the most simple of pastes left, for *that*, being made of white bread and milk, needeth *clean hands*."

Another angler tells us that " assafœtida, oil of polipody, of the oak, oil of ivy, oil of Peter, and gum ivy, mixed up as paste, will wonderfully increase your sport."

Now, of all the abominable stinks assafœtida is the worst. But if the fish like it, the credit due to the angler in providing it for them, in spite of all objections, is great. It is produced from a species of *ferula*, in the dry stalk of which we are told Pro-

metheus brought fire from **heaven.** *Polipody*—almost
as filthy in smell as the **preceding—will** be found
under the class Cryptogamia, amongst the **last** and
lowest of vegetables. It **is of the fern** tribe. The
oil of ivy is the tear which exudes from the stem of
that parasite when the limb is wounded. We are **not**
sufficient chemists to determine what **is oil of Peter,**
unless it was **some** preparation, secret or otherwise,
of a mediæval **"Peter of the** Pool," or that of St.
Peter's wort.

This reference occasionally **to the flesh of** whelps,
in combination with oils, as a lure for fish, recalls a
passage in the life **of** the great **French** chirurgeon
Ambrose Paré, in which he dwells upon the difficulties
he had to encounter during two whole years of self-
imposed retirement from his business, to obtain from
a professional contemporary at Turin (*temp.* 1536) his
secret of curing wounds made **by** gunshot. He
writes—

" It fell out **that the Marshall of Montejan, the King's**
lieutenant-general, then **in Piedmont, died ; wherefore I went**
unto my chirurgeon, **and told him that I could take no plea-**
sure in living there, **the favourer** and Mæcenas of my studies
being taken away ; and that I intended forthwith to return
to Paris, and that it would neither hinder nor discredit him
to teach his remedy to me, who should be so far remote from
him. When he heard this he made no delay, but presently
wished me *to provide* *two whelps,* **one** *pound of earth-worms,*
two pounds of oil of lilies, six ounces of Venice turpentine, and

one ounce of aqua vitæ. In my presence he boiled the whelps, put alive into that oil, until the flesh came from the bones, then presently he put in the worms, which he had first killed in white wine, that they might be so cleansed from the earthly dross with which they are usually replete ; and then he boiled them in the same oil so long till they became dry, and had spent all their juice therein ; then he strained it through a towel without much pressing ; and added the turpentine to it, and lastly *aqua vitæ ;* calling God to witness that he had no other balsam wherewith to cure wounds made with gunshot, and bring them to suppuration. Thus he sent me away as rewarded with a most precious gift, requesting me to keep it as a great secret, and not to reveal it to any."

Ambrose **Paré** was surgeon in ordinary to Henry II. in 1552, a post which he also retained under the three succeeding kings, Francis II., Charles IX., and Henry III. It is therefore not a little curious to find " Monsieur Charras, apothecary royal to the late French king, Lewis the Fourteenth," coming out with recipes of a similar nature as " unguents for the certain taking of divers kinds of fish." It may be that M. Charras, as apothecary, was entirely in ignorance of the original application of " whelp oil," and that, finding it, probably with the directions for its composition after the death of this surgeon, in a peculiar box, for its better transit upon the field of battle, drew an inference therefrom, that it was intended for some sporting pursuit, and if so, that it would not apply to any other than angling. Or—as even incidents travel in circles—that the hoax played upon Ambrose Paré by **the** original compounder, probably as a punishment for the excess **of** his curiosity, cropped up in the guise **of** a joke for which **the** credulity of the anglers of that age had evidently prepared the victims.   It is clear, however, that it served to assist the chemists and druggists in disposing **of** their oils, etc., for at least two centuries, and that the fishermen were pretty handsomely mulcted in the purchase thereof.   The fact of dipping the earth-worms into white **wine to** *kill* **them will not** escape the notice **of the intelligent angler, who will recall** Oppian's allusion **to the** uses of wine-lees in fishing, and **the several** prescriptions **of other old** writers upon angling, whereof wine is **an** ingredient for a paste in which to dip or place the worms or gentles for a *short time only* previous to the use of them : this doubtless to aggravate their writhing, and make them **more** " **lively** upon the hook."

Approaching **a literature nearer to our own day** (1740), John **Richardson, Gent.,** thus expresses himself " as to ointments or unguents :"—

" Many ingenious anglers **esteem** them so, **for** the effectual furtherance of this sport, that **they** affirm they will not only *allure* but even *compel* fish to bite. For my own part, I honestly confess, that though I have found them in some measure *advantageous* to my recreations, yet in far from so **high** a degree as has been pretended. However, it is worth every sportsman's while to be acquainted with some of them, that if they **are** willing **to** be at the expense and labour of a

trial, they may select those for their daily use which on experience they shall find to be best. One or two of those that are most highly commended, would, I own, be more pleasing to me were they more simple, and less superstitiously compounded. In particular this by Monsieur Charras, apothecary royal to the late French king, Lewis the Fourteenth :—
'Take of man's fat and cat's fat, of each half an ounce ; mummy, finely powdered, three drams ; cummin-seed, finely powdered, one dram ; distilled oil of aniseed and spike, of each six drops ; civet, two grains ; and camphire, four grains : make an ointment according to art. When you angle with this, anoint eight inches of the line next the hook. Keep it in a pewter box, made something taper ; and, when you use it never angle with less than two or three hairs next the hook ; because if you angle with one hair it will not stick so well to the line.'   .   .   .

"Gum ivy (not the oil of ivy) is of a yellowish-red colour, and of a strong scent and sharp taste. To get it true, drive several large nails into thick ivy stalks, and having wriggled them till they become very loose, let them remain, and a gum will issue out of the hole. This gum is excellent for the angler's use : perhaps nothing more so under the form of an unguent."

Then we meet with other writers who have each in turn some favourite nostrum : now it is oil of olive, now chymical oil of lavender or camomile :—

"But for a trout in a muddy water, and for gudgeons in a clean stream, the best ungent is compounded, viz.—

"Take assafœtida, 3 drams ; camphire, 1 dram ; Venice turpentine, 1 dram ; beat altogether with some drops of the chymical oils of lavender and camomile, of each an equal quantity."

That the refined trout should be induced to partake of this precious compound in dirty water, and a gudgeon in clean water, is perhaps intended to illustrate the wide difference in the intellect of the two fish.

Then follow instructions how to know the true camphire and how to keep it :—

"The Bornean camphire is best ; choose that which is white and clear like crystal, strong-scented, will easily crumble between the fingers, and, being fired, will scarcely be quenched. There is a counterfeit or factitious sort, which, put into a hot loaf, will parch ; but the true will melt. It will keep many years in flax-seed, if it be not exposed to the air ; otherwise it will evaporate and consume to nothing.

" Assafœtida—chuse that which is pure, fine, clammy, and smelling almost like garlick.

" In the absence of gum-ivy, take ivy berries and express them ; put some of the infusion into a box, and when about to use gentles put them therein for a few minutes.

" Dissolve gum-ivy in the oil of spike, and anoint the bait with it. Mr. Walton prescribes this for a pike."

The oil of spike must not be confounded with the oil of spikenard, often mentioned in old books upon angling. The former is alluded to in Hill's *Materia Medica* as an oil extracted from a smaller species of lavender—" The oil of spike is much used by our artificers in their varnishes, but it is generally, adulterated ;" while that of spikenard (*Spica nardi*, Lat.) is a plant which grows plentifully in Java, and appears to have been known to the medical writers of all ages ; indeed it is thus men-

tioned in the Scriptures (Mark xiv. 3); while the
Spectator says: "He cast into the **pile** bundles of
myrrh, and sheaves of spikenard, enriching **it with**
every spicy shrub."

In some of the many recipes in which oils are **used**
we find **that of comfrey** alluded to, which **in Baily's**
Dictionary is given as "an excellent **wound herb**;"
and the celebrated J. J. Rousseau, **in his** *Letters on the
Elements of Botany*, speaks **of it as the** *symphytum
officinale Linnæi*, being common **by** watersides.
Galbanum, **a** strong-scented gum, **is likewise fre-**
quently mentioned; and herein is a strange contradic-
tion of opinion in reference **to its odour, for** while we
find in the Apocrypha, **"I yielded indeed a** pleasant
odour, like the best **myrrh; as** galbanum" (Ecclus.
xxiv. 15); Hill, the chymical author, whom we have
before quoted, says "its smell is strong and disagree-
able."

"Some advise to take the bones or skull of a dead man, at
the opening of a grave, and beat them into powder, and to put
of this powder into the moss wherein you keep your worms;
but others like **the** grave earth as well."

"**Man's fat**" is very often alluded to in the old
books, and we are directed "to any **surgeons**" **for it !**
"Cat's fat" is likewise strongly recommended, **and**
that fat from a heron's leg. Now we know that
herons and cats are fond of fish, and that although a
cat has an almost insuperable aversion to the wetting

of her feet, the sight of a fish will induce her to take
to the water, and that when once she has, otter-like,
pursued fish in this way with success, she becomes
one of the most desperate of poachers. But man is
not always fond of fish, and the fat of a fellow who is
no ossophagist might tend to drive the fish away
rather than to induce their presence, and if such be
the case, we fear there will become a great demand
for the adipose of an angler, and he who in dying
carries so tempting a bait may be followed to his last
resting-place by the brethren of the rod in a humour
rather of joy than of sorrow! This is certainly a
grave view to take of the question, and naturally
brings us to an end :—

> " All arts, all shapes, the wily angler tries,
>   To cloak his fraud, and tempt his finny prize :
>   Their sight, their smell, he carefully explores,
>   And blends the druggist's and the chymist's stores
>   Devising still, with fancy ever new,
>   Pastes, oils, and unguents, of each scent and hue."

And in Jones' *Oppian* :—

> " A paste in luscious wine the captor steeps,
>   Mixed with the balmy tears that Myrrha weeps,
>   Around the trap diffusive fragrance rolls,
>   And calls with certain charms the finny shoals ;
>   They crowd the arch, and soon each joyful swain
>   Finds nor his labour nor his care in vain."

G. F.

T

THE TWEED AT DRYBURGH.

A MORE appropriate resting-place for our great national minstrel and novelist could not have been selected than the cloister-grounds of Dryburgh Abbey. They lie within the circle where his brother enchanter, Sir Michael Scott of Oakwood, is traditionally asserted to have set to task his clamorous familiar, and through its agency

> " Cleft the Eildon Hills in three,
> And bridled the Tweed with a curb of stone."

Thomas of Ercildoun, also (the Rhymer as he was called), spun his boding octosyllabics within a horn's sound of the sacred precincts. Melrose and the nameless den haunted by the "white ladye of Avenel," whose draped figure, moulded in *alto relievo* centuries ago, embellishes the roof of one of the banqueting apartments at Gala House, are not far off; and on the slope of a conspicuous height stands erect—the cynosure of all eyes—Smailholm Tower. In regard to its more immediate accessories and points of attraction, Dryburgh Abbey, as a ruin, carries the palm among the four great religious edifices which, three or four centuries ago, formed the strongholds of Christianity on Tweedside. It wants the ornateness and beauty, both of design and workmanship, which characterise the Gothic structure at Melrose ; it does not pretend to cope in altitude and stern simplicity with its Norman sister at Kelso, nor yet does it affect a comparison with the massive and still tenable walls and coping which appertain to its Jeddart colleague; but being more impressively **a ruin** than any of them, **it** has that which none of the others have, **or are** ever likely to have—surroundings which befit its character, elevating **as well as** adorning it. Yews and ivies are here in profusion, and venerable orchard trees, the products of which it is allowable to imagine were partaken of by monks and devotees, not to say reivers and Southron invaders, in the olden days. And there are oaks of course (for the site of the Abbey is said to have been that of a Druidical shrine or city—the name itself supports this tradition), and other growths showing foliage of varied hues, in abundance. But the grand attraction—that which no doubt moved most the soul of Sir Walter Scott when still in the body, to desire as a restingplace this God's-acre—was the elbow of the river which clasps it. Climb with me, tired angler, to the Braeheads, as **they** are called, which form the rear ground of Lessuden village, and look down upon the landscape. A more enjoyable wind-up to your day's sport you cannot have. On Tweedside, which is crowded with scenic attractions, I know of no spot that so powerfully commends itself to the eye, and is more adapted by its associations to invite to soothing reverie.

The charms which belong to this view-point are no doubt greatly enhanced in the angler's estimation by the character of the river. The curve or bend here taken by the Border-stream embraces a series of rocky pools and gravelly stretches, which in their harmonious combination present themselves at once to his mind as the cherished lurking-places both of salmon and river-trout ; not that they excel in this respect the ranges of water in their immediate neighbourhood, but forming as they do a prominent feature in the picture, they add to the interest of it in the eye of a certain class of onlookers, and really deepen and make more imposing the general effect.

Since the communication by railway was established betwixt Kelso and St. Boswells—a station on the North British line situated at about a mile's distance from the Abbey—I have taken opportunities, two or three at least every season, to pay a visit, rod in hand, to the bend in question and the portions of the river adjoining it. Sometimes, for variety's sake, I alight at Maxton Station, three miles further down, and fish up towards Dryburgh. In that case, I rarely wet line until I pass Benrig and come within view of Mertoun Bridge, **a short** way below which **runs a section** of water which, **to** the **eye** of an experienced trout-fisher, is irresistible ; **not** to say that **in the** Maxton range itself there **are no holds of** equal promise, only, were one **to** commence **upon such** in earnest, he must make up **his mind to stick to** them, and leave unaccomplished, **for that day at** least, an intended pilgrimage **to St. Mary's shrine.** With this in **view therefore, and a** meditative **lounge on the Braeheads** behind **Lessuden, I skip o'er the Benrig pool and** its superintending stream, and **begin operations** with fly, minnow, **or** worm, according **to** the condition **of** the river, near **the** base of a small island which subtends the bridge above mentioned. There, where Tweed is rejoined **by a run of** diverted **water** which **has done** service at Mertoun Mill, I seldom fail, **in the months of May,** June, **and** July, **to** bring to bank **a dozen or two of fine trout,** ranging in size from **half-a-pound to one and a half pounds.** On June 11, **1855, I find mention made in my** diary of my having **taken, chiefly at the point** indicated, forty-two trout, which **weighed in the** gross **close** upon 20 lbs., and on the **27th of the** same **month** and year I encreeled thirty-four more which **turned the** scale **at 21 lbs.** On the occasion last referred **to the** river was small and clear, and the day intensely **hot.** Well-scoured worms were the lures principally **employed by me**; but I also gave the stream **a run** over with the par-tail, and captured several **of my** largest fish with that bait, using the ordinary three-hooked tackle described by me in chapter 7th of the *Angler's Companion*. It is my impression that **had** I persevered for two or three hours longer, **I should have** added very largely to, if not doubled, the amount specified. **A** recent attack of lumbago, however, had inculcated the propriety of taking wading-exercise in moderation ; **and not having an** assistant with me, I came to the conclusion that **it was** high time to leave off; a burden on **the** temporal shoulders of twenty pounds and more, **gradually** made up, being equivalent at least to that **which** Christian **in** Bunyan's famous parable carried **about** with him on his spiritual shoulders at the outset of his pilgrimage.

Passing under Mertoun Bridge towards the back of the mill-cauld, I come to a stream of rapid character, which is celebrated among trout-fishers as the scene of several extraordinary captures made with minnow and par-tail during the dusky hours—the late **John Younger of St.** Boswells, well known in that **quarter as a** writer upon fishing, etc., taking pride in exhibiting the sketch of a " swallow-smolt" of five **pounds** weight which was **secured,** along with others of proximate ponderosity, by his son, one summer's night, some ten or twelve years ago. Higher up lies

the Mertoun Mill-Cauld, in the Long Stream, as it is
called, heading which I have often done satisfactory
execution. The salmon-fishings on the upper portion of this stream belong to the Dryburgh estate,
and are situated about half-a-mile from the Abbey
Here, on the 10th of April 1861, I hooked, played,
and landed several large salmon-kelts, the joint
weight of which exceeded sixty-four pounds,—a well-
mended, strong-running twenty-pounder topping the
lot. There is nothing worthy of mention **in** the in-
cident itself ; and I only refer to **it** because it is
associated with the circumstance of my having spent
the remaining portion of the day, and of the night
that followed, at the mansion-house of Dryburgh,
which, along with the shootings and fishings on the
property, was rented by a friend of mine, whose kind
invitation to take a cast for salmon on the river I
had accepted.

My sleeping apartment on this occasion **was**
situated on the wing of the building nearest **to St.**
Mary's Aisle, that portion of the Abbey in which,
in virtue of Sir Walter's claims as a descendant from
the ancient family of the Halliburtons—once the
proprietors of Dryburgh—his remains, and those of
his family, including Lockhart, lie interred. While
in the occupation of this apartment, during the witch-
ing hour, it was only natural to summon up thoughts
bearing upon the illustrious dead, with whose relics I

stood in comparative proximity ; and it was but
natural too, having disparted the shutters and raised
the blind, to gaze out, if not by moonlight, by starry
influences of a purer order, in the direction of the
Abbey. More conspicuous than even the outline of
its mouldering walls were the stately yews that keep
sentinelship in **their vicinity.** The effect imparted
by them heightened greatly the solemn interest of the
scene, but not more than did the moaning of the adjacent river, and the hooting at intervals of an **owl**
which had left the monastic ivies, and sate perched
high up among the plumes of one of the aforesaid
sentinels, within fifty yards of where I stood. Not
readily shall I forget the impression produced upon
me under this appropriate combination of circumstances ; but to describe how the emotions were
worked upon until they lapsed into the condition
best expressed as a state of reverie, **is not easy.** To
me, when a mere boy, and during my attendance at
the Edinburgh University classes, Sir Walter Scott
in the flesh,—the towering figure, not ungainly in
itself, but made so to a slight extent, in the view of
the distant observer, through the medium **of a** mal-
formed limb—the peaked forehead—small but saga-
cious eyes, which were given effect to by their shaggy,
singularly shaggy brows,—all were familiar. As
one of the deputy-clerks of Session, sitting in his
place before the First Division of the Court, I had

often regarded him and formed conjectures as to the
visions that were passing before his active mind,—
how foreign they were to and totally separate from
the mechanical duties of his office. The grave reti-
cence,—the gaze into vacancy, which wanted recognition of the object it was seemingly directed **to,**
—the hurried jotting down with the pen of passing
thoughts,—all betokened a spirit wrapt up in a higher
mood of contemplation than that which engages a
mere recorder of judicial utterances ; and to observe,
on his discharge from the Parliament House, the
stalwart Borderer hurrying down the Mound on his
way to Castle Street, latterly to Shandwick Place;—
the very recollection of my having often done so is
worth looking back upon. Everyone knew him, but
even his most intimate friends seldom used the freedom to interrupt his progress by addressing him ;
not that had they done so the interruption would
have been otherwise than cordially met with ; still,
there was an air of abstraction in his look that de-
terred from any advance on the part of the passer-by
beyond the offering of **a** respectful token of recognition. All these reminiscences of the Great Unknown
naturally enough flashed across me on the occasion I
speak of, and combined to raise to the highest point
of solemnity to which the feelings can attain my contemplation of the scene under review. I am not a
believer in ghosts, but I believe in the power of the

mind to summon up from the world spiritual shapes and shadows which shall characteristically people those places belonging to the world material, which, under certain aspects, produce a powerful effect over the imagination ; nor in this instance was it possible to exclude the *genius loci*, moulded out of living remembrances, from playing a part in my reverie.

But we have gone off at a tangent from the **river** to the poet's shrine—an episode which will be excused, when the relationship of Tweed to the ruins it environs is taken into full consideration. We now return to our fishing-ground at the point where **we left it—viz.** the Nether Cast in the Dryburgh water, **as it** is termed. Superintending the Long Stream already referred to, flow the Lessuden Haughs, which, although they form a good hold for kelts in March and April, especially after a freshet, are in better repute as trouting water. Here, during an easterly wind in June, I have frequently, when the river was low and clear, met with excellent sport. Above the Haughs lies a killing run, termed the Birkie Heugh, the fishing of which with the salmon-fly requires some management on the part equally of the boatman and the rod-wielder. I have taken fish on this cast both with fly and minnow ; the term fish, be it understood, on Tweedside, is applied solely to salmon. **Higher** up, at the termination of that bend or curve, which forms on the north side a natural protection to

the Abbey grounds, occurs a short cast called the
Throat, the inclination of whose casual occupants to
favour the salmon-fisher is usually determined in the
course of half-a-dozen throws. Above the Throat, at
a fascinating pace, ambles the Burn Stream. From
both of these holes I have educed *salares* in the shape
of well-mended kelts. It is rarely indeed that anything better nowadays is to be got out of them.
The shallows below the Throat, however, and those
heading the Burn Stream, abound in fine trout ; and
in the worm-fishing season—that is in June and the
early part of July, after the starry-sides have had
their surfeit of winged insects—I recur to them annu-
ally, as places associated with sport of a first-rate
character. It is not always, however, on such occa-
sions that I have had the good fortune to find the
trout in a taking humour—or when they are so, to
secure to myself a reasonable stretch of intact fishing-
ground. The railway and the Mackintosh water-
proofs have assisted, to an extraordinary extent, to
increase the numbers of waders that resort to Tweedside ; and nothing can be more annoying to the skilled
worm-fisher anticipating a great day's take, than to
find the range of river determined on by him on the
previous night as the scene of the morrow's sport,
pre-occupied by a brace of tyros ploughing their way
thigh-deep, down, instead of up the streams—through,
in fact, the very centre of the margins where, at that

season of the year, the trout, under the operation of heat and light, are accustomed to feed—scaring to the right and left the realities in the shape of pounders and two-pounders of your visionary expectations. It cannot be helped, however, for there is no reasoning with mar-sports of this sort, who have been tutored to look upon the artificial fly as the only legitimate means of capturing trout ; and so, on some of the English rivers, no doubt, it is very properly regarded ; but Tweed is different, and will bear, as an important salmon-stream, to be treated under a line of policy, in respect to its fresh-water trout, much less conservative.

Directly over the Burn Stream, on the south bank of the river tower the Braeheads, the descent from which is steep and hazardous, but partakes more of the nature of a *scaur*, being composed of loose, shifty earth and gravel, than of a precipice. Further up Tweed, on the same side, we come to the Hare Crag, a rock of some height which juts out into the river and overlooks a fine salmon-hold that is seldom or never without its tenant. I have taken a fish or two here, and a perilous spot to commit the tackle to it is, on account of the submerged rocks which lie in conjunction with it. The most difficult of the *salares* to deal with, under this peculiarity of shelter-ground, is a boring kipper or brown male, which has become familiarised with its quarters—in other words has been an occupant of the pool for three or four weeks ; and the hazard, be it noted, is always greater when **the river is at** its *minimum* size than when it is full and discoloured. In the former case, the fish may be supposed to have acquired an acquaintance with the strong and secure points round about its temporary residence, and be in a condition **to avail** itself **of them** accordingly ; whereas, when there is an extra pressure of water upon the hold, and the medium through which **the salmon's powers** of vision have to be exerted happens to be **altered** from transparency to semi-opaqueness, the effect of **these** changes upon a hooked **fish, after the first burst,** is to bewilder and dishearten it, or at any rate to render improbable its bringing to bear any resources, save its natural strength and activity, against the skill of the well-appointed angler.

Immediately above the Hare Crag, we come upon a piece of shifty water enclosing an islet, or rather an accumulation **of gravel,** studded here **and there with** stunted willows, which occupies space to the extent **of two** or **three** acres. There the principal force of the river **is** directed towards the south bank ; but the **branch in** question is of too rapid a character to admit of being fished successfully before the end of **May.** It is not salmon water, nor is it fished as **such ;** but no doubt, in the lower part of it, a migratory fish is occasionally taken by means of trout-

tackle. I once caught a splendid creelful of river-
trout here in the month of June with worm and par-
tail, the stream being low and the day warm and
sunny. Above the islet stretch what are evidently
the remains of an old cauld-dyke, which we are at
liberty to assume did service in its day in connection
with the monastic establishment at Dryburgh. The
pool formed by it is overhung on the north side with
crag and scaur, and possesses all the constituents of
an excellent salmon-hold. Some portions of it are
deep, and a large fly is required in order to do it
justice ; that **at** least is the opinion of the local
fisherman, Fox, whose patterns approach in dimensions, and are assimilated in colours—blue and yellow
prevailing—to the salmon-flies used on the Shannon.
From this pool, tamely termed nowadays the Boat
Hole, I once took **in** autumn, using one of Fox's
loudest persuaders, a fine salmon of 17 lbs weight,
which róse from a depth of twelve feet and upwards
to the surface, not by any means a usual circumstance. Above the Boat or Ferry Hole runs, or rather
ambles, bounded on the south side by a lofty scaur,
the Bridge Stream, celebrated equally as the choice
harbour of salmon and as the abode of fine river-
trout, **many** of which attain the weight of two or
three pounds. This stream has acquired its present
name from a wire suspension-bridge thrown across it
by one of the Earls of Buchan—an eccentric character

who, among other devices, caused to be erected in the **way** of ornamentation to the Dryburgh estate a huge ungainly statue in honour of the Scottish hero Wallace, and a dome or temple dedicated to and graced by the figures of the muses ; not an unclassical work of art by any means, but sadly out of place, and in consequence reduced to a ruinous condition, partly through want of means on the part of the possessor, and also—I feel pained to add—of propriety on the part of visitors. The bridge, which is contiguous in its way to these curiosities, has **not** been used as such for forty or fifty years, and the skeleton portion which remains had better be removed altogether than left as it is, to call forth queries and emotions of a painful nature. Immediately under this dissolving structure, some years ago, I hooked, played, and after a severe run of nearly half-an-hour, landed a fish of 19 lbs. weight. Above the Bridge Stream occurs a salmon-cast, known by the designation Munsey. I recollect educing from under the shadow of an ash-tree, on the north bank **of** the river, by virtue of the snipe-wing, an immense kelt from this piece of water ; and out of its superintending flow, which is really magnificent salmon-ground, I have, once and again, taken fish of great mettle. **The** highest salmon-stream on the Dryburgh water, and perhaps on the whole one of the most likely for a clean fish to take up quarters in, is termed the

Battery, probably from its being walled in or fortified on one side. It is very rapid, and can only be fished with success when Tweed is in a reduced state. The minnow on this cast is **an** acceptable lure both to trout and salmon. Heading it expands the famous Monk's Ford, which, get a mild easterly wind to ruffle it in May or June, may be fished without fear of the result. The water, being in prime order, two stone weight of trout (it is purely a trouting range of water) would not be considered anything very extraordinary **in** the way of a take—the average weight of the individual captures approaching, if **not** exceeding, half-a-pound.

Irrespective of the interest attached to it in con-**nection with** the Abbey grounds, Dryburgh water, as **a** stretch of Tweed stored with finny wealth, and **moulded** by nature to the angler's liking, possesses peculiar attractions. I shall not say it is unsurpassed, either as a succession **of** salmon-casts or **as a** trouting-beat, by the divisions of the Border **river conter-minous** to it ; but it excels them in variety **of char-**acter, and **is** enhanced in the estimation of **its fre-**quenters **by the** circumstance that, owing to this variety, **let** the **general** taking humour, whether by **trout or** salmon, on the river, be **what it** may, the chances are greatly in favour of its affording sport.

To the greater part of **the** range **of** water above sketched the fair trout-fisher has always **been** permitted ready access, both by the various proprietors on its banks, and the lessees **of** the fishings; the Abbey policies, in fact, which extend to nearly a mile on the south side of the river, being the only portion **from** which the public are excluded, and *that* from considerations with which their superiority in the way of commanding sport with the **rod** has little or nothing to do.

Leaving the Dryburgh casts, which **are** crowned by the Monk's Ford, the angler, pushing upwards, enters forthwith upon the Bemersyde fishing-grounds, which, in their alliance with those of Old Melrose on **the opposite bank, form** a fascinating combination of river-scenery high in order with salmon-holds and trouting-water of established celebrity. I do not know, throughout the whole course of Tweed, from its sources in Tweedsmuir down to the mouth of the Whitadder—a course of nearly **a** hundred miles in **extent—of a spot** where this combination is maintained so admirably. For more than twenty years it has been **my delight, two or** three times every **season,** to visit it, rod in hand; and a personal acquaintance with the proprietors and occasional lessees of the salmon-fishings as well, has given me not a few opportunities to test its excellence as sporting water. **Besides** a score **or** two of kelts, I have abstracted from it several **fish** which **I** may be permitted to affirm were clean and seasonable. As to their having

U

the tide-lice **on** them at that distance **from** the sea, that was out of the question ; but **although** slightly browned **outside,** they betrayed **no great develop-** ment of milt or roe, and showed at table red and curdy ; nor as to their richness and fine flavour could there be any dispute. **Of** the superiority of the sport occasionally met **with by the** trout-fisher **on the** Bemersyde and **Old Melrose** waters, some idea may be formed, when I mention that on one occasion (June **4,** 1855) I captured in the course **of three** hours, out of the Gate-heugh streams, eighteen trout, which weighed upwards of **19** lbs. The toppers were nine in number, and turned the scale at $14\frac{1}{2}$ lbs., which speaks to their being **on the** average a pound and a half apiece. They were all taken with the worm, in very rapid clear water, **with a** fine single-gut line, well shotted. Out of the lower trouting-casts, about a month after, I took thirty-four trout weighing five-and-twenty pounds, also with the worm, but chiefly from the shallow margins and with tackle very lightly weighted. A difference in temperature of about **ten** degrees occurred on these two occasions—a scorching heat, which affected largely both air and water, pre-vailing in the latter instance.

T. T. S.

FLY-FISHING, AND HOW IT SHOULD BE DONE.

FLY-FISHING has always been, and we believe always will be, the favourite method of angling; and deservedly so. Few who have once owned its sway are capable of resisting its attractions. What golden memories of the past it recalls! What bright visions of the future it portrays! And when May comes, that month pre-eminently the fly-fisher's, with its bright sunny mornings and soft southern breezes, once more, unencumbered with anything save a light rod and small box of flies, the angler wends his way to some favourite stream. Once more with elastic tread he climbs the mountain's brow, and having gained the summit, what a prospect meets his gaze! There, far as the eye **can** reach, rises into the blue sky summit after summit of the heath-clad hills, while underneath lie the grassy slope and luxuriant meadow, the green corn-field and waving wood, and, glittering and circling among all like a silver thread, winds the far-stretching stream in its beauty. There is nothing **to** break **the** solitude save the plaintive bleating of the sheep **or** the cry of the moorcock.

As the angler descends, the music of the song-bird meets his ear from every bush, and the groves resound with the cooing of the wood-pigeon or the soft notes of the cuckoo. And now he approaches the scene of his anticipated triumph. There is the deep rocky pool and racing shallow, the whirling eddy and rippling stream—now foaming over rocks, and now meandering slowly between green banks. Now it pauses as if to enjoy the glory of the prospect, then rushes impetuously forward, eager to drink in the grandeur of some new scene. Everything seems endowed with life to welcome the return of summer, and the very river is alive with leaping trout. No wonder that with Sir Henry Watton he finds " fly-fishing " a " cheerer of the spirits, a tranquilliser of the mind, a calmer of unquiet thoughts, a diverter of sadness."

And then the art itself is lively and graceful. Look at the angler as he approaches some favourite spot. See him as he observes the monarch of the pool regaling himself on the incautious insect that sports in fancied security upon the surface. Inwardly he vows that it shall be avenged. Cautiously he approaches, concealing himself by kneeling, or keeping behind some bush, lest by any chance his expected prey should discover him and so be warned. Gracefully wheeling his long line behind, he lays his flies down softly as a snow-flake just above the desired spot. **A** moment **of** expectancy succeeds ; the flies approach the very **place** where **the** trout was last seen. **Look** at the angler how with keen eye he watches, to strike with alert hand the moment he either feels or sees the least movement. **There** is a stoppage **of** the line and an instantaneous movement of the angler's **wrist, and the trout is** fast. **At** first he shakes his **head** as if surprised and bewildered **at the** unwonted interference with **his liberty, but** gradually awakening **to a sense of the** danger **of his** position, he collects **his scattered energies, and makes** a gallant fight **for liberty. Frequently he will leap in the air** several **times as if to ascertain** the character **of his** opponent, **and** then make **a** frantic rush ; but the figure on the bank follows **him** like a shadow, **and at** last, strength and hope both exhausted, he turns on his side and becomes an easy prey, leaving the angler to congratulate himself on having achieved such a feat with a tiny hook **and** tackle **like** a gossamer.

The victory, however, **is not always** with the angler—more frequently the other **way.** Often at the last moment, just as he **is** putting out his hand to secure his prize, the trout makes a bolt, and is gone, leaving the disappointed artist the picture of blank dismay, and in a very unenviable frame of mind ; indeed, **of** all the trials of the temper which occur in the ordinary course of life, there is none to compare

with that of losing a good trout at the last moment,
and anglers have various ways of giving vent to their
pent-up feelings, depending upon their peculiar
idiosyncrasy. But of all the different means of relief
there is perhaps none at once so satisfactory and so
reprehensible as that referred to by a late great
humorist who, if not an angler, was the friend and
associate of anglers :—

> " **The** flask frae my **pocket**
>   I poured into the socket,
> **For** I was provokit unto the last degree ;
>   And to my way o' thinkin',
>   **There's naething for 't but** drinkin',
> When a trout **he lies winkin'** and lauchin' at **me.**"

Everything, we say, combines to render fly-fishing
the most attractive of all the branches of the angler's
art. The attempt to capture trout which are seen to
rise at natural flies is in itself an excitement which
no other method possesses. Then **the** smallness of
the **hook and the** fineness of the tackle necessary for
success increase the danger of escape, and consequently the excitement and pleasure of the capture ;
and for our own part **we** would rather hook, play,
and capture a trout **of a** pound weight with fly than
one of a pound and half with minnow or worm, where
the hooks being larger, there is less chance of their
losing their hold, and **the** gut being stronger, there is
less risk of its breaking. Fly-fishing is also the

cleanest and most elegant and gentlemanly of all
the methods of capturing trout. The angler who
practises it is saved the trouble of working with
worms, of catching, keeping alive, and salting min-
nows, or searching the river's bank for the natural
insect. Armed with a light single-handed rod and a
few flies he may wander from county to county, and
kill trout wherever they are to be found.

But besides being the most attractive and valuable,
artificial fly-fishing is the most difficult branch of the
angler's art; and this **is** another reason of the preference accorded to it, since there is more merit, and there-
fore more pleasure, in excelling in what is difficult.

But there is one great error in fly-fishing, as
usually practised, and as recommended to be practised
by books, and that is, that the angler "fishes down"
stream, whereas he should "fish up."

We believe we are not beyond the mark in
stating that ninety-nine anglers out of a hundred fish
down with the artificial fly; they never think of
fishing in any other way, and never dream of attri-
buting their want of success to it. Yet we are prepared to prove, both in theory and practice, that this
is the greatest reason of their want of success in clear
waters. In all our angling excursions we have met
only one or two amateurs, and a few professionals,
who fished up stream with the fly, and used it in
a really artistic manner. If the wind is blowing up,

anglers will occasionally fish up the pools—(as for fishing up a strong stream they never think of it)—but even then they do not **do** it properly, **and** meet with little better success than if they had followed their usual method. They will also, if going to some place up a river, walk up, not fish up to it, their plan being to go to the top of a pool and then fish it down, never **casting** their **line** above them at all.

We **shall now mention in** detail the advantages of fishing up, **in** order to show its superiority over the old method.

The first and great advantage is, that the angler **is unseen by** the trout. Trout, as is well known, keep **their heads up stream ; they** cannot remain stationary **in any** other position. **This** being the case, they see objects above and on **both** sides of them, but cannot discern anything behind them, so that the angler fish**ing down** will be seen **by** them twenty yards off ; **whereas the** angler fishing up will be unseen, although **he be** but a few yards in their rear. The advantages of this it is impossible to over-estimate. No creatures **are** more easily scared than trout ; if they see any **object moving on** the river's bank, they run **into deep water,** or beneath banks and stones, from **which** they will not stir for some time. A bird flying **across the water,** or the shadow of a rod, will sometimes alarm them ; and nothing connected with angling is **more** certain than this, that if the trout see the angler, they will not take his lure. He may ply his minnow in the most captivating manner, may throw his worm with consummate skill, or make his flies light softly as a gossamer—all will be unavailing if he is seen by his intended victim.

The next advantage of fishing up we shall notice, is the much greater probability of hooking a trout when it rises. In angling down stream, if **a** trout rises and the angler strikes, he runs a great risk of pulling the flies straight out of its mouth ; whereas, in fishing up, its back is to him, and he has every chance of bringing the hook into contact with **its** jaws. This, although it may not seem of great importance to the uninitiated, tells considerably when the contents of the basket come to be examined at the close of the day's sport ; indeed no angler would believe the difference unless he himself proved it.

Another advantage of fishing up is, that it does not disturb the water so much. Let us suppose the angler is fishing down a fine pool. He, of course, commences at the top, the place where the best **trout,** and those most inclined to feed, invariably lie. After a few casts he hooks one, which immediately runs down, and by its vagaries—leaping in the air, and plunging in all directions—alarms all its neighbours, **and** it is ten to one if he gets another rise in that **pool.** Fishing up saves all this. The angler commences at the foot, and when he hooks a trout, pulls it down, and the remaining portions of the pool are undisturbed. This is a matter of great importance, and we have frequently, in small streams, taken a dozen trout out of a pool, from which, had we been fishing down, we could not possibly have got more than two or three.

The last advantage of fishing up is, that by it the angler can much better adapt the motions of his flies to those of **the** natural insect. And here it may be mentioned as a rule, that the nearer the **motious of** the artificial flies resemble those of the natural ones under similar circumstances, the greater will be the prospects of success. Whatever trout take the artificial fly for, it is obvious they are much more likely to be deceived by a natural than by an unnatural motion.

No method of angling can imitate the hovering flight of an insect along the surface of the water—now **just** touching it, then flying a short distance, and so on ; and for the angler to attempt by any motion of his hand to give his flies a living appearance, is mere absurdity. The only moment when trout may mistake the angler's fly for a real one in its flight is the moment it first touches the water ; and in this respect fishing down possesses equal advantages with fishing up. But this is the only respect, and in order to illustrate **this,** we shall give a brief description of fly-fishing as usually practised down stream.

The angler, then, we shall suppose, commences operations at the head of a pool or stream, and, throwing his flies as far as he can across from where he is standing, raises his rod and brings them gradually to his own side of the water. He then steps down a yard or two, repeats the process, and so on. Having dismissed the idea that the angler can imitate the flight of a living fly along the surface of the water, we must suppose that the trout take the artificial fly for a dead one, **or** one which has fairly got into the stream and lost all power of resisting. A feeble motion of the wings or legs would be the only attempt at escape which a live fly in such a case could make. What then must be the astonishment of the trout, when they see the tiny insect which they are accustomed to seize, as it is carried by the current towards them, crossing the stream with the strength and agility of an otter? Is it not much more natural to throw the flies up, and let them come gently down, as any real insect would do?

In addition to drawing their flies across the stream, some anglers practise what is called playing their flies, which is done by a jerking motion of the wrist, which imparts a similar motion to the fly. Their object in doing this is to create an appearance of life, and thus render their flies more attractive. An appearance of life is certainly a great temptation to a trout, but it may be much better accomplished

by dressing the flies of soft materials, which the
water can agitate, and thus create a natural motion
of the legs or wings of the fly, than by dragging
them by jumps of a foot at a time across and up a
roaring stream. Trout are not accustomed to see
minute insects making such gigantic efforts at escape,
and therefore it is calculated to awaken their suspicions.

We believe that all fly-fishers fishing down must
have noticed that, apart from the moment of alighting, they get more rises from the first few yards of
their flies' course than in the whole of the remainder ;
and that when their flies fairly breast the stream
they seldom get a rise at all. The reason of this is
clear : for the first few feet after the angler throws
his flies across the stream they swim with the current;
the moment, however, he begins to describe his semi-
circle across the **water,** they present an unnatural
appearance, which the trout view with distrust.
Experienced fly-fishers, following the old method,
who have observed this, and are aware of the great
importance of the moment their flies light, cast very
frequently, only allowing their flies to float down a
few feet, when they throw again. We have seen
some Tweedside adepts fill capital baskets in this
way ; but as we have before stated, it will only
succeed when the water is coloured, or when there
is a body of clear water sufficiently large to conceal

the angler from view; and even then he may have much better sport by fishing up. The angler drawing his flies across and up stream will catch trout, and this is the strongest evidence that trout are not such profound philosophers as the notions of some would lead us to suppose. But though he does catch trout, they are in general the very smallest. Indeed the advantages of fishing **up** are in nothing more apparent than in the superior size of the trout captured. We believe they will average nearly double the size of those caught with the same flies fishing down, and though generally not so large as those taken with the worm, they are not much behind them, and we almost invariably kill a few larger trout in a river with the fly than with the worm.

Though our remarks in this article have principally reference to angling in small rivers, where fishing up is *essential* to success, the same arguments hold good in every size or colour of water in a less degree, as even though the trout cannot see the angler, the other advantages which we have mentioned are still in his favour.

If we were fishing a large river when it was dark-coloured, and required to wade deep, we should fish down, because the fatigue of wading up would, under such circumstances, become a serious drawback. In such a case we fish in the following manner :—

Throwing our flies, partly up and partly across from where we are standing, we allow them to swim down a yard or two, when we cast again, never allowing them to go below that part of the stream opposite us. But though the angler gets over the ground as quickly this way, and casts as often, as if he were fishing up, yet he has not the same chance, because if a trout catches sight of his flies just as he is lifting them, their sudden abstraction may deter it from taking them on their again alighting ; whereas in fishing up the angler casts a yard or two further up every time, so that every trout may see his flies at the moment they alight.

The reader must not suppose, however, that fishing up is all that is necessary for success ; on the contrary, the angler may throw his flies up stream, and know less of the art of fly-fishing, and catch fewer trout, than his neighbour who is fishing down. The mere fact of an angler throwing his flies up stream is no proof that he is a fly-fisher. Of those who fish down stream, some catch more and some less, and in like manner with those fishing up, one may catch three times as many as another, depending upon the particular method they each adopt ; and unless the reader pays strict attention to the details referred to in our *Practical Angler,* we are afraid he will not derive much benefit. Fishing up is *much more* difficult than fishing down, requiring more practice, and a better acquaintance with the habits of the trout ; and we believe that a mere novice would, in a large water, catch more trout by fishing down than up, because the latter requires more nicety in casting. But to attain anything like eminence in fly-fishing, the angler *must* fish up, and all beginners should persevere in it, even though they meet with little success at first, and they will be amply rewarded for their trouble.

The only circumstances in which fishing down has the advantage of fishing up, is when the water is so dark or deep that the fish would not see, or if they did see, would not have time to seize the flies, unless they moved at a slower rate than the stream. We think that this rarely applies to angling for river trout, as when inclined to feed upon flies they are generally on the outlook for them, but it does apply to salmon and sea-trout fishing. Both these fish lie in strong deep water, and as they are not accustomed to feed upon flies, they are not on the outlook for them ; so that if the salmon-fisher were to throw his flies up stream, they would come down at such a rate that the salmon would never see them. Besides which, it is obvious that whatever salmon take the angler's fly for, they cannot take it for anything they have seen before, and therefore there is no reason for supposing they can detect anything unnatural in its motion.

We have devoted this article principally to the **errors** of fly-fishing as generally practised, and we hope we have succeeded in convincing the reader of the truth of our observations; but as we have frequently endeavoured in vain by *viva voce* demonstration to persuade anglers to fish up, we have no doubt numbers will adhere to their own way. As no amount of mere argument will convince such, we offer **to** find two anglers, who, in a water suitable for showing the superiority of fishing up, will be more successful than any three anglers fishing down after the ordinary method.

We have just given the same reasons for fishing **up** stream **as in** the first edition **of** our *Practical Angler*, because upon this point there can be nothing **new ; and we** are as ready as ever to find anglers who are prepared to do battle in their behalf, on the terms just stated ; but while one or two have come forward to dispute the theory, none have accepted our challenge and come forward to dispute the practice. One reviewer—the only objector we can remember who gives a reason—says, "that so long as streams run down, carrying the food of the fish with them, so long should anglers fish down." While, however, his premises are undeniably correct, **we** entirely dissent from his conclusions. Streams certainly run down and carry the food of the trout with them, but along with that food they do not carry an apparition in the shape of an angler with rod and line upon the bank ; and as nothing will familiarise them to such an apparition, we draw the conclusion that that apparition had better keep out of sight and fish up stream. Moreover, the fact that the natural food floats down is anything but a reason that the artificial lure in imitation of that food should be pulled up.

We must confess, however, that fishing up stream with fly has not been adopted by a large portion of the angling community, **and** that for various reasons. In spite of the strong manner **in** which, in **our** *Practical Angler,* we **cautioned our** readers about the difficulties of fishing up stream, numbers who read the arguments for it, and were struck with the soundness of the theory, thought they saw at a glance the cause of their previous want of success, and that in future the result would be different. Having equipped themselves *à la* Practical Angler, and even taken a copy of that excellent work in their pockets, they started with high hopes on their new career, **but** the **result** was not different, and after one or two trials with **no** better success, not a few have condemned fishing up stream as erroneous and ourselves as impostors ; though we imagine the fault lies with themselves. We have met anglers fishing down stream—and this is no supposititious case, but one which we have seen **over and** over again—with a copy of this said volume in their pockets, who complained that they had got

X

everything therein recommended, and were getting no sport. On pointing **out to them** that there was one important mistake they were committing, in **fishing** down stream instead of up, they stated that **when** they **came to** a pool they fished it up—that is **to say,** they first walked **down** the pool and showed themselves to the trout **and** then commenced to fish for them.

> " **The trout** within yon wimplin' **burn,**
> Glides swift, **a silver** dart :
> And safe **beneath the shady thorn,**
> Defies the **angler's art."**

John Younger objects to this as incorrect, but we rather think that Burns is right, **and** the angler wrong ; as it is evident the poet alludes **to** a trout that has caught sight of the angler, and safe he is, at least *pro tem.*, as our pupils who first frighten the fish by walking down 'a poolside, and then **fish up it,** will find to their cost.

Others object to fishing up stream, as requiring too frequent casting, being too fatiguing, and because they **have been** accustomed to fish down, **and would** prefer fishing in that way, even though they **do not** catch so many trout. If any angler prefers catching five pounds weight of trout, fishing down stream, to ten pounds weight, fishing up, we may wonder at his taste, but it is no concern of ours.

W. C. S.

ON THE THAMES.

WE have lately read and heard much of "Social Science," and we have had it dinned into our ears how necessary fresh air and exercise are to the well-being of all good folks, be they inhabitants of town or country; but there is one outdoor sport which I think has not been mentioned at all by any of the professors of public health, yet which, to my mind, is worthy of being seriously noticed—I mean "angling," or, if you please, "fishing." The impure air of London necessarily creates a feeling of debility and oppression, and, as a remedy for this, the gin-shop is but too often applied to. Fresh air, be it observed, is a much cheaper and much more wholesome stimulant; and this can be obtained in abundance, and at a cheap rate, by going out fishing. How, for instance, is the poor artisan, by nature a Nimrod, by profession a tailor, to gratify his instinct at a small expense of time and money? He cannot hunt; he has no horse, and if he had, *quære* would he remain long on the animal's back were he mounted? He cannot shoot; he has no gun, and if he had he could get nothing better than hedge-popping; but he can fish. When.

where, how ? Have we not **our** noble river, the Thames,
close at hand, **and are** there not thousands of fish in
it whose destiny, **sooner or** later, **is to** be caught ? **A**
small **sum** expended **will take** the angler to Richmond,
Teddington, Sunbury, Kingston, **or** Windsor, where
fishing may **be had** in abundance. I do not say the
angler will return with a ten-pound trout every day,
but if he has luck he may **get a good basket of** pike,
perch, or gudgeon.

Angling, moreover, especially Thames angling, is
most admirably suited for ladies. It requires **no**
exertion, **no** moving about—simply neatness of finger
and **quickness** of eye ; and I therefore cordially recommend **it to the notice** of the ladies.

Now **the first attempt at** angling will probably
prove a failure ; it is an art, a science, that requires
ingenuity, neatness, quickness **of** thought and action,
and, above all, patience. **If** we listen to a lecture
from a learned professor upon the brains of animals,
he will point out the human brain as being at the
highest end of the scale, the brain **of the** fish at the
lowest. Holding up the brain of **a fish,** beautifully
prepared **in spirits of** wine, he **will say** : "There,
gentlemen, is an example **of a** badly-developed brain.
The creature to which it belonged is proverbially dull
and stupid." Yet the **next day, if we** look over Rich-
mond-bridge, we may behold the same learned but
sportless professor puzzling his well-developed brain

to catch the creature which but yesterday he was asserting had so little brains. The brain of the fish is quite sufficient to keep him off the professor's hook, angle he never so wisely. For my own part, I have often been laughed at for bad sport. Returning from fishing one cold winter's day, when the jack were *not* on the run, I met a foxhunter coming home from a run across country. "Why," said he, "Buckland, you never bring home a fish, and you are always fishing: it is very extraordinary." "Not **at** all," I replied; "you are always out hunting, my friend, and I never yet saw you bring home a fox."

There is a species of harmless monomania peculiar to anglers, which others, who have not been bitten by it, can by no means appreciate. The angler will walk miles, and then fish all day; he will go through all sorts of hardships and difficulties for the sake of catching fish; and when he has got them, and *shown them*—for this is a great part of the fun—he often does not know what to do with them, unless, of course, he happens, lucky man, **to be in a trout or** salmon country. Again, there may be often plenty of fish, and *they won't bite;* alas, how often does the angler sing this melancholy song! The Cockney fish about London have had their noses pricked by the hook too often, and know the smell of cobbler's wax **and** varnish too well to be caught by anybody who holds a "wand," as the Scot calls a fishing-rod. Some-

times, however, the fish are "all on the feed." I knew
of a party of four who, relying on such news as the
above, came to a quiet retreat near Windsor. They
got out of their beds at half-past two in the morning,
and fished away in their punt till half-past nine, and
when they came back to breakfast they had captured,
the four of them, one gudgeon and one roach. What
a contrast this is with a professed angler of my acquaintance, who has caught two hundred-weight of
fish—barbel, roach, perch, etc.—in one day, and **who**
has come home "with the punt-well so full that all
the fish had turned up"—*i.e.* died of exhaustion. **I**
believe his story, as he is a great professor of the
science. It is a treat to see him get ready : he punts
quietly up the river, as silent as a red Indian, peering
deep down into the water. All at once in goes **the**
rypeck (the pole used to fix the boat) and over slides,
without a splash, the junk stone (a heavy stone weight,
having a cord attached) and the punt swings across
stream into "the swim."

"This will do, sir." Then out comes the tackle :
a few hanks of **gut, a** few loose hooks, and a very
rustic-looking float, or more often a quill from the
wing of a **swan ;** and then the line, not a great thick
cart-rope, but a delicate **silken** cord, fit almost to
make ladies' purses or hair-nets. "Fish is artful
things," **says** he ; "you **can't** fish too fine for 'em."
Most anglers imagine that fish can neither see nor

hear; can't they, indeed? What bird may be best taken as the type of the angler? Look at yon heron, how quietly he sits, and what a sober-coloured coat he wears; *but what fine sport he has!* When anybody accomplishes difficult feats which others fail in doing, it is always said, and always will be said, that he has some charm, some scent, some hidden device. Rarey was stated to give his horses a drug to tame them; a successful angler had his worm and bait boxes examined when his back was turned, to see what scent he used; and the poor heron has not escaped, for he is said by many, even at the present day, to have an oil in his legs which attracts the fish, and I have heard of anglers being foolish enough to shoot or buy a heron, and endeavour to extract this oil from the bird's legs to be applied to their own base purposes. All three cases—Rarey, the angler, and the heron—are alike; there is no conjuring, no charming, except the charm of gentleness, patience, and quiet; hence we see anglers generally silent men, not inclined to quarrel. Dear old gossiping Izaak Walton was of these, and the following might have been a part of one of his discourses addressed to the friend who was lucky enough to be in his company :—

> "Say, canst thou tell where eels in winter hide,
> Or where the swallows' vagrant race reside,—
> How salmon yearly quest th' accustomed main,
> Or wintry frogs their foodless kind sustain ?

> Say, canst thou tell how eels of moisture breed,
> Or pike are gendered of the pickerel weed,—
> How carp without the parent seed renew,
> Or slimy eels are formed of genial dew ?"

I wish I could be by old Izaak's side, to tell him what various investigations have, since his time, been made in these subjects ; how man has been overhauling the mysteries of nature with the probe of science and the lamp of the microscope. How he would stare to hear of pisciculture, Dutch eel and carp breeding, the French oyster-nurseries, the new salmon and trout fisheries bill, etc.! I thought of all this as, not many weeks ago, I made a pencil *facsimile* of the old man's **autograph,** which he cut on the tomb of his friend Casaubon, in Westminster Abbey. There, in Poet's Corner, still remains the old man's handiwork, and his autograph scratched in the marble—"I W 1658." "What," writes a gentleman, commenting on my *fac-simile* of the old man—"what more likely to have occurred than that, after the lapse of years, Walton, then a grey-haired old man of sixty-five, should in one of his retrospective moods have sauntered pensively down the grey aisles of Westminster Abbey into the place of tombs, and that there, seated by the monu-mental slab **of** Casaubon, while the memories of **old days and** of good and great friends thronged anew **through** his heart and made his eyes dim, he should have traced, half-absently, on the stone that simple

and faithful ' In Memoriam ?'"   Old Izaak is buried
in the cathedral at Winchester; and should the
reader ever take himself there to catch Itchin trout,
he should go and look at Izaak's monument, for it
will assuredly bring him luck.

But to return to the Thames.—

The first day of June is to the Thames angler
what the first of September is to the partridge-shot, for
it is on this day that the former can begin his angling
operations without let or hindrance, either from fear
of laws piscatorial, or from qualms of his own conscience.   It is true, indeed, that but very few fish can
be caught in the beginning of June; but still there
is something in trying to catch them.

Accordingly, one fine first-of-June morning found
your humble servant and his poetico-piscatorial friend
P. being punted through Chertsey Bridge by the
stalwart and clever fisherman, John Harris of Weybridge, both hard at work putting new tackle together
and in as high spirits as two Cockney anglers could
have been on the first day of the season.   We first put
together our trout-tackle in order to try the weir ; but
when we got there, alas ! two punts with two anglers
in each were moored in the only two likely places,
and we heard from Harris a most exciting account of
the trout of the year that had been—of course—captured " the day before yesterday," and that by some-
body who, as far as sport is concerned, had no business

to catch him—who had in fact the worst of skill and the best of luck.

“ It’s no use going to the weir,” we simultaneously exclaimed ; “let’s try for a jack.”   “ In a year or two, Harris,” added I, “if all goes well, we’ll try for a salmon.”

“ I don’t see why you should not,” said Harris ; “the reach just above the lock used to be a famous place for salmon. My family have been fishermen here and at Laleham for the last hundred and thirty years ; and I heard the old people say that my grand-father caught a salmon weighing forty-seven pounds between this and Laleham, and eight one morning at a single sweep of the net below this very bridge ; and if you gentlemen at Hampton continue to turn them out, some of them will most likely come back up the river. They would soon get through the dirty water at London—that is, if they can stand the gas, and they would be up here in no time. The old people used to calculate that a salmon would come up to Chertsey from the mouth of the river in about twelve hours.”

“ Look out !” cried my friend, who was meanwhile fishing away. “ I’ve got him.”   “ What is he ?” “He’s not very heavy.” “ Pull him up, then.” The line came home far too easily to be agreeable to the angler. “ Is that all ? a little foolish one-year-old jack, about as big as a small table-knife. Little goose

he is to have tried to swallow a fish half his own size.
Let's put him on a flight of hooks, and use him as a
bait for his larger brethren, for if there's a bait better
than another for a big jack it is a little jack ; or no, on
second thoughts let's mark him and turn him in again."
Accordingly I marked him by a process which I believe will be effective, and, if so, of very great use to
salmon-breeders. "Harris, should you know this
fellow again now he's marked?" "Certainly, sir."
"Very well, then, here he goes into the water again ;
and look you, if ever you catch him, he's my fish. Recollect the date of marking is June 1st. But now let's
be off down stream. Oh, bother, there goes a punt
before us, spinning all the way." "Never mind,"
said P. ; "I have got my new tackle on, and it's
painted green, so that the fish can't see it. *We* are
sure to have them." "All right," said I ; "go on."
So we floated down the river, spinning and chatting
and chaffing, for about half-a-mile.

  " Did you not say something about green just now,
friend P. ?" "Yes, I **said** my tackle was green, and
upon my word I think we are of the same colour as
the tackle, for you've not had a run, and I've caught
nothing but a dead dog, and had a good shot at a
swan—the spawn-eating vagabond—with my flight of
hooks. Oh, it's not the fault of my tackle that we
don't catch fish, it's the weather, of course it's the
weather,—isn't it, Harris?" "Yes, sir," said Harris ;

"it's the weather, decidedly the weather, sir," and we all relapsed into silence.

"Did you ever see ladies fish?" said I. "Fish?" said P.; "ladies fish—what for?" "For fish, of course; could they possibly fish for anything else?" "Ah!" groaned P., "don't talk about ladies fishing, it's a sore subject, it's so very expensive taking ladies out fishing." "How's that?" "Why, last season I betted away a small fortune in gloves, and one day when we were gudgeon-fishing I got positively furious, and laid an even dozen pair that a certain young lady would not catch eleven gudgeon out of twelve, nibbles included. She caught the dozen right off, that's a pair of gloves for every gudgeon. I very seldon win myself, and when I do I never get paid. Another thing, recollect—never let ladies out of the boat. One day the ladies got out to gather flowers, whilst we men went on fishing. All of a sudden the spooney who was with me dropped his rod, jumped up, cried out, 'There goes Lucy!' and walked straight over the gunwale into the river, and was very nearly drowned. Holloa! what's that? it's music." "It's only Tityrus 'playing a rustic song on his slender pipe,' or rather **his penny** tin whistle. I wonder if Virgil's 'Tityrus' was like this English musical shepherd. If you want to see a real live Tityrus, you will meet them in the London streets, dancing insanely for coppers on the pavement, and blowing into the leg of an inflated pig-

skin ; he must be very excitable to dance to such
porcine music.   Play up, boy," we cried ; "never
mind the cows."   An answer rude, and decidedly not
classical, from our Chertsey Tityrus, put an abrupt
end to our conversation.   We then anchored for lunch
under a bush.   While washing a glass I saw an apparition in among the weeds, not six inches from us, in
the form of Master Jack, who lay, apparently half-
asleep, and I am sure laughing at us.   " Well, that *is*
impertinence.   Look at the fellow ; we have been
fishing for him all day, and now the rascal comes to
lunch with us."   " Of course he does," said P. ; "the
fish about here are wonderfully well-bred and highly
civilised I assure you ; they require introductions before they make friends. I like a good rustic fish now—
regular unsophisticated fellows that don't know what
a hook is, nor yet the smell of cobbler's wax, or fishing-tackle makers' varnish.   But see if he'll eat veal-
pie . . . ungrateful brute, he refuses it—he's off.
Never mind, *we* will eat it.   This is very pleasant
though ; I feel quite poetical.   Give me another glass
of sherry, Harris.   I say, do you recollect Tennyson's
charming lines about the brook ?   How well they describe this little gravelly shallow—

> " I wind about, and in and out,
>   With here a blossom sailing,
>   And here and there a lusty trout,
>   And here and there a grayling." . . .

I **wish** I could recollect the words." "The gent as
wrote them verses didn't live about these parts, any
ways," growled out Harris ; " but I think we'd better
be off, gentlemen, if we're to catch any fish to-day."
So away we float again down stream.

"**P.**," said **I**, "**the** author of *Piscatory Eclogues,*
who wrote about **fishing a hundred and** thirty-four
years ago, must have been **in a fix on** just some such
hot day as this, when he wrote—

> " Then vainly waves the angler's reedy cane,
> And costly baits allure the drove in vain ;
> Ofttimes he views, awarned by adverse skies,
> **His** fly, or sportless cork, with hopeless eyes."

We were still floating down, when Harris said :
" This is Doumney ; I wonder if Mr. Buckland knows
the meaning of that." " No," said I, " what is it ?"
" It's one of the places where the Romans crossed the
Thames, and the soldiers at Chobham was going to do
the same thing one day with their pontoons (soldiers
is always soldiers, sir) ; but there's another place where
they crossed close to Walton-bridge, and they dredge
up curious things sometimes. The other day a **man**
told me he had dredged up a marble image like, and it
lay about in the barge a long time, and then the man
said he would take it home, **and** put it in the garden
for an ornament." " Harris," **I** said, " where's that
garden ? Don't disappoint me ; **we'll** go there instantly." " Well, sir," said Harris, " the man never

took the image to his garden at all, it was chucked overboard again by one of the boys." "What Goths these dredgermen are!" said I ; "are they not, P. ?" "Don't see it," **said P.** "Don't bother me about your Romans and your dredgermen—

"Her eyes are ——

Confound it all! you've put the words out of my head *again.* I wish you would not disturb me when you **see I'm** thinking." "But you must be disturbed ; here's the place **where** the jack are. It's no use your saying 'What a bother it is fishing !' when you are out **fishing.** Get up and fish, you lazy poet. You'll get **an** idea for your new edition of 'Puck on Pegasus.' I shall go and try yonder back stream while you remain here." So off I went and caught nothing, of course, but I saw whole nurseries of little fish on the shallows, and was watching them to see what I could learn and bring **as** evidence *in re* "the-grand-turning-out-of-young-fish question now being argued in the High Court of Pisciculture."

A shout from the distant poet,—"There he is ! **It's** the spoon that has done it." "So I perceive," I shouted in return ; "I thought *he* would." On my re**turn** P. explained in the most kind manner that "'the **spoon'** was the bait he had put on his line for the **sake of** giving the jack a new sensation." So we all put **on** spoons and fished away, but the sensation had passed away, and the jack would not have it a second time.

" It's near dinner time," said the poet, "and we must be off ; but we must have one cast in Weybridge Weir.   Can't you give us one more bit out of that wretched old angling book you are so fond of ?" " **Yes,** friend poet ; **here's to our** next merry fishing trip, and better sport, though I can't say more agreeable company.   Harris, just take that last cool bottle out of the live-bait well, if the fish have not been at it, will you ?   We will drink to the truth of this—

" ' Happy the fisher's life and humble state ;
   Calm are his hours, and free from rude debate ;
No restless cares he knows of sordid gain,
   Nor schemes that rack the toiling statesman's brain ;
Fearless in shades he takes his healthy dreams,
   And labours mild amid refreshing streams.' "

F. B.

FISHING AND FISH-HOOKS OF THE EARLIEST DATE.

MANY have been the writers who have indulged themselves and their readers in describing the pleasure to be derived from the arts of taking fish, and who have thus obtained as much gratification from delineating the methods by which they have ensnared their prey **as** in putting these arts into successful execution. But in referring to the history of this pleasing pursuit no one has ventured to travel back into very primitive times, as if not expecting to find in the earliest ages of the world any authentic notice of the art, and perhaps concluding that in primitive ages the people were altogether ignorant **or** careless **about it. Yet there** is evidence that such **was far** from being the case ; **and on close** inquiry **into the** habits of life of the people who lived even before the flood of Noah, we are able to discover that ingenuity **had been then** exercised—and that too by men of high eminence in science—for the same purposes, and to **as** large **an** extent, as we find in our own day ; in which case we may believe that they experienced as large an amount of pleasure as ourselves in the same

Y

pursuit, and we believe also with a far higher degree of benefit to **the** world at large. The arts then invented, as we shall see, were highly valued in many successive generations, and have never ceased to **be** employed down to our own times.

The natural historian Pliny knew nothing of the remotest history of the world ; but he records a tradition which he must have copied from some ancient writer whose works are lost (b. iii. c. 5, 7 ; b. v. c. 13 ; b. vii. c. 56), that Joppa had been a city situated **on** the coast of the sea before the date of the great flood that was spread over the earth ; and that the west border of Syria at that remote date was a coast of the **sea,** is more distinctly affirmed by the Phœnician historian Sanchoniatho, to whose narrative we are indebted for further interesting particulars.

The earliest inventions and amusements in the arts of life, as also in elegant improvements, were by the reprobate son of Adam and his near descendants ; and perhaps it was as combining both these characters that we are told how a boat was first formed, which was for the pursuit of fishing, by the father of Vulcan, and who was called, by a Greek accommodation with such as were more ancient and of another lineage, Halieus—a name which fixes his employment as being conducted on the sea, where his first attempt at seamanship was only such as is practised in our own times by men possessing the lowest amount of skill iu shipbuilding, and to whom the present age is a prehistoric time. This earliest fishing-boat was hewn out of the trunk of a tree ; but we are not informed **of** the nature of the instruments—whether nets or otherwise—with which the fish were caught ; and it remained for the higher genius of Vulcan, who, beyond doubt, is the Tubal Cain spoken of by Moses, and who, as Sanchoniatho informs us, was the son of Halieus, to bring the invention to its much higher degree of perfection. There were giants in the world in those days, and the floating **tree** may have been suitable to the stature of its builder ; but as is the case with most men who have been distinguished for eminent mental qualifications, this remarkable inventor appears to have been of even small stature, and to him, therefore, the less unwieldy vessel, the prototype of the coracle, built of planks, would be more appropriate. But as well as being of small size, he may even have been deformed ; for, added to the fact that by the more modern mythologists he was represented as a cripple, Herodotus refers to something peculiar in his appearance as recorded by those whose traditions are the most authentic, the Egyptians and Phœnicians. This writer, in alluding to the actions of the Persian Cambyses in Egypt, says that he forced an entrance into the temple of Vulcan, which was regarded as royally sacred, and derided the image of the god there worshipped ; which, indeed, resembled those Phœnician figures that were placed on the prow of their ships and were called Patæcians, not exceeding the stature of a pigmy. He likewise went into the temple of the Cabirian gods—so named from the Cabiri, Phœnician deities according to Sanchoniatho, the statues of which, with caps on their heads, were only about a foot in height, as described by Pausanias. Tubal Cain himself was so called, as signifying that from his skill the world derived profit, and the name of the Cabiri was significant of the might of these deities ; but the connection between them is proved from the conduct of this madman conqueror, who commanded that the deities in the temple should be thrown into the fire because they so much resembled the statues of Vulcan, from whom they were reported to be descended. It is certain that the personage here spoken of was highly reverenced in Egypt, even as one of their greatest gods, under the name of Phtha, although confessedly of Phœnician origin, and that the kings themselves were specially his priests.

It was this Vulcan or Tubal Cain who in the business of fishing was the first inventor of the line and baited hook ; the hook, as the Phœnician historian informs us, being made of iron or copper, and, we will venture to affirm, of a better shape than those which are represented in a later age by Dame Juliana Berners in the Book of St. Albans. But these primitive fish-hooks, as instruments of great good, may

have been made of gold ; for Vulcan himself also bore
a name equivalent to Chrysor, from the works he
executed in that precious metal ; and we are borne
out in this last conjecture by the fact, that a golden
fish-hook has been found·buried in the sand of a small
trout-stream in Cornwall. We will not affirm that
this is of Phœnician origin, although a metallic ball
found in that county may lay claim to that distant
parentage ; and still less will we venture to say that it
may have come from the skilful hands of Tubal Cain
himself, who was otherwise called Hiphastus and
Zeus Michiris, which last word signifies the "god-
mechanic ;" but it is of skilful workmanship, and is
preserved for its curiosity in a museum in its perhaps
doubly native county.

But in bringing again before the public these long-
buried reminiscences of ancient times, we must not
overlook the fisher-girl, whose elegant appearance was
such as to have formed the ideal of the Goddess
of Beauty. It is to the associations with the pursuits of her family that we can trace the origin of
the opinion that the Venus of antiquity was a produce of the ocean—in corroboration of which there
exists an ancient representation of her as seated on a
sea-shell and borne above the sea by marine beings.
This sister of Tubal Cain was called Naamah, which
so much in sound resembles Nemaus, who was said
to be the wife, or one of the wives, of Chronus or

Ham, that Bishop Cumberland has no doubt of their being the same person ; and it may have been from this alliance with the family of the great artist that this son of Noah found himself in possession of a larger amount of knowledge in antediluvian science than were his brothers, and perhaps with an inclination to the same pursuits. At any rate it is certain that his early descendants had recourse to the same employments on the sea that had formed so prominent a characteristic of the former inhabitants of the same regions. At an early date—at least after the dispersion of the families from Babel—a little town of fishermen was built at Sidon, and this soon extended itself to other stations as colonies, of which an important **one was Tyre or** Tzur, where fisheries were also carried on ; and the near connection of these with the other descendants of Ham appears from Melkart or Melchrat—which name, as Selden informs us, means " the strong king"—and who, although termed the Tyrian Hercules, was reverenced in a very ancient temple in Egypt. Melchart's eminency is said to have been derived from his voyages and discoveries at sea. He formed a settlement at Gadir or Cadiz, where a temple was erected, it seems, to his memory, and in which, according to ancient custom, were two famous pillars, the reputation of which, in course of time, was transferred to the neighbouring mountains at the entrance of the Mediterranean Sea. But it was to one sovereign of Sidon especially, and that a woman, that is to be ascribed the great advancement which was made in the comfort and prosperity of the people by the regulation and protection of the fisheries. Her name was Gatis, and afterwards, by what appears to have been a higher title of honour, Atergatis. She was the author of an edict by which it was enacted that no one should eat fish without a licence from her, and that every fisherman should bring to her the fish he had caught—a claim which, as Selden believed, was intended **to** imply that she was so far the sovereign of the neighbouring sea that no one should be permitted to take fish in it without a licence from herself. That this was not an act of severity to her own subjects, but was rather intended to protect them from the encroachments of strangers, appears from the high favour in which she was always held by the former ; for after death, according to the theology of these ages, she was regarded as a goddess, and fishes of gold and silver were dedicated to her—even from districts that were situated at a considerable distance— and in some places people abstained from eating fishes in honour of her. This circumstance is to be ascribed **to** the fact that the image which represented the goddess Atergatis—who was also called Derketo— was made in the form of a woman with a fish's tail, and in some instances with the head and arms only **of a** woman, but the whole body of a fish.

Coins are even now known which have this representation; and within not many years past a structure representing the same object was found on board and stolen from a Chinese fishing-boat. By the men of this boat, beyond doubt, it had been esteemed a protecting deity to their pursuits. Later still, a figure **of a** similar kind, formed perhaps of the head and shoulders of a monkey united to the body and tail of **a** fish, was carried to America from **Japan** under similar circumstances. It is probable **that the great** god Dagon of the Philistines, mentioned in the Bible, and which was a male deity, and was reverenced even in Etruria, **although** with a more emblematic image, **may** have been either the husband or the son of Queen Atergatis, since some difference was made in the statues which represented them, and that of Atergatis bore a female form. But it might have been in either case only the restoration of what had been recognised in the ages before the flood; for a tradition is recorded by Sanchoniatho that a Dagon was known in **the** same manner at that early date. And it is to be further observed that in the former case, as perhaps also in the latter, these first fishermen had directed their attention to the improvement of the arts of agriculture, which **may** account for a double signification of the name. The word Dagon signifies a fish divinity; and accordingly in the history given of him by the judge-prophet Samuel only his arms are mentioned ; but the name also conveys the idea of a produce of the soil. That the knowledge of this compound deity should have spread, as modern observation has shown, to the extremity of Eastern Asia, **will** appear the less remarkable when we are told **that** the people of Babylon were also worshippers of such a god; and the reason assigned for it is, that he —perhaps in the person of some learned priest of that faith—had taught them many valuable truths, of which, beyond doubt, something **of** the art of **fishing formed a part.** This **deity** of the Babylonians was called Odokon; **and on the** reverse of a coin bearing the figure **of** Dagon is that of a horse. **It** would be strange if we could discover that to the earliest nation or sovereign **of** fishermen we have been indebted for the first taming of the horse to human dominion.

J. C.

z